CODE: JO962
THE SEAL

J.D. BRIDGEFORD

Code: JO962, THE SEAL
Copyright © 2019 J.D. Bridgeford

ISBN-10: 1727322541
ISBN-13: 978-1727322545

DEDICATION

...to Harris; my Dear, may you rest in peace...

ACKNOWLEDGMENTS

This book was inspired by events that happened a long time ago, places I know, and by people who entered and left my life by serendipity. The book found its life through those memories.

CHAPTER 1

IT HAPPENED A WHILE AGO. My friend Penny told me this was a very strange time of her life and I believed her. She was something else, she was someone else, lived her life with no holds barred, and, in-between, let me watch her dog Damien. Her past had caught up with her and she had to deal with it the best way she could. Love would come and go, and the past would re-enter her life in a very serendipitous way. She told me her story and I listened, and this is the way I understood her...

It was early morning on Touchstone Drive and the street was laying quiet and empty. The first orange rays of sunshine had just started to touch the hill behind the homes, and, in the street, a few early risers were straggling along.

Inside the English style townhome, Penny was laying in the bed stretching herself and yawning. It was her day off, and yet it was not in her demeanor to lay around; it was wasteful in her mind.

Damien, her Doberman, was next to her and looking with begging eyes for Penny to let him go out in the backyard. She looks at him then gets up reluctantly and opens the French doors to let him out. She leans against the door frame as she watches him run outside to take care of his pressing needs. She can feel the cool breeze flutter up and it creates a shiver throughout her body, and the next moment goose-bumps surface on her arm and the hair stands straight up.

While watching Damien, her attention is being distracted by a moving black drone circulating above her backyard. The drone makes a sudden stop and watches Damien; he suddenly notices the drone and starts to run towards it barking so the entire neighborhood can hear him. The next moment the drone turns towards Penny. She raises her voice and starts to yell commands in a soft and direct manner to Damien, but he's not moving his focus off his target.

"Damien! Damien! Damn it, get back in here!", he reluctantly comes back while he is looking behind him to cover his six and runs back inside. He turns around immediately and tries to press his head through the crack of the door as Penny closes it shut.

"Damn it, you know better, what's the matter with you?" She stops herself just for a second to take another look at what was hovering outside. She separates the venetian blinds and can see the drone linger for a brief second before flying off. Penny crawls back into bed and Damien follows like he was stuck to her with glue.

Despite the incident, it was a beautiful early morning, and she watched the light sneaking in between the slats as she lay there all alone with Damien, contemplating life and how she had ended up where she was.

The thoughts from the past were coming back to remind her of what had happened the last day in Jordan. The loud noise of a voice echoed in Arabic from the speakers for morning prayer, and cars and mopeds zipped by outside. It was the morning hustle in Mafraq, and it was the last day she would have waking up to the sounds and smells of Middle Eastern fare. She had tried to forget, but the unequivocally unfortunate situation was all she could remember. It had been chaotic and almost like a bad dream that she was waiting to wake up from, but she never did.

This was the day Penny and Howard, her husband, were going home. They would replace the dusty sandbox with Colorado's beautiful green hills—that is, until the bomb went off and changed everything in a moment. Finding her husband injured among others on the ground and the stressful journey to Heidelberg VA hospital was agonizing to remember. In her mind, it was like a silent movie on loop.

After the funeral, Penny's life was permanently changed, no longer protected by anyone. She was alone, she had nothing to go back to, and she made her decision at that point: she was going to take a trip around Europe before going back to deal with the remains of what was left of the life she had once had with Howard. As if things had not been life-changing enough, they would change again when she met Harris.

Penny took the train to Ljubljana, capital of Slovenia. This was her escape; even if it was only brief, she needed to clear her mind. It was on the border of Eastern Europe, a gem, a hideaway in which to relax, away from the watchful eyes of everyone.

She needed the rest—she knew that—but she was a restless soul, and she knew that wasn't going to happen back in the States. Too many questions, and too many people who thought they knew what she needed but ultimately didn't.

Arriving at the Ljubljana train station, she stood out like a sore thumb. Penny's demeanor, and how she carried herself was distinctive, and people took notice of her. She demanded attention unintentionally, but all she wanted was to be left alone and to blend in, but she knew it was not to be.

That rest that she'd planned on and was desperately needing was going to be diminished, unbeknownst to her.

She checked in late that afternoon at the Hotel Slon, the nineteenth-century Elephant Hotel. It was notorious for its unique history, and she decided to stay a couple of days to explore the city at her own pace and head to the coast later. That was the plan, and she had barely got herself settled when Harris entered the picture. Little did she know that her innocent attempt to relax with a drink at the bar down the street was the moment the universe would change its course.

It was a bomb-shelter bar hiding in plain sight, and it opened its doors at night. The metal doors were sunken into the ground during the day and were unnoticeable. That changed at night when the street traffic had died down. In an unobtrusive way, they opened up to stand like angels' wings. A staircase became apparent and mysteriously welcomed patrons. The temporary wooden stairs seemed like they were from the long-over prohibition period, and its railingless and spiral way made each step a balancing act. It was a stark reminder of the multiple wars that had recently passed through the country. The city had always been prepared for the next battle, and now was no different.

When she arrived, Harris was sitting at the bar sipping his cocktail, just an ordinary chap with glasses, nonchalantly looking around. However, under the veneer hid a maverick journalist, ostensibly a war correspondent, but in fact an MI6 Intel who was on a mission to cover the Balkan war, which she unexpectedly found out later. She was the one who had lost direction of where life was taking her next, as she roamed with no map and no coordinates.

Penny was a magnet who would automatically draw people to her and almost perforce she could open up uninitiated conversations. This was how her acquaintance with Harris had started; it was he who had approached her.

The interesting conversation that had developed ended up with a simple question by him, and the next moment she had signed up to head into no man's land as an interpreter. The plan was for her to use her linguistic talents to help those who were helping the innocent victims of the unasked-for war. Her thoughts had wandered off to the place she had processed repeatedly; it was something inexplicable that would rest.

Penny turned in the bed when a subtle sound came from the living room, but she couldn't be bothered to investigate. Then, a loud noise made Damien sit straight up, the hair on the back of his neck standing up. She sat up and looked at Damien: she knew he wouldn't be acting like this unless... She got out of the bed and walked toward the living room to see what had made the noise. She looked around and felt goose-bumps on her arms as she continued, only to find a picture frame that had fallen down in a corner. She sighed with relief as she walked over to the frame to put it back up. She straightened the photo of her and Howard.

She looked around as if this was some form of omen and then saw Damien, who was staring down the hallway. She tapped him on the head to walk with her as she continued to the bedroom, and she called out to him, but he was lingering. At a second call, he ran back into the bedroom, jumped onto the bed, and laid his head on her abdomen.

"What were you looking at?" she said to him as she stroked his head and his eyes closed in contentment. Penny looked over at the time. She was going to have to get up and get going, but it was her day off, and she needed to do something constructive and not just lie around in bed.

She got up, walked into the bathroom, and did a double take at herself in the mirror. "What do I want out of life? I have a great job, a career that takes me places..." she said to her reflection.

She was fulfilled career-wise but not emotionally. She had tried dating a few years back, and thought she had found Him, but something was off. Her clairsentient radar had told her that something was wrong; still, she had been drawn to him for some reason. She was fighting her better judgment. She wanted him, and he wanted her, but his excuses and lies had placed a wedge between them. She knew that it was not the right time for them, and yet she did not know why he was in her life. She would push him away, and he would come back like a boomerang over and over again until she ignored all his pleas.

She wanted someone who was like Howard; a loving man, a man who was protective of her and, yet, allowed her to be who she was, and accepted her strength. She needed the feeling of a man who loved her unconditionally, and he had not been that man.

Penny falls back into deep thoughts and looks back in time, and how they met. It was through work, he came for a fire inspection at her place of business; he was the fireman, a lieutenant, and an EMT. He was a man who walked with authority and exuded charisma. Once their eyes met, it was all over. He could not stop looking at her, and he devoured her with his eyes.

He was persistent and finally she let her guard down, but she later discovered that it was more than a strong fireman who was standing in front of her. He was a man with so many secrets, that was clear, she could sense that as it gave her goose-bumps when she was around him. However, she was equally as intrigued by him, as he was about her.

He was the man who looked at her with passion in his eyes, and unexpectedly would say for no reason, "You are so beautiful!"

The first time they had met, there was this chemistry between them and a fire spark that would not fizzle out, but the more time progressed, the more she was seeing his true side, and the lack of integrity was where she drew the line and ended their relationship.

Now, years down the road, all she had was comforting morning showers, and that had become old. She knew that it was time to become serious and find the man in her life who she was going to grow old with.

She looks over at Damien, "This thing sleeping in my bed has to change.", she says to him as she looks at him stretched out on his back as comfortable as he could be. Her executive position at PEGC was constantly changing, and she didn't mind it, but they were the type of changes that came with the steep price of working long hours and never having enough time for a life outside work.

Penny takes a closer look in the mirror, *'Oh, shit, my hair is showing a few streaks of grey!'* she thought to herself. This was surely the sign of the sad fact that she was no longer 'that thirty something' anymore, and it was time to fix that. She turns around and pulls the coloring kit out of the cabinet, Cappuccino brown hair coloring, to be precise. It was time to turn up the volume before going out for breakfast.

She turns to Damien, "What do you say pup? Let's turn up the heat today!" and Damien responds with several small barks. "I'm assuming you are agreeing with me." she says as Damien lifts his head up and then lets it slowly sink down in front of his paws as he silently looks on her pending task while she colors her hair. She was going to do her best to clean up her act, and, hopefully, the spring feelings would come out to play.

Penny walks down to Broadway to Lucy's Coffee Shop to get some breakfast. People were standing in line to get in and there was a wait. Damien's impatient demeanor did not warrant the wait in line, so Penny continues to walk over to the other side of the street to get a Starbucks. At the crosswalk there was this tall man, close to 6'3", not too bad looking, in his late 20's, maybe early 30's. Who knew these days, people were looking younger while they were older, as she was looking 10 years younger herself, she knew that things could be deceptive.

He had a scruffy bad boy look, five o'clock shadow, and his left arm and shoulder were hiding a secret as his left shoulder was covered with a tattoo resembling a water dragon. She observed him behind her shades. He was certainly someone she wanted to get to know better.

The light turns at the crosswalk and she proceeds to cross the street while she was thinking about what her next agenda was going to be. Damien was following Penny, doting along next to her when she suddenly stops in front of the coffee shop. She ties him to a tree and turns quickly as she bumps into the man from the crosswalk.

"Oh, I'm sorry!" Penny exclaims apologetic. Damien starts to bark, and the man snaps his fingers and Damien quiets down. Penny looks surprised back at him.

"What's your name?" she asks him curiously while at the same time intrigued by how he managed to command Damien like that as Damien would only listen to her or Jennie.

"Marcus." he responds back and looks at Penny for a response.

"Oh, I'm Penny." she says as she takes off her shades, and she looks right into his clear blue eyes while she gives off a smirk as she shakes his hand. The handshake lingers, and Penny finally catches herself and pulls her hand away. Penny turns her attention to Damien, "Be a good boy now." she says as she gives him on last pat before she turns back around and follows Marcus inside.

Penny senses this normalcy as if she knew him from somewhere, and, yet, it did feel right, but she wasn't feeling any passionate chemistry, just a feeling that she could see him being a friend to start with. Oddly enough, she felt as if she knew him from someplace, and, yet, she couldn't place her finger on it.

Marcus was standing in front of her in line, and she didn't mind; it gave her the chance to observe him without him knowing it. Hmm, he really was tall and big, but the question remained, what did he do for a living? Curiosity was second nature to her, and she was constantly analyzing and trying to figure things out.

"Penny, it's your turn." Marcus says reminding.

"Oh, ok.", she manages to fumble out. She could feel him watching her, and her finger was tapping on her lips as she thought about what she wanted, *'come on Penny, pick something.'* the thoughts internally pressed her for a decision. "A Caramel Macchiato, please." she said as if it was a last resort decision.

"What's the name on it?" the clerk asks.

Marcus chimes in, "Penny, and put it on my tab."

She looks at him confused, and he smiles back at her, "That is the least I can do for you, since we walked over here together."

He certainly was taking charge in a bold way, and she knew he didn't have to, and, yet, she wondered if he did it out of kindness or if there was an underlying agenda. Penny knew all too well how to play along, she was eventually going to find out and continued to watch him pay for both their drinks.

"Well thank you." and she smiles back at him while he watches her with his studying eyes. "I will have to repay you one day." she continues.

"You can start by enjoying the coffee with me, give me some company." he replies. They grab their coffees and walk outside where Penny gets Damien. She turns to Marcus, "Down the street just 100 feet there's a park." she says while pointing into the direction.

Marcus and Penny find a place to sit close to the walkway, and Damien lies down by her feet completely content. Pedestrians and runners were using this park frequently; it was a great place to people watch.

"I guess you like your coffee brown?" Marcus says to break the silence and makes a nod with his head as he hints at Penny's cup.

"I like my coffee brown and sweet the way I like my men." she snickers and makes a joke of his comment.

Marcus responds quickly, "And I like my women with a sense of humor." as he gives off a smile while he sips on his coffee.

"Well, I can tell you there is more of where that came from." she counteracts in a witty way; yeah Penny had a sharp wit that some men could shave with. Inside that sharp brain was this bottled up comedian that, at times, just wanted to come out and play. Penny knew that was one thing that Howard had been attracted to. Today Penny realized that maybe she had the perfect partner to banter with, and she couldn't stop thinking that things happen for a reason.

She knew nothing about this man, he could possibly be someone who was a mercenary. Yeah, Penny could take things to the extreme as her life had been nothing of the ordinary. She could never be too sure what people did for a living, just like she knew herself, she knew the fireman himself had secrets that she had yet to unveil. Marcus had tattoos all over his body, and you hear all the time that people had day jobs and another life on the side, just like she suspected the fireman. She starts to smile to herself as her mind was racing with all sorts of scenarios.

"What's so funny now, if I may ask?" he says.

"Oh, I was just thinking how this rendezvous happened today." she lied. She was thinking how crazy her thoughts were and she had let her thoughts carry her away to the extreme, but she wasn't going to tell him that, hell no, she was going to lie, because 'people lied all the time', that's what Dr. House always said. It was true, she just had to look at Dee, the fireman, as he was a walking testimony to that.

"So, what do you do?" he asks as he's breaking the pause in the conversation.

"I'm working for a bank downtown, but today is my day off and I am going to try to do some errands as tomorrow is a working day. Yeah, I'm not being delusional. If I know something; today will still be there tomorrow, so I am just postponing my work load to tomorrow." she says as she takes a large gulp of her coffee.

"I work over there." he says, and points toward a construction site with a crane moving a load of construction materials.

"Oh, I see, that explains your..." and Penny stops herself as she gestures his body size.

"Well, it's a way to keep in shape, I use to be in the military." he says as he takes his last sip of the coffee and gets up from the seat then walks over to the trash can.

Penny's mind is now all over the place, she wants to see him again, but how, "Can I ask you something, are you handy, I mean can you do remodeling?" she says with a tone of a proposal growing behind the question.

"Well, I can take a look at it, and you can tell me what you're looking at having done." he says, as he was reading between the lines of what she was asking. "So, if I can have your number, I can call you…" he says and stops to wait for her answer to his suggestion.

Penny stands up and pulls out a company business card from her wallet and a pen that is stuck in the checkbook slot. She writes her number on the back of the card. "Here, take this and call me, and we can set a time." she says business like as she was.

He studies the card and looks over at her. "I'll call you… maybe we can do dinner?" he says as he made a point of inviting himself, and Penny smiles back at him.

"Yeah, why not." she says and gives nods of goodbye in military style, tugs the leash at Damien, and the two walk off.

Marcus is left standing there with the card in his hand, and he is overwhelmed with a feeling that Penny was a woman of a different caliber than he was used to. He knew he had to get to know her better, as she was a woman of few words, yet she intrigued him, and he was not the last one to experience that perception of her.

CHAPTER 2

WITH DAMIEN'S SPEED THEY were back at the house in no time. Penny starts to look for projects that she could think of having done; kitchen was something that had been eye sore. She walks up to the computer and pulls up the Photoshop program, then walks back into the kitchen and starts taking pictures. She had always hated the kitchen, it felt too small, and she looked at it with measuring eyes. Damien stood next to her bobbing his head, left, and then right, and then he looks up at her and gives up a bark.

Penny looks down at him, "It's high time to do something about it, right?" she says to him, and returns to the computer and uploads the pictures. She looks at the save button, she thinks for a second, and saves is under 'Marcus'. That was going to be his project, or was it that he was going to be a project for Penny?

Penny's starts to think, what did she want in her kitchen? What was important? She logs online and starts to browse for ideas as the phone rings, "Oh how annoying!" she exclaims. She lets it go to voicemail, then, a few moments later, the voicemail chime sounds. "Oh, another voicemail, great." she says facetiously. She shakes her head as she stretches her arm out to reach the phone.

"Let's see who called me, Damien.", she says out loud. Damien just lays there and doesn't move a muscle, his head is still, but his eyes are following her every movement. Penny smiles to herself, it was Marcus. He wasn't wasting any time, and neither would she.

He wanted her to call him back, but she didn't want to seem too eager, she would let him wait just to keep it interesting. She was going to give herself more time to browse on the web for ideas before she would call him, and, of course, sound very casual. It was obvious, the small butterfly flutters started to build up within her and made it hard for her concentrate.

Penny gets up from her desk and opens the double French patio doors that face the backyard. Damien is quick to run out, and then he disappeared at the far end where she loses sight of him. She sits down on the step and her thoughts were again revisiting her time with Harris. Marcus had reminded her of Harris with his comment of being an ex-military.

HARRIS HAD WOKEN HER up early the following morning after their encounter in the bar. It was around 3 am when the ride to the war zone started and she remembered the small Yugo he had proudly presented to her, *It was going to be the most comfortable ride she would ever experience.* 'The 1.3-liter motor sounded like a revved-up Singer sewing machine.

They had endured through rough terrain for 6 hours, and this explained a lot about the condition of the struts, they had seen better days, wobbly and bouncy like a trampoline at times. By the time they reached the old farmhouse, Penny was ready to get out; she should have recognized that his facetious statement was something she would be reminded that it had merely been a joke, by the aches she was experiencing.

Harris had stopped in front of a barn, he got out and opened the barn doors, and jumped back in and pulled the car inside. Her body ached as she stumbled out feeling square and stiff. Harris moved quickly, and in no time, he had covered the car with a tarp and then followed up with piles and piles of hay. She could tell this was not the first time he had done this.

Penny was stretching herself and she could see the haze and the fog building up, while dogs and chickens were running around barking and clucking intermittently. Harris had told her they were going to stop on the border between Croatia and Bosnia, and that there was a man who would safe keep the vehicle until they came back.

This was it; they were at the frontline of the war and were about to enter the war zone. As they walked past the main building, a man came out of the house and waved at Harris. It was obviously understood at that moment the dynamic of the arrangement. Harris told her he paid the man handsomely to park it in his barn, and it had never been a problem so far, but those things could quickly change as that had been evident in the past.

They got on the road and started walking. Penny had

conveniently enough brought Howard's combat boots in her luggage, this was all that was left of him that the VA hospital allowed her to keep. She was still trying to wake up as they walked down the pebbled country road where horses and carriages were passing them by.

The only lifeline Harris had brought with him was a satellite cell phone in case of emergency.

CELL PHONE, YES, Penny reminded herself, she had to return Marcus' call. She gets up and she looks for Damien as she turns and walks back inside. She grabs her phone and hits the return dial button on the last incoming call.

It's ringing, "Hello.", she hears.

"Hello, can I speak with Marcus?", she asks.

"This is him." he says.

"Oh, it's Penny. I am returning your call." she says with a business-like tone in her voice but feels a bit nervous at the same time.

"Oh, hi." he says with a sweet voice, "I was thinking, I mean, I wanted to ask you if you were busy tonight, maybe."

Before he could finish his sentence, Penny responds. "Sure, why don't you come over around eight." she says, and she can hear him laugh.

He didn't expect that answer she could tell, and Penny blurts out her address. This was going to be the test of who he was; if he was a man with integrity or just the regular fuck boy. Eight pm was a few hours away and Penny still had time to handle her private business matters.

She had just finished the conversation with Marcus when she could hear Damien's hound-like bark, and then he came running back into the house, his tail was wagging like a whip and he was barking up a storm, and then he turned around and raced back out again.

Penny walks back out to the yard to see what was going on that made him all excited and nervous at the same time. It was the drone, it was back. Penny walks back into the house, "Enough already!" she says out loud irritated. She walks up to the desk drawer and pulls out her loaded gun, she cocks it and walks back outside.

The drone was still hovering back and forth along her windows, and then it turns toward Penny and stays still as if it was watching her intently. She doesn't move, instead she prepares herself mentally to take it down and raises the gun swiftly, aims, and two rapid shots are fired. It all goes so quick that the drone had no chance to move out of range.

The drone hits the ground, then Damien runs up and grabs the remains and drags it back under the patio awning. He chews manically on it, and the sound of crushing plastic can be heard.

Penny looks at it and hopes that this would be the end of it. Someone was watching her and was now clearly aware to stay away from her, and again she couldn't understand why someone enjoyed being a nuisance. She had no enemies, at least that she was aware of.

She walks back into the house and gives the room one quick glance. Damien's toys were scattered all over the place, one would think she had a toddler in the house. She puts the gun down on a table and starts to clean up the place. Every now and then Damien would run to the door looking at her and what she was doing while he was wiggling his tail and would dash back out to the leftovers of the drone. He was a forever puppy and Penny's only companion that stayed faithful.

The time ticked on quickly, between the cleaning up in the house Penny was making phone calls and conducting her business matters. She suddenly glances over the clock, and it was six already. She walks into the kitchen; she opens the refrigerator, it's sparse, all she had was bottled water, juice, eggs, some lunch meat, peppers, and a few bottles of salad dressing. She opens the freezer drawer and some frozen scones were staring back her along with a few bagels and the faithful double vanilla ice cream for a rainy day. I guess this was what it looked like to be a single household with one dog, she sighs heavily.

She could not remember the last time she had guests over, she nearly never had time because of her busy schedule. She was going to have to order in some food as it all came out of left field unexpectedly.

She walks back to the bedroom and she looks at the bed, she hadn't made it, but it was time for a fresh set of sheets, that she knew. Penny rips the sheet off the bed, and walks over to the hamper and drops it in. Her eyes catch Howard's combat boots, and she stops and leans against the wall, and she sinks down on to the floor and grabs one of the boots. She looks at the boot and flashbacks from the last time she had worn them were like a fresh wound inside her.

SHE REMEMBERED THEY HAD ARRIVED IN SARAJEVO around noon that day. At first, they started off on foot and walked for a couple of miles, then a British convoy came up behind them. They were coming from Split and were heading to Sarajevo. Harris, with his credentials, had managed to hitch them a ride with the convoy. Penny observed the soldiers while Harris had chimed in the conversation and laughed with them, typical men's humor. Harris had told her very little about the trip except that he had made a connection with a military person from the local resistance organization and they were going to be interviewing a person of interest.

Once they had arrived at the outskirts of Sarajevo, they walked off the main road and up onto a deserted small country trail. The homes were riddled with bullet holes telling a tale of terror; they were shattered from the cannon fire of tanks. The images where etched inside Penny's memory and were not going to be diminished any time soon.

The further they walked; the more homes were appearing to them in the same condition. Then, abruptly, Harris stopped, and they were just standing there in the middle of nowhere waiting, and, without a moment to react, armed militia came spewing out from the surrounding ditches.

The next thing Penny knew they were being escorted into the village with firearms pointed directly at them. This was how they did it, Harris said. However, she was not surprised or scared; there was nothing to gain or lose as she'd already lost what was dearest to her and if this was the time to meet him on the other side, so be it.

Penny had understood that things happened for a reason, and that there was a purpose for her being alive and spared from the Jordan incident, and now she was going to translate for a good cause.

When they walked into the patched-up house that was the headquarters for this resistance militia, Penny could tell this was the heart of the organization. They were greeted by a young woman, and they were both strip-searched. Then the woman brought them to the second room where people were busy discussing strategic moves and gesturing wildly with their hands as they were pointing at the maps that covered the table in the center of the room. Radio chatter was going on in the back room but was too faint for Penny to be able to discern anything.

Suddenly, a tall man comes out of the back room, he greets Harris like a long-lost brother. These were war times, so all friendly interactions were welcomed. Penny quickly surmises that the man appears to be a high-ranking officer.

The meeting had barely lasted an hour before chaos started to break out. Penny paid close attention to the side conversations and learned that they were expecting enemy forces to enter the village.

Penny warned Harris that they had to leave right away, and, before they were able to leap outside, rapid gunfire was heard all around. Penny threw herself on the floor, covering her head from falling debris. She laid there completely still, not moving a muscle as she could hear bullets bursting through the walls from all directions. There was no telling where exactly they were coming from. She looked for Harris and could see that he had been struck several times by bullets gracing him. He was having someone watching over him as they had been stopped by his Special Forces vest.

Penny was hugging the floor waiting for a cease-fire and Harris was a few feet away from her and was not moving. She had to crawl up to him, she knew that. Penny was determined that she wasn't going to lose him. She slowly crawled across the debris covered floor as she made her way to Harris' position. As she got closer, she made eye contact with him; he was looking at her, but said nothing, just gave her thumbs up.

She had made a quick assessment of the room and could see the front door was closed, but the back door was wide open, where their militia hosts had made their escape. She saw that there was only one dead person on the floor who didn't make it. Penny moved slowly without making so much as a sound, and she could hear voices outside looking for survivors. She signaled to Harris to start moving towards her into the adjacent room.

The dead body was blocking the entrance to the room, so Penny dragged the heavy body away from the door and freed up the passageway. She frisked the dead man for weapons, on his side she could feel something hard, so she dug deep under the man's clothing and pulled out a gun that was tucked in a holster. A Makarov pistol, she recognized, this was not what she had been used to, she had done some military training when she was young and what she had been used to, was a Glock 17. This was a Russian handgun that most security and police forces used. She had heard of them and seen pictures, but never been up close to one.

She takes the gun and follows Harris into the adjacent room.

Penny immediately notices that there is no other way in or out other than the door they just crawled through. The lone window in the room was boarded up and had shafts of light poking through its bullet holes. Harris and Penny were now stuck in the room with nowhere to go. They were trapped, and it felt like they were in a waiting room just waiting for death to find them.

It was nerve-wracking as the two remained absolutely silent and prayed that no one would find them. Waiting for the military convoy to pass through the town was excruciating as it was dragging on and on like waiting for a seemingly endless freight train pass by a railroad crossing.

Penny was sitting pinned to the wall listening to the sounds of the military vehicles as they disappeared into the distance. Finally, after what felt like an eternity, it was completely quiet.

Penny looked at Harris and waved at him to come over to her. He tenderly got up on his hands and knees, and Penny could tell that despite Harris' protective vest, he was still hurting.

PENNY'S EYES WERE CLOSED as she sat there in the closet

recalling her situation in the Balkans with Harris while holding on to her late husband's boot. Still deep in thought, she started feeling wet licks on her lips which was confusing because she did not remember anything like this from her meeting with Harris. Suddenly, Penny realizes that the licking she's experiencing is not part of her reminiscing, so she forces herself to open her eyes and, there he was, wagging his tail, wiggling his body, and licking her face: Damien. Penny was now back to reality with Damien standing there in front of her, and his leash on the floor next to her.

"Oh, I see, you are trying to tell me something." she says and pats his little head gently. This was her responsibility these days and Damien wanted to go for his run, and that was the best way to get him calm for the rest of the evening. "Let's go out for run at the park." He starts jumping up and down like his feet are made of springs and runs back and forth while letting out small howls. He was a happy boy.

"OK, OK, I'll get my running shoes on." she responds to his impatience.

The sun had started to go down around seven o'clock; however, it was still light outside. Spring had come early this year and the weather was getting warmer every day; yet it allowed for relaxing nights outside on the terrace.

Their run took them through the park, that very same park they had visited earlier in the morning, and forty minutes later they were back at home, tired, sweaty and content.
Damien's tongue was hanging lose like a limp tie and foaming off the sides. They both needed water, and for Penny that meant both on the inside and on the outside.

She pressed the key into the lock and turned it and gave one precautious casual look as she opened the door and let Damien in. Penny then entered the house and closed the door behind.

She walks up to the cd player and hits play then starts to walk away, but she stops as the music starts; it's Jennifer Paige. This strikes a chord in her as she had not heard these tracks for a long time. After a few brief moments of listening, she continues walking back to the bedroom as she takes off one sweaty garment at a time. When she reaches the bedroom, she hangs them on the back of the chair.

She looks over at the bed and it dawned on her that she had forgot to make it, it was still stripped. She bends over and opens the linen chest and pulls out the sheets and quickly makes the bed, and finally pulling the cover over it.

Damien is walking around and whipping his tail happily, watching her make the bed. He jumps up on the bed as soon as Penny lifts her hand off it. He lays flat with his paws holding up his head, and stares into the bathroom as Penny makes her way in for a much-needed shower.

She turns on the water and gets ready to get in when she hears the doorbell ring. Damien jumps up and starts barking ferociously. Penny grabs a towel and wraps it around her and heads to the front door. She quietly approaches the door and looks through the cat eye, Marcus had already arrived. Penny hesitates, she looks over to the large clock hanging on the wall and it was ten to eight. She opens the door. "Hi." she greets him as she blushes bashful since she is standing there in just a towel that's wrapped around her body.

"Well... Hello..." Marcus says and seem to be at a loss for words.

"Come on in." she says. Damien is glued to her side and his posture tells Marcus that he's protecting Penny.

"He is not happy to see me this time." Marcus says and looks at Penny.

She looks down at Damien, "Well, you are on his territory now." she says and looks back at Marcus, "I was about to take a shower, we just got back from a run." she says and walks away, leaving Marcus with Damien. Penny gives off a loud whistle and Damien comes running on her command. He catches up to her and Penny walks into bathroom and closes the door. Damien is placed to stays outside and guard the door.

She smiles to herself as she jumps into the shower and lets the water pour down her décolletage and her face, it's a great sensation. The relaxing feeling of water running down her tired body was priceless, she could stay there all day, but she is reminded by Damien's bark that there is no time to waste as Marcus was left alone with Damien.

Finished with her shower, Penny hurries to get dressed, she gives a quick look in the mirror. Drying the hair? Who has time for that she contemplates, as she grabs the brush off the counter and gives the hair a few brush strokes and folds it back.
She continues to walk out to the living room and finds Marcus standing there admiring the artwork on the wall; it's an oversized painting of a female face. The painting is 4.5' x 3.5'

in size, where tears are cascading down the cheeks which is surrounded by feathers.

"I see you're admiring the art. Do you know much about art?" she asks inquiring.

Marcus turns around quickly, as if he was caught off guard. "Nah," he says while continuing admiring the painting, "I don't know much about art, but when I see something I like, I buy it." he continues.

He seems to relax after the initial scare he had moments prior, and the conversation has calmed things down. She can tell he is a little nervous; first the greeting at the door, and now she comes out with wet, combed back hair and verbally startled him. She was showing a side that he was not expecting, and yet he came across loving the surprise.

He studies the picture a little longer, then he turns to Penny, "I brought some takeout for us, I hope you like Chinese."

Penny smiles and nods agreeing, and then she brings him back to the kitchen. "This is your project..." she says as she folds out her arms, her way of breaking the ice. He looks around, nods agreeing. It calms down the atmosphere which makes everything finally start to feel just right, like a normal situation, a new, but positive normal.

He puts the bag on the counter. "I got a little bit of everything."

Penny starts to poke around; he had literally brought a little bit of everything. "You really went all out..." she says and looks at him and can see he is assessing the space. Penny smiles and dives back into the bag. "...and you even thought about the dessert." she says under my breath.

"Say again." he says.

"Oh, no I was just thinking to myself."

"I know I invited myself over here today and I felt bad thinking you were going to make something for us, so I got here early hoping that you had not gone out of your way to..."

Penny interrupts him, "Shh, you don't need to explain." she says and puts his mind at ease. "I think we should take all this out to the back terrace." she says and pulls out a tray, some plates, and San Pellegrino water from the refrigerator. She loads everything up and, before she grabs the tray, Marcus steps in.

"I'll take that, you lead the way." he says like the true military gentleman he was. He follows Penny to the back terrace where the loveseats were placed facing each other. He places the tray on the table and watches Penny turn on the outdoor lanterns. The sun had gone down, yet it was a warm evening, but Penny knew that it would eventually change.

They sat there for a moment and looked at each other. Finally, Penny breaks the silence, "I was thinking about showing you what I wanted to have done afterwards." and she points at the meal he had brought.

"Sounds great, I'm very interested, how about I make you a plate?" he asks and points at the tray of Chinese food containers.

"Please, help the damsel in distress."

He busts out in laughter and does a double take with his eyes in a flirtatious way, "I bet. You really look like you need to be rescued."

Penny blushed and laughs at his comment, then Damien comes out sniffing around, his nose had a discriminating pallet and could smell good food miles away. Penny sends him off, and after a few strolls around the yard, he lies down to rest, and falls asleep.

CHAPTER 3

PENNY TAKES A BITE OFF HER FOOD; she gives off a look of satisfaction that is spreading all over her face. Marcus looks at her with a smile as he takes a bite and understands the pleasurable expression in Penny's face.

"Yeah, this was really good!" he says and awaits Penny's response.

"Mmm." she says as she finishes her food. She continues to eat quietly, and she looks at him, he had told her that he had been in the military.

"So, tell me…" she says and pauses and takes another bite of the food, and she churns on her thoughts as she chews.

"Tell you what?" he responds and looks puzzled by the sudden question that Penny never finished.

"You said you were in the military… please forgive my curiosity, but what did you do in the military?" she says as she continues to eat and wait for his response. It's quiet for a moment as she chews and looks at him as he is finishing his bite.

Penny can sense that this was a sensitive topic for him, "You know you don't have to..." and he stops her.

"Let me tell you, I think it's better that I'm being an open book with you regarding to my past, it's nothing that I want to hide." he pauses for a moment, and then continues, "I have PTSD from my time in the Army, I was in Jordan the last part of my deployment." he says and quiets down.

She could see his face giving off an embarrassed yet humble expression. He was trying to be open without scaring her away. Penny leans over and grabs his hand.

"It's ok, you can tell me. I lost my husband in the middle east on an assignment." she says.

He looks up at her surprised, "Oh, he was military too?" he asks, and his eyes perk up.

Penny retracts her hand, "No." she says, and she can feel the hurt bubble up as this was the first time she had mentioned to anyone that she had been married before. Not even the fireman knew about Penny's prior life, she had let him think she was a single woman.

"I guess you don't want to talk about it." he says as he puts down his plate and looks at her with compassion. She looks up from her plate, as she is chewing and contemplating to whether she was going to tell him.

"To be honest with you, I have not told anyone this before, but it was a while ago." she says, and she finishes her last bite. She looks over at Damien and can see him stretch his front paws, and she reaches down to pet him, "You see, Damien has been my companion since my husband passed away in Jordan." she says as Marcus moves in his seat.

"So, what happened? Uh... that is if you don't mind me asking." he says and gets intrigued by moment.

"My husband wasn't a troop, he was an FBI agent and SWAT member, and he had been in Jordan on an assignment. He didn't tell me much about what he was doing, it was something about a troop going rogue." she says and looks up at Marcus, she could tell he was showing an interested ear.

"So, did he find him... I mean, did he find the person in question?" he asks curiously as he was looking down at the plate and grabbing a new bite.

Penny thinks back, "I remember the conversation vaguely and I recall we were going home that day and he said he'd found him, but all I wanted was to get out of that sandbox."

"Then what happened, was there something..." and he is interrupted by Penny.

"Yes, I was at the marketplace getting a few things that I was going to add to my luggage, and that's when it happened..." she says and quiets down; her eyes had frozen, but just for a brief moment, and it was as if her mind had taken over the conversation, and she went into a mode of being lost in time. She could see vivid pictures replay themselves, and she continues, "There was this blast..." she pauses, "...people were running, and chaos presented itself with people's cries and screams of terror. They were running towards me, but I was running towards the explosion. It was crazy, I pulled up my phone and called his cell and I could hear it; I was searching for the sound amongst the injured and I could hear the ringtone go off over and over again. Had it not been for his phone in his pocket, I would not have recognized him." she says as she stops herself and looks up at Marcus and notices that his jovial facial expression had change to a more somber and wondersome look.

Marcus understands very well that this was a time she had tried to process, but it was still fresh as she was unable to talk about it without getting emotional. He knew that he had to divert the conversation to something else. "Why don't you go and get the laptop." he coaches her.

Penny gets up quickly as she seizes the opportunity to regroup and walks into the house and grabs her laptop computer off her desk. She walks back out and hands it to him.

"Come and sit down over here" he says as he taps on the seat next to him.

She gets up and walks over to his side; he leans backward on the loveseat and places his left arm across its back, resting it. He looks over at Penny, "What was your husband's name? I mean, I'm just being curios." he says as he looks at her with gentle eyes.

Penny looks at him and she can sense he is the 'good guy'. "Howard." she says after she had her second thought.

"OK." he says as he nods acknowledging and starts up the computer. Penny points at the program she used, and he opens it up and she starts to elaborate as she points at the different pictures she had downloaded as ideas.

"Well, what I wanted to have done to the kitchen was something with more of an open approach and more streamlined."

He looks at the computer screen and then he says, "Can you email the pictures to me so I can do some drawings and suggestions for how we can change it for the better?"

"Sure, I'll do it right now." and she pulls the laptop onto her lap, and she looks at him, "Um, what's your email address?" she asks.

He blurts out his address almost automatically.

"Ok, consider it done." she says concluding. "So, tell me one thing..." she starts to ask.

"What would that be?" he says quickly before she has a chance to finish her sentence.

"Why did you call me today?"

He looks at her, "Why am I not surprised that you would ask that question?" he continues, "Well ... I felt why waste time, I mean the sooner we got together and figured it out we could get the wheels in motion."

Penny can sense there is a sort of chemistry building up and she needs to distract herself. "Let me put away the laptop and I will be back." she replies with confidence in her voice. She gets up from the seat, but suddenly she loses her balance and falls back into the seat and into his arms where he catches her.

"Oops, how did it go?" he says and smiles, and she smiles back embarrassed at him as he is helping her to get her bearings back.

It had been a minute since she felt a man's touch. She had to get away from him for a moment as her face was starting to change colors and she was feeling the heat buildup. This was not like her, and she didn't want to tip her hand, she was the woman who was always so poised and composed, and here he was a man who made her weak in her knees.

"Let's put away the stuff in the kitchen." she says as she needed more time to get her senses clear.

He follows with the tray; she places the laptop on the desk and turns the CD back on that was in the changer. She turns around and watches him put the dishes away, not that it took long but it was enough time to give her an opportunity to study him from a distance. Who was this man? She wanted to know more, and she had just scratched the surface.

She stands in the doorway waiting for him; Marcus turns around and has strawberries in his hand. "Shall we?" and points to the strawberries.

"Oh yeah." Penny says with immense childish desire. "I can't wait."

They walk back out; Penny lays down on the sofa on the opposite side from Marcus with her legs sticking out resting on the arm rest. She piles up the pillows behind her back, and he holds out the strawberries to her as the gentleman he is, and she grabs a handful. She slowly devours them one at the time by holding on to the stem and taking bite size pieces while making a humming sound of content. They are both quiet, and enjoy the silence, and slowly the strawberries were diminishing off the plate one after another.

"So, how long have you lived in Seattle?" Marcus opens up the conversation by asking cautiously.

Penny thinks how much information she should give him, her life was not cut and dry as most, it was more complicated, and she was someone who was hiding in plain sight. "A few years, I moved here just because of the work." she says as she stretches on the sofa, and yawns big. She tries to sound as casual as possible, and she masks it by her next move as she pops another strawberry in her mouth to pause the conversation. She was chewing on it slowly as she was thinking, and her mind was trying to be a step ahead and have natural answers to the potential future questions coming from him. She was a mix of a Leo, Sagittarius, and a Taurus; the Mercury in Capricorn, the analytical person, she was the 'everything should be nice, but don't fucking tell me what do' personality. The crazy Sagittarius with a drama free queen mannerism snatched from an act of Aubrey Hepburn's.

She had been Penny for quite a while and only now was she reminded that she had been someone else when she was thinking of being married to Howard. Only one person knew who she really was and that was Harris.

"I think I missed introducing myself properly." he says as he wipes his hand on his pant leg and stretches it out to Penny as she sits up and grabs it, "I'm Marcus Scott." he says proudly.

She smiles and in a goofy manner as she responds, "Penny Bridge, at your service."

They both laugh at each other's introduction, as this was almost the ultimate ice breaker.

As they were laughing, Damien gets up from his position and starts to give off his own noise as if he could speak. Marcus gives out another burst of laughter and looks over at his watch. "I guess this is my queue to leave, I can tell." and he points at Damien, "He spoke."

Penny pets Damien and consoles him and she feels a little disappointed, but she knew tomorrow was another day and she had to get up early. She gets up from the couch and walks Marcus over to the door, with Damien in tow. "Thank you." she says softly and smiles at him. "It's been a while since I enjoyed myself."

He looks at her with an intense look and quickly bends over and kisses her on the cheek. "No, thank you, for letting me come to see you tonight!" he says quickly, then turns around and walks out the door.

Penny lingers in the doorway and watches Marcus walk down the sidewalk. Damien walks up to the door, presses his head through the doorway looking out, and then he taps his paw on Penny's leg and she reacts and closes the door.

Marcus gets into his truck and lingers for a moment before he starts it up, his mind was back in Jordan. The conversation he had with Penny brought his own demons back to him, but he had managed to process them better than she, he had thought. His pondering wouldn't give him a break even though he was driving, he tried to distract himself and focus on the road ahead.

He recalls that on his last day in Jordan, he had spoken to his superior, coincidentally, his name was Howard but not Bridge, instead Grant. He had been killed in the blast that Penny had talked about. It was all so conflicting to him what she had said. Was there a second person with the same first name as her husband? He was now confused, and his memory wasn't the best because of his symptoms. If it had not been enough that he had PTSD, he suspected that he had CTE. He had done enough research and it was clear that he had had enough blows to his head throughout his years in the army that he was showing symptoms.

He pulls over and stops the truck as the thoughts were all too consuming, and he starts to think about the conversation he had with Penny tonight. There was something very familiar with her and yet he was not certain if that was something he had just felt because she made feel him at ease, or if there was something more to it. He knew he would need to spend more time with her and get to know her, maybe then it would reveal itself.

Marcus still had connections in the army, and he was going to find out if there was more than one Howard who was in Jordan the same time as he was. He had to follow his gut feeling on this, as it wouldn't give him any rest, the thoughts were agonizing.

Marcus pulls out his phone, scrolls down on his list of contacts, and stops at **Q**, for Quentin. He pushes for the text message box to open and begins typing, *'Q, tell me, was there another Howard at the time when we were in Jordan?'*

He stops for a second and leans back in his seat; he remembers the last conversation he had with his good old friend Howard. His last mission had been a covert matter and he was going to be released and move on to the next mission, but that never happened instead he ended up going back home as a disabled vet.

He remembers the conversation, strangely enough, clear as a day.

"I know who he is now, thank you Weaver, I owe you big time." Howard says as he grabs his shoulder.

"No, we did what we had to do, I would do it all over again." Marcus says proudly.

"You'll have to come and visit me and Jackie in the Colorado mountains when you get back home."

"Yeah, where is she, your woman? I haven't met her yet, Howard."

"You will, believe me you will, she is something else Marcus. Promise me that if something would happen to me..."

"Nothing will happen to you, stop talking shit."

"No, I mean it! If something happens to me, promise me that you'll keep an eye on her, OK?"

"OK. OK! But I'm telling you it won't, so I'm not going worry about it. You're going home tomorrow, you and Jackie. Then I'll be close behind." and Marcus laughs it off.

"OK, I will hold you to it."

Marcus closes his phone and straightens himself back up and starts up the truck up and takes off, all while his head is having questions circling in his mind, and he was hoping that Q would have an answer to his question.

BACK AT PENNY'S HOUSE Damien has jumped up on the bed where he's faithfully waiting for her. He was the one who protected her and the only companion she completely trusted.

Penny comes out of the bathroom and shuts off the light, and she crawls in under the covers. Damien has placed himself on his back totally stretched out and without any worries. Penny grabs her phone, looks over the latest emails, and then looks over the missed phone calls. She had a missed call from, "Harris?" she says out loud questioning.

Penny listens to her voicemail, *'Hey, Penny luv, call me back as soon as you get a chance, we need to talk, cheers.'*

She looks over at the time, it was too late to call him now. She knew that it sounded urgent, but she would have to call him in the morning on her way in to work. There was something in the message that felt troublesome and she couldn't stop thinking about the tone he had given off; it didn't sound good. She puts down the phone on the nightstand and pulls the cover over her shoulder and shuts her eyes.

CHAPTER 4

HARRIS IS SITTING AT HIS DESK finishing his last notes, and he stops for a second as he thinks of Penny, and why he had not heard back from her. He turns off the computer and reaches out to turn off the desk lamp when he recognizes a reflection of headlights lighting up the hallway. He looks over at the time, it is 02:30. He wasn't expecting any visitors, and his radar goes off as this was almost expected, but he wasn't expecting it so soon.

He turns off the desk lamp and gets up from the chair and walks out to the hallway and towards the stairs to the second floor. When he reaches the landing the lights are off, he peaks out the Tudor style windows facing the front, and he can see the outlines of two individuals sitting in the car. They had stopped one hundred feet away from the house where the tree line met up with the avenue. Something told him that the uninvited guests weren't there with any good intentions. A feeling creeped up that the battlefield had managed to find its way to his front door.

He walks back down quickly, and stops halfway, and presses open a hidden door in the wall panel. He turns on the only light that sheds light for direction going down the stairs. He pulls the door shuts behind him and, with swift steps, he reaches the downstairs of the house.

Harris lived on an old estate in Haddington, on the outskirts of Edinburgh in Scotland, and the downstairs parts of the house were never in use. It was a part of the house that had secrets that were out of sight and out of mind. Just a few dim lights were revealing the condition of this untouched dark part of the house. The rooms seemed have been left over from another era.

Harris walks into what looked like a dated kitchen and grabs a case that is resting against the wall. He places it on the table, opens it, and takes out his Enfield sniper rifle. He looks at it and stops briefly for a second, his mind was going over the scenarios of what he needed to do. He never thought he would have to use it, or these measures, but he had no choice, it was him or them. The rifle had belonged to his father, who had been an ex-military man, and Harris' admiration for him had made him follow his steps, but with a different direction.

He quickly assesses it, and loads the 10-round magazine, then locks it in and cocks the rifle ready. As much as he wanted to be ready, he knew that this wasn't going to be over by a long shot.

He quickly looks over at the table. Was he missing something? He sees his worn-out cap, his so-called talisman that had seen better days, and puts it on and turns it clockwise backwards. He reaches over and grabs the binoculars that were sitting on the table and puts them around his neck, he gives a quick adjustment to the scope on the rifle before he walks with steady steps to the other side.

He stops at the end of the hallway and waits for a second at the door as he listens for voices to make sure no one was standing by the door, before he slowly opens it quietly. He takes one step out and looks to the left and then to the right as he moves up another step when he suddenly hears the car start to move. They are slowly moving along the front when the car's tires hit the gravel, and it's noticeable how close they are.

Harris walks slowly towards the corner of the house and peaks around. The car had rolled all the way up to the front of the house, and he knew this wasn't good as the only advantage he had was the darkness. He could tell they were facing east by viewing them through his night vision scope. The grounds were in pitch-black mode, but the binoculars were his eyes and he watched every move that was being made.

He slowly lays down flat and gets into position as he puts his aim in the direction of the parked car. He couldn't help himself feeling curious, at the same time he knew this could only end up one way. He was ready, holding the sights on the vehicle as he surveyed the vehicle.

The passenger door suddenly opens, and a man dressed in dark clothing gets out and walks back to the trunk of the car. He can't define his features, and quickly looks around and scopes the north side, back and forth. A second person gets out and they are both now speaking a language Harris was very familiar with.

He can sense this was now or never, as the second person sticks his head back into the car to get something, he makes a split decision. He quickly fires off a shot without hesitation, and it hits the man in the car with a sharp sound and a crashing sound of breaking glass. Unexpectedly, the man by the trunk of the car turns rapidly and Harris fires off one more round. The bullet hits its mark and the man falls backward into the trunk.

The first shot had penetrated the car's window and killed the first man, and the second man met his bullet face on. As quickly as it became a potentially dire and out of control situation, it ended before it even had had a chance to start. Despite of the elimination, Harris wasn't sure if he was he alone. He waits in the shadowy darkness, holding out to see if there were more waiting out there.

"Hmm, it was either me or them," he mutters to himself as he wanted to justify the end with the means. He wasn't the person who lightly snuffed out the light in a human. He was the ultimate humanitarian who fought injustice from foreign governments and military operations involving oligarchs, but deep down inside there was still this buried renegade who came out and became the inadvertent cleaner.

He's scoping the area in the dark with his binoculars, and once he's satisfied that there are no more visitors hiding in the darkness, he secures the rifle and leans it against the wall. He slowly walks up to the vehicle's driver's side and reaches inside to see what the man had been looking for. He had fallen back under the dashboard; the body was heavy and immobile. It was no surprise to Harris; he didn't expect him to be breathing as this was a precision killing and he had only one chance to make it right.

He pulls his head back out of the car and assesses the area behind him, he couldn't be cautious enough. Harris walks back to the trunk where he finds the second man slouched over on his back with his eyes as wide open as the opening in his frontal cranium lobe where the bullet had penetrated. Harris moves him over and beneath his body the revelation was made clear; the car was full of C-4 explosives. It looked like it had a set up for multiple detonations, lined up as Christmas lights on a string, and would have had devastating results. He knew that he had made the right the decision. He looks at the house and back at the explosives, he knew by looking at the set up that they were there to rig the place.

He takes two steps back and grabs the man's legs that were resting outside the trunk and drops them into the trunk. He walks back to the driver side and grabs the other man by the legs and pulls him out of the car, and his head hits the ground with a thud. Harris drags him back to the trunk and drops his body in next to his partner. He closes the trunk and sighs heavy and exhales, "I am getting too old for this shit!" He gets into the driver seat, starts up the car, and drives it to the side of the house where he parks it out of sight from the front door. He had to get rid of the car, this wasn't the end he knew, there were going to be more people looking for him as soon as they do not hear back from the first 'team'.

He walks back and grabs his rifle and gives one last surveying eye on the area. It was silent, not a sound could be heard. He walks back inside through the side door that he came out of and walks into the kitchen and places the rifle back in the case and closes it.

He leans on the table with his knuckles, and his mind is reflecting on the work he had done in Sarajevo. It was finished a long time ago, but somehow, they were still looking for him. The story seemed to never end, war crimes would never die, and neither would the memories of the victims. The justice for the crimes that had victimized so many were pale in proportion to the magnitude of what had really happened. Harris was the one who had managed to expose the truth and hunted down the proofs while putting his own life on the line, the uncomfortable and ugly side that had a human face to it. Now he was made aware that the suspicions of him being a target were very much real and he knew that if they had found him, they also knew about Penny.

Harris walks back upstairs and into the bedroom, his thoughts were going back to the situation that had just happened, he repeated the event over and over in his mind, as the thoughts floated from the current situation to the day he and Penny had been in the crossfire in Sarajevo. He remembers escaping the house they had been caught in during a firefight, and the muddy affair when hiding in the ditches as they were staying low and covered by the terrain.

They had occasionally been walking on the road to get to the next village, and they met others on the road taking the same route. His vision was saturated with pictures of Penny talking to locals, and her face smiling back at him sporadically. Then, out of nowhere, they were again faced with a hostile military helicopter that was letting off a rain of bullets. People were falling like timber as Penny and Harris were pushed to the ground while they tried to follow the people who were running like scared animals, and who were falling victim to the bullets.

Harris and Penny were laying on the ground, shielded by the lifeless bodies of the victims of the attack. While lying under the fresh corpses and acting like they were dead, they could hear soldiers walking past and talking as they were looking for survivors.

Harris walks into the bathroom and turns on the light, he takes a good look in the mirror, he had certainly aged. His lifestyle was showing signs of aging in his appearance. He couldn't help himself from thinking of Penny, it had been a while since he had seen her. The last time he recalled was years ago, and he couldn't stop thinking of how lucky they'd been as they had managed to get out of Sarajevo with a UN convoy and back to the border.

He walks back out to the room and he looks around; he remembers her staying with him. She was the woman who won his heart so strangely, to him this was serendipity, but it only lasted for so long as she had to leave. He thought of her as someone who was to be reckoned with, and even though the trip was over, the threats poured in from various sources.

Penny had not been safe, and she reluctantly wanted to involve the FBI. She wanted to live a normal life and that wasn't going to happen, she knew; not as a Grant. There was no other way but to change her name, it had to take place to keep her life safe, and that's how she went from Jacqueline Grant to Penny Bridge.

Harris had pulled favors and he had handpicked the name, it was an innocent sounding name, something that would allow her to surf under the radar.

After all these years as a sleeper, she was again a topic of interest. The prosecuted war criminals had, yet again, new trials in the Haag and it was far from over, and tonight the problem had knocked on his door and reared its ugly face.

Harris gets into bed, and places his glasses on the nightstand, it was going to be difficult to relax, he knew that, but he was going to close the eyes and hope that it would be enough and eventually he would fall asleep

.

CHAPTER 5

THE ALARM GOES OFF AND PENNY GETS UP and walks into the kitchen. "What a night, woo!" she says while exhaling and stretches her arms up to the ceiling while yawning big. Damien is mimicking her action and gives up a large yawn. He continues watching her from his positioned in front her, and his tail is whipping across the floor.

She leans on the counter and turns on the toaster oven to 375°. She turns around and opens the freezer and eyes the scones and pulls them out. Damien is watching her and moves along like a K9; every move she makes his head follows, not missing a beat. She notices his observing her, "Oh, you want one too, huh?" she says while looking at him and places one extra scone on the baking sheet.

She grabs the Italian espresso maker and fills it with water, and then pulls out the Cuban-style coffee and fills the filter with the fresh ground coffee, tamps it down, and screws on the top and places it on the stove. She stops herself and falls into a daydream, but quickly snaps back to the present with the feeling of a cold, wet nose on her leg, and she looks down, "Alright, alright, I am making it." she tells Damien who has brought her back to the present.

There was no time for that this morning, she had to get ready and be out the door in the next hour. She hears the coffee percolate and she grabs a cup and fills it with the fresh coffee, she quickly glances at the scones through the glass door, they still had time to go.

Penny runs back to her room and pulls her clothes and shoes together, in her peripheral view she eyes her cell phone, and grabs it and drops it in her bag, as she walks back to the kitchen. Damien has located his leash and has walked up to the front door and dropped it on the door mat.

The timer on the toaster oven is going off, at the same time the doorbell is ringing. Penny hustles to pull out the scones, and in the next she speed-walks to open door, and there she was, her faithful friend and dog sitter, Jennie.

"Look at you, in a hurry as usual." Jennie cracks as she grabs the leash and Damien is whipping his tail frantically and making happy dance moves on the vinyl floor, he was ready to go without any doubt. Jennie and Damien had routines and he loved them as much as he loved sleeping in the bed next to Penny.

"You know me, always trying to get things done in the last minute." Penny responds as she was pulling everything together. She grabs her to-go cup and pours the coffee into it and then bags the scones in a paper bag while giving Damien his scone.

Jennie attaches the leash to Damien's collar and walks out the door, and Penny slips her feet into her shoes and follows her. She gives the door handle one last shake before she continues to walk over to the car that was parked by the curb. Penny glances quickly over to her left before walking out into the street and gets into the car. She pulls off from the curb and slowly cruises down the street, the window is rolled down and she holler's, "Hey Jennie, I will call you later from the office."

"OK." she responds and waves acknowledging, and watches Penny speed away.

Penny drives along the street as her mind was all over the place, work, the new acquaintance she made, and Harris. "Damn, Harris!" she exclaims annoyed. She should have called him, but now that would have to wait until she got to the office. Penny swerves along the road as she can't get to work fast enough, and there was one thing she was going to do first.

Penny walks in and people are already working. She walks by her assistant and she doesn't even notice her. She drops her bag on the desk and pulls out her phone. She walks over to the window as she looks up Harris number. Her eyes are resting on the view of buildings; she looks west, and can see the crane rom the construction site, then she hears the dial tone go through, once, twice, three times and it goes to voicemail.

Penny walks back to her desk and puts the phone down. She was puzzled over the voice message he had left her. She grabs her glasses, and turns to the computer and logs in. Suddenly there is a knock on the door. "Come in." Penny calls out as she is resting her eyes on the screen.

The door opens, and it's Spencer. She looks up from behind her glasses, "Ah, it's you." she says as she really didn't have time for him.

"Well, good morning to you too. I guess that day off wasn't enough." he says sarcastically, "Maybe I should send you off on a little longer vacation," as he gives her a look that a parent would give a child that they were less pleased with.

Penny continues to work and lingers a minute before she can think of how she is going to answer his snarky comment. She stops what she is doing and puts her glasses down, "Ok, good morning to you. Now, what can I do for you?" she says as accommodating as possible and giving him her complete attention. She had all the work that was left over from yesterday that she had to finish, and now she was forced to give up a positive attitude while this was the last thing she had in mind, considering her workload. She knew Spencer wasn't just coming in to say, 'good morning', it was something else she could tell. She looks at him with eyes telling him to spill the beans.

" Yea...there are two visitors here today from the Texas corporate office. I'm not sure what they want, but they wanted to talk to you specifically." Spencer says curiously and she can tell he is pondering on what it is all about.

"Do they have names...?" she asks and gestures with her hands openly while she shrugs her shoulders and shakes her head, as she is expecting more information.

Spencer takes a sip from his coffee cup, "Taytum and Neal..." he says and nods with his head, " I don't have a good feeling about this… but if it is about the work you have done, then I am more than pleased and happy that you work for me."

She sighs loudly as she had enough of the political civility. "You know what Spencer, I can't wait to parade around with these two ten-gallon hats and try to educate them about what needs to be done just to find out later on that they didn't give a shit about my ten cents. It's just a fucking show and pony ride, that's what it is Spence. You'll see, a circus, but remember they are not my monkeys."

Spencer is grinning behind his cup as he takes a sip of his morning coffee, he is happy to have her back, that he knows. Penny's spin on things were a comedy act to say the least.

She puts her glasses back on, looks down back at the computer screen, and without even looking at him she says, "I know Spence, its ok. Sometimes you have to let the steam out, otherwise it just gets bottled up inside and then comes out like a champagne cork."

Penny opens her email box, "Of course!" she exclaims, "I'm gone for one day and 72 emails in the email box, just brilliant, but I guess that's what this position gives, more money and more responsibilities and zero friends."

Spencer leaves the office quietly on that note, and Penny doesn't even notice him exit.

Time ticks away quickly and she manages to clean out her email box when she hears her cell phone ringing. She grabs it and looks at the screen and answers it, and on the other end she hears, "Hey, my luv.", and there is no mistake that it's Harris who has returned her call.

"Hi." she says with her satin sounding voice as her eyes land on a picture of Harris that's sitting on her desk. She listens attentively as she gets up from her chair and walks over to the window where she is looking out while pondering on the meeting and listening to Harris with a half ear.

"Oh, have I missed that voice." Harris says enticing, and then the tone changes, "Penny luv, I'm not calling you..." and Harris stops. How was he going to tell her what he had discovered?

"Yes, go on, I can sense this isn't a social call, I figured as much from hearing your voice message." she says, as she already knew it was not good news and she continues to look out the window.

"Remember Sarajevo and the war criminal we tracked down, and the evidence we provided...?" he quiets down. He knew that this was the last thing Penny wanted to hear. It had been a long time, but the scab that had covered the wound had not yet fully healed, and he knew it was being ripped off the moment he had brought it up to her.

Penny walks back to her desk and sits down in the chair as she is now paying full attention to what he's saying. She leans back in her chair while resting her eyes on his picture. She takes off her glasses and throws them on the desk then rubs her eyes from strain. "Yeah, go on." she says with a heavy feeling weighing on her.

"I've been writing an article about the new trial at the Haag with the same individuals we put away..." he pauses, "...and last night I had some uninvited guest at my house."

"What! Are you OK?" she exclaims and moves herself back up from the resting position. He had suddenly grabbed her complete attention.
"I am, but it was a close call. I think we need to get together because they are not going to go away."

"So, you took care of it?" she says referencing the visitors.

"Yeah, they are done, but I need to have the trash picked up, and I have a solution, don't worry." he says and pauses, "When these individuals are not returning calls, or show up, they will come looking and there will be more than two next time."

"Listen, I want to talk more, but I have a meeting I have to go to, let me call you back as soon as it's over." she says assuring.

"Yes, just call me back. I am going to be home." he says confirming. "If something would happen to me, just know... you mean a lot to me." he says, and the call is disconnected.

Penny gathers her paper pad and pen, and then she gets up from her chair and walks out to Julia's desk. Before she gets the chance to say anything Julia quickly utters, "They are in the conference room waiting for you."

Penny nods to Julia acknowledging her, then she walks over to the conference room and stop just outside the door; she can hear two voices having a heated discussion. She walks away, and she continues to Spencer's office, knocks on the door and she hears, *"Come in."* from inside.

Penny walks inside and sees Spencer at his computer, and the next second he turns around quickly.

"Hey there, feeling better?" he says and smiles.

"Yeah... So... tell me, what do you know about Taytum and Neal? I mean, what department are they from?"

"Whoa, I really don't know. I mean I just got an e-mail from Chätt telling met they were visiting, and that they requested to speak with you, but, if it has to do with the numbers, then I guess it's all good, maybe a promotion? Who knows..." he says and tries to keep a positive spin on it.

Penny always knows what goes on, and this visit came out of left field. "Promotion? Don't be stupid. Promoting me to what? We both know that there's nothing here that's a step up, unless they're asking me to go back to Texas, and that's really not my plan." she says with a tone that she had no intent of cooperating in any geographical change.

She walks over to the window and rests her hands on the windowpane. "I love this city... feel at home here." she says, and he can tell she was in her own thoughts. She turns around and leans back against the edge of the windowpane and folds her arms in to a resting position, then she looks at Spencer with a look that she was thinking about other things.

"Well, I guess I will just walk in there to poke the bull to see if I will get hit with the horns." she says as she walks towards the door.

Spencer stops her, "Hey..." he pauses, and Penny turns around, and he continues "...I know you were out yesterday, what happened? You seem different."

"Nothing, just another day... not enough time to ..." and she stops because she did not have time to elaborate her thoughts as Taytum and Neal were waiting for her in the conference room.

"I know that there's something going on, but you know you can always come to me and we'll talk about it." he says.

"I know, believe me, I know." she says, gives him one last look before she pushes the door handle down and walks out.

Penny walks with steady steps to the conference room where she walks in without knocking. The two men stand up as she walks in.

"Hi, please sit... I'm sorry if I am late, I was called in to a last-minute meeting." she says excusing. "I was told about this request for this meeting just today, so please forgive me if I come unprepared."

"Ms. Bridge, may I call you that?" Taytum says.

"Yes, of course... I'm sorry, I didn't catch your name." Penny says as she wasn't sure who was who.

"My name is John Taytum, and this..." he gestures, "is my associate Robert Neal."

"Ok," she says and observes them both with a measuring eye, "I don't remember you guys from the last meeting at the corporate office."

"Ah, well, I worked for another bank and Chätt, I mean, they got me onboard... Why are you asking?" Taytum asks and he doesn't know if she was just being curious or if he should feel offended.

She continues observing their behaviors.

"I didn't expect to get the third degree..." Taytum says and chuckles and tries to lighten the atmosphere in the room. He looks at Neal, and Neal chimes in laughing.

Penny continues to observe the men and breaks up their self-indulgent laughing, "So, please continue. What can I do for you guys?"

"Well, we have something that, well, how can I say, a bit of a risky situation. We have something that needs to be picked up, it's classified." he says with a tone of reservation.

"Ok, so where do I come in?" Penny says and looks confused; she wasn't a delivery boy for anyone.

"We know that you speak multiple languages, and it's beneficial in this instance. You're working in the department with lending and acquisitions, and we, well I mean, I believe you're the person to bring it back safely." he says with almost an amateurish delivery, and not before Penny had noticed that his eyes were moving side to side as if he was having a condition of some sort, but now they were moving frantically like a mad eye moody. The demeanor sets off Penny's sixth sense and she could tell this was not what he normally did, and his persuasion skills were off course.

"Bring back? What do you mean, where is this information?"

"It's in Geneva." Neal says and takes over the conversation.

"OK, so? I mean, we're here on a Friday discussing this..."

"Well, we would like to have this taken care of immediately. It's all taken care of... Your flight leaves tonight."

"Whoa, whoa, wait a minute! You expect me to get up and go on the drop of a dime?" Penny is taken aback by the suddenness of this.

Neal looks at Taytum and back at Penny, then he stands up and places his hands on the table. Penny can sense this was not up for discussion and braces herself for what was to come next.

"What we would need for you to do is to fly out to Geneva and bring back important papers for us that are being prepared as we speak. We want them to be brought back by our own people. They cannot be sent with a mail courier and they have to be retrieved from an attorney's office in Geneva. I hope that you understand that it is of the utmost importance that we get the documents to the States." he says as he looks at Penny with a calm facial expression while he tries to convey the importance of this assignment. He can see that Penny has reservations about this.

"So, I will be going alone to pick up the papers. Now what is this pertaining to?" she makes this confirming statement that she is yet to be convinced.

"It is a new business proposal that is going to change this bank's future and we don't want it ending up in the wrong hands." Taytum says with a strategic selling method; he has recognized that she is not easy to be persuaded and continues, "Listen, I know this is last minute, but at this point I'm not asking." and Taytum pushes a manila envelope toward Penny. "Instructions are inside the envelope; tickets, credit card, etc. Are we good?" he says as he is confirming while waiting for an acknowledging response from Penny.

"I guess I don't have much of a choice..." she says and looks down at the envelope.

"I've already let Geneva know that you're on your way." he says, and smiles. He hesitates for a second, and then says in broken French, "Heure de rafraîchir votre français."

Oh yeah, Penny was going to freshen up her French. What she needed was a drink to wake up; something stronger than tea was what she needed. Her head was spinning as she was thinking of what Taytum said; she also had her suspicions that this was not just about some papers, but something more serious.

Taytum concludes the matter after giving Penny her directive. He signals to Neal, who follows Taytum, and the two men leave the room without saying another word.

Penny, still sitting at the table, looks at the envelope and the over to the open door, "Fucking assholes..." she mutters to herself.

Penny grabs the envelope, gets up, and walks out of the room and over to Spencer's office. She knocks on the door and then just walks in, not bothering to wait for his OK to come in.

"Hey, busy?" she says as she notices Spencer's sitting with his back to her as he is typing on the keyboard.

"Nae, what's up? Come on in..." he says without turning around.

"You wouldn't believe this shit..." Penny says and sits herself down in a chair facing the desk.

"What happened...?" he says as he turns around looking concerned as he places his glasses on the desk.

"Those mothers just dropped this envelop in my lap and told me to drop everything I've got going on just to baby sit some papers from Geneva to the US."

"Can't be that bad... I told you earlier that I needed to send you on a longer trip. See this as your opportunity to go." Spencer looks at Penny with a sarcastic look on his face.

"Really, Spence... Listen..." Penny looks at Spencer with a look on her face that he has never seen before, and this gets his attention. "I have a bad feeling about this, this comes way out of left field, and to pick me of all people, nae, try again... It doesn't sit well with me."

Spencer is looking up and down between his papers on the desk and Penny, while listening at the same time, he is quiet and is waiting for her to finish her venting.

"I'm sorry, but had I felt this was a free vacation, I would have been doing jumping jacks celebrating, but this, nae, nae, this is no vacation!" and Penny lifts the envelope up in the air as she makes her statement clear. Spencer looks at her now and is giving her all his attention.

"This is work." Penny gets up from her chair, walks over to the door, and opens it as she looks back at Spencer. "I'll be back next week." she says as she walks out before Spencer can respond to any of what she had said.

The door shuts hard and Spencer jumps a little in his seat, this was not what he had expected, and he wasn't sure of whom they were as he had never seen them before. He suspected they were new employees, but that was all he seemed to know.

ON THE OTHER SIDE OF TOWN Marcus is walking into the UPS store. He greets the clerk as he walks up to the mailboxes. He sticks the key into the lock and opens a mailbox, he reaches in and pulls out an orange manila envelope.

He lingers as he looks around, then he opens the envelope and pulls out a folder. He gives it a brief look, then closes it and puts it back in to the envelope. He locks the mailbox and walks out, waiving back at the clerk as he exits the store.. Marcus pulls up his phone and makes a call. "Yea, I got it Q." Marcus says.

"The information is vital; we can't have it come to completion. So, Weaver, it is important that you get a hold of it before anyone else." Q instructs.

"Yeah, I understand... Just make sure the payment is ready when it's done."

"Money is not a problem, but more important is what you need to bring back. Make sure you clean up behind you."

"OK got it. Hey, listen, now to something else..." he pauses, "Did you get my message about Howard?" He says cautiously.

"Yeah, I looked into it, but nothing comes back except our Howard. Why are you asking?" Q asks.

"I was just curious, simple as that." he says as if it wasn't important.

"OK, now just get me the docs so we can close this matter." Q says commanding and ends the call.

Marcus looks around and checks his bearings as he puts away his phone.

IT'S LATE NIGHT IN DALLAS and most of the employees have left PEGC corporate office on the 42nd floor on Elm Street. The streets around the building are almost desolate, not many people are left in the Renaissance building. Only a few guards are patrolling on the ground level, letting people out as they're exiting after hours.

On the 42nd floor light is coming from the threshold of the door
of the south corner office, and occasional shadows in the light
provide a sign that someone is still lingering in the corporate
office. Inside the office a man is placing a rug and beads down
on the floor along with a green book embossed with gold Arabic
lettering. He positions the rug facing North East. He puts down
the book in front of him then opens it and continues to place
the beads next to it in a ritualistic manner. He turns around
and grabs a Kufi and Galabiyya that are placed on a nearby
desk and puts it on. He positions himself in front of the rug as
he raises his hands up starts to chant "Allahu Akbar!"

He holds his hands folded over his chest, recites the first
chapter of Qur'an in Arabic and raises his hands up again.
"Allahu Akbar!" He bows while reciting. "Subhana rabbiyal
adheem Subhana rabbiyal adheem Subhana rabbiyal adheem"
The man continues with his prayer, as this was his normal
routine.

CHAPTER 6

PENNY IS BACK IN her own office, the clock on the wall is pointing at 18.00, and she can't stop pondering on the two men who had paid her an unexpected visit; something was not right. She felt compelled to call the Dallas office. She wanted to find out if there was someone who had some inside information about what she had just been assigned to take care of.

After hesitating for a few brief moments, Penny picks up the phone and dials the corporate number. Her call goes to a voicemail recording stating that is the office was closed for the day. This was not her way of starting her first day back at the office and now she was bound to leave again.

MARCUS IS PULLING OUT HIS duffle bag and drops it on the bed. He stops for a moment as he ponders on what to pack and it then hits him, "Penny!" he says out loud. He had not spoken to her today and he felt a void because he had not heard her voice and he wanted to see her before he left. Marcus had yet to read the fine details of his assignment, but that didn't matter as he knew he would get to it, but first he wanted to talk to Penny. She was the first woman in a long time who had caught his attention, there was something about her he liked, and he couldn't put a finger on it.

He grabs his phone, dials her number, and a couple of rings later he can hear her soothing voice. "Hey, Penny girl, are we still on for tonight?" he asks and waits on her reaction, as he knew damn well that they didn't have any plans.

"I didn't know we were. Are you telling me or asking me?" and she gives up a laugh as she is just being funny.

"Well, a guy can try." he says with a little confidence and sass in his tone.

"Well...I have to go out of town..." she says, and her voice has changed from being upbeat to disappointment and that something wasn't right. "I won't be back until next week."

"Oh, ok, can you tell me about it, where you're going?" he asks, and he was a little surprised now as he didn't expect her answer.

"Man, you're curious... well it's not a national secret, I need to go to Geneva to pick something up." she says less than enthusiastic.

"OK, will I see you when you get back?" he continues with more questions

Penny starts to feel it's too much. Too many questions, and why so persistent. Penny wasn't used to a man wanting to see her, Dee had been the opposite as she had been the one to chase his calendar to pencil in a simple face to face. "Listen…" and she stops herself; no, she didn't want to sound annoyed or irritated, it wasn't his fault that she was in this situation and she did want to see him, and she quickly changes her tone. "Yeah, we can, but, know this, I really didn't plan this trip, it was just sprung on me. I can't tell you any more than that, so no more questions, please." She says pleadingly and hoping she had been diplomatic enough and not hurt his feelings.

"I understand, no more questions." he says and sounds a little reserved. His thoughts brought him back to his own reality that he had things he needed to do, and this was the best time to do it as it allowed him to not have to explain anything since she was going to be away herself. "You just call me when you get home, I'll be here." he says with a tone that he couldn't wait for her return.

"OK, I can't wait to be back." she says and snickers a little before she disconnects the call.

Marcus pulls out the folder from the manila envelope, he looks at the first page, destination 'Geneva'. "Hmm, what's the chance of us going to the same place?" he says out loud. He grabs his phone and scrolls over the contacts and makes another call.

"I need the plane ready early in the morning; 04:00 at Renton."

"Yes, Mr. Weaver, and it's the regular as usual?" the man says.

"Yes, John, you know it." and he ends the call. Marcus pulls the duffle bag open and starts to put a set of clothes into it, he had to travel light. It was a quick extraction and no trail to be left behind, and no casualties, that was his MO. He drops the manila folder and his tablet in the bag. He looks over at his nightstand and grabs his faithful money clip with his battalion seal on it, he rubs the seal as he was thinking of his men. This was his lucky charm and he went nowhere without it, especially on his assignments. He drops it in the bag on top of the other items.

Marcus was a sleeper just like many other soldiers that had left the army, ready to be called in on delicate matters that had to do with national and international securities.

PENNY IS TURNING OFF her computer and is starting to clear things up when it dawns on her that she needs to make arrangements for Damien. The whole day had been absorbed by work and she had not had a chance to check in on Damien. She picks up the phone and dials Jennie.

"Hey there… what are you guys doing?" Penny says cheerfully, although she wasn't, and she hated to ask for help because of her independent streak, she was so used to doing things on her own. It was her defense mechanism, how she protected herself.

"We are good, aren't we Deedle Beetle!" Jennie says as she calls out to Damien, and Penny can hear him pant and make noises as if he was trying to speak. "So, when are you coming to pick him up?" she asks casually.

"Well… that's just it, I need you to help me this once." Penny says in a lower speaking voice as it was almost painful for her to utter those words.

"What's happened?" Jennie says in worried tone while she is asking.

"A lot of things; I have been assigned a 'pick up' assignment, but if you can't I can ask another friend of mine, I am sure he wouldn't mind doing it." Penny says accommodating.

Jennie can read between the lines that she needed to keep Damien a little longer. *"No, I am OK, of course I want to take care of him, he is my buddy."* Jennie says as she is petting Damien.

"OK then, I'm leaving tonight, and I should be back by in a few days. You have my number if you need anything."

"We will be OK, just take care of your business and call me when you get back." Jennie says.

Penny ends the call and gets up from her chair and stretches her stiff body. The sun had gone down, and it was dark outside. She stops for a second in her tracks, and her thoughts are wandering off to Marcus. She rests her arm against the window as she watches the hazard light on the crane across the way and a smile creeps across her face as she was contemplating on how she wanted the simple life and still be excited about the future. She wanted to do something that she enjoyed, that was more like a hobby yet getting paid for it. The job she was having was satisfying, but it was not worth it, the stress, and the money she was making was not offsetting any of it.

She no longer wanted to be single, and he, well he maybe was the future, he was so different from Dee she could tell instantly on one hand, and then he had Howard's qualities and that was

what made her feel so comfortable. He talked, and he wanted
to hold a conversation, contrary to Dee who always suspected
someone in wrongdoing, a true reflection of his own actions.
Penny knows that it is too premature to even think in those
tracks, but for now she was going to have to go home and pack
down a small bag and head to the airport to catch the flight
that she was booked on and get back as soon as possible to get
it over with.

She grabs her coat, and turns off the light, and walks out and
closes the door to the office. Penny drives through the city in an
almost autopilot fashion as her thoughts were all over the
place, and without much thinking she arrives home. She sits
for a second in the car and thinks about the facts and that she
was going back to familiar territories. She exits the car and she
stop for a second to listen, it's quiet in the street. She gave her
regular scope of the surroundings before proceeding to the front
door, this was her regular routine, never left anything to
chance.

She walks up to the door, and she can smell the signs of spring,
a fresh wet grassy smell. She sticks her key in the lock, she can
hear the click as it unlocks, and pushes it open. There was no
Damien greeting her like she was used to, and it was bothering
her. She could sense a strong ominous feeling was making itself
present and the hair were standing straight up in the back of
her neck.
She continues inside and lets her hand slide on the wall, and in
the next the porchlight was turned on and she closes the door
behind her.

She walks through the house in the dark with just the natural light from the outside lighting up the place, as she passes through the living room into the bedroom. She lunges the bag onto the bed and continues into the closet and stops herself for a second to assess what she was packing and then she pulls out a bag and opens it up.

Her eyes suddenly catch her portable fireproof safe that was screwed into the floor. "Yeah, the passport." she says out loud, and then she sits down and pulls out the keys. Penny opens the white sentry safe box and grabs the first passport on top and looks at it. It reads *'Jacqueline Grant'*, she continues to rummage through the box and pulls out another one, she opens it up and she looks at it, *'Penny Bridge'*, she puts the other one back, but, before she closes it, she sees the dog tags with her late husband's name on them. She places her right hand over them and lets the hand linger before picking them up. She holds them tight in her hand as she closes her eyes. The pictures flashes by her as she recalls the last time she had seen them on him, he was on the stretcher. There were no doubts, Penny missed him, and it had been a while since she had to go through the box and her memories. They had lately started to haunt her again and surface like an old ghost, and why was that, she wondered. She could sense a change in the atmosphere, a change was heading in from over the horizon and it was coming on slow, but without a doubt she could sense it coming towards her.

CHAPTER 7

PENNY PULLS INTO THE LONGTERM PARKING and scurries to the elevators. She walks up to the counter and hands over her passport to the agent, and checks in her luggage. He looks at her, and back at the passport, all while she glances over to her left and watches the other travelers. Her eyes suddenly catch what she thinks is a familiar face. She looks back at the agent and listens to the information that is given to her. Penny is tired, and it had been a long day, but it wasn't over yet. She looks back to take a second look at the individual she saw moments ago, and he is gone. She could swear that she saw Mr. Taytum.

Penny is handed her boarding passes, and she takes them all while her attention is elsewhere and she slowly heads to the security checkpoint. On the way she looks around to see if she could spot the individual she had seen minutes before while was checking in. Penny starts to pull out her phone when someone bumps into her, she turns around. A black man looks up at her, "Oh, I'm sorry." he says and gives up a bashful smile.

She smiles back at him and turns around and continues to look over her phone for messages. Penny can sense the looks from him staring at the back of her neck. She can smell him, and she recognizes it, it was Dee's favorite fragrance. The black Varvatos and it brought back memories when things were good between them, but she knew now his interest in her had just been 'fake'. It wasn't real, except he was really interested in what he could get out of the relationship on self-serving terms.

This brought back childhood memories, the memories of being the youngest sibling of six sisters to a single mother. Everyone was fending for themselves and everyone was acting out of self-serving purposes. It was that survival mechanism that kicks in when you are in the jungle, but this one was made of concrete. She knew all too well what is was like being poor, and not having enough, and she had been determined to leave those conditions in the past and not look back.

Growing up, her mother never took time to give anyone any motherly love or attention, it was just a daily grind to get through the day. It was clear why Penny had not been able to hold on to a man until she met Howard. Her life had been a domestic prison, with her mother as the warden, but without the true motherly love. Not feeling that she was loved had made her develop trust issues and if someone said they loved her she would ask why. She knew people said they loved, but how many people meant it, people tended to say things for self-serving purposes, so she asked. She wanted definition, it wasn't good enough with the words, and when she heard them say *"I don't know"*, she had the superior feeling that she was right, yet again she was Ms. always right. The trust issue was with men, and it wasn't strange, her father had made threats of kidnapping her as a young girl, and if she wasn't confined at home she was living under an assumed name in school. After her father had abandoned the idea and her as a child, she was still living under these conditions of being watched and any kind of normal childhood was eradicated, and she grew up fast in more ways than one.

There had been this routine of waking up, and dealing with the days as they hit you, and that was the normal life for Penny. In all reality it had never been normal, but for her, she had nothing else to compare it with. Arguments and fights that went from verbal altercations between her and her sisters to physical fights.

Penny's heart had hardened during her childhood years, she had created this shield in the form of a wall surrounding her like an impenetrable fort. She had been receptive to other's information and soaked it up like a sponge, and she had mastered how to keep the conversation stuck in a one-way direction. She knew how to make the other person the center of attention and she did this to avoid letting anyone ask her questions. She had learned to interact by giving information around the topic of conversation just to make the other person feel she was sharing, but it was not on a personal level, more of an opinionated one. There was no doubt why Penny had chosen the psychology degree as her first major, she already mastered it in her daily life. Finance had been her minor because of her easy understanding of numbers, which would be something she was able to later fall back on.

She remembers the day she had left her childhood home and moved in with a friend. Conveniently enough the person was never home, so the place was basically empty. It was her safe haven, her escape, and that had been her life since she was 17, a long escape. She had fended for and defended herself since she was a young child, and escaped her dark days growing up. No one knew this about Penny, no one except Howard. That was why Howard had been the love of her life, she had been able to open up to him and she felt safe with him, but that had been abruptly ripped from her and she was alone again.

She was a strong independent woman, and she had proven that by finishing school and attaining a graduate degree on her own. She owed no one any gratitude, it was by hard work, determination, and tenacity. The memories were constantly reminding her of the time she was trying to reconnect with her mother. The proud moment of presenting the accomplishment of her degree, not even then had her mother shown any admiration or motherly love or even said anything remotely positive; there was this concealed sense of contempt, a sort of jealousy that Penny had managed to do it, and her mother had not. It had been a response of a simple, *"Oh, ok.".*

"It's your turn." she hears a soft-spoken voice say.

Penny turns around. "Oh, I'm sorry, my mind was elsewhere." she excuses herself and proceeds to go through the security checkpoint still in autopilot mode. She had been moving along through the security checkpoint line mechanically all while rewinding her life story in her mind. She felt a little embarrassed that she was been so absent minded.
She hurries and grabs her shoes and carry-on bag from the conveyer belt, and walks to the gate while continuing to feel

occupied with thoughts but now they had shifted onto the assignment she was given.

The sense that there was more to it than just simply 'bring home the document' was overwhelming. It was Taytum's demeanor that set it off from the beginning and his response to her asking questions that had presented a red flag. He didn't seem to like how he was questioned by her, and his way of telling her just to do it was not sitting well with her either.

She can see that the boarding has already started as she is approaching the gate, and while she's slowly walking up, she's passed by the man who was behind her earlier. He seemed more in a hurry than she was, and she watches him stop at the very same gate that she was going to. She smiles at the situation of how people travelled these days; hurry, hurry, and... wait. Like with everything else, things had to be done quickly, and then it was this wait that one couldn't escape.

Penny reaches the desk, hands over her boarding pass, and slowly walks down the jetway where she comes to a halt at the entrance to the aircraft. The man who had been behind her was now in front of her. She can't help but smile, they were at the same point and yet she had taken her time.

Penny finally gets to her seat, and it was in the first-class part of the plane. She places her coat in the overhead compartment and sits down in her seat. She could hear the door to the plane shut, and she knew that they would shortly be up in the air. She pushes the window cover up and looks out at the dark tarmac. Lights were lit up and a few men were running around getting the plane ready for departure.

Penny is tired and her head and eyes are demanding rest, she closes them for a second and suddenly she can feel the plane is making a jerking motion as it starts to be pushed back from the gate. She can hear the flight attendant talking about safety precautions; the words are slowly fading away and becoming background noise until Penny's fallen into a deep sleep.

Almost as soon as she's fallen asleep, she's being nudged by the attendant who asks, "Would you like a blanket to cover yourself up?"

Penny looks up in a daze and smiles back while she nods agreeing and grabs the blanket. While she covers herself up she can see the man who she had in front of her earlier heading toward his seat. He looks up and meets her eyes and gives up a smile again. Penny forces a smile and she can sense the cheeks temperature rise, she was blushing right back at him, there were nowhere to escape his looks now, and he was aware of her presence.

Penny closes her eye's and falls back to slumbering, she needed just a few hours of sleep just so she could feel a little better when she woke up. She needed a more coherent mind for what she was about to do next.

The nine-hour flight had almost come to an end, and Penny had been watching the sun rise over the horizon and set high overhead. It was almost noon in London, but Penny's watch was pointing at 15.00. She looks out the window and can see the movement of the plane as it starts to turn and descend through the clouds. As the plane comes through the clouds, the

Captain makes an announcement that it was already 11:00 local time.

Her thoughts are back in Seattle, thinking of Damien and of Marcus. She had never felt so adamant about getting the information and hurrying back home. There was a longing for exploring this new-found acquaintance she had discovered, and this trip was putting a wrench in the original plans. She closes her eyes for a second and Harris crosses her thoughts. Their last conversation and the call she hadn't been able to make was bothering her, but she would, when they landed, she would call him back.

The apprehension and prosecution of war criminals they were liable for had been a high price for Penny, she had to go underground and this was not something she had wanted because she knew that a past of this caliber would eventually come back, and it was just a matter of time that something was going to give.

She remembered the day when Harris had told her that he had got wind of information that she was compromised, and her identity had been revealed:

"We are going to have to change your name, change everything." Harris said.

"What do you mean, everything?" Penny asks.

"You can no longer be Jacqueline Grant, we need to give you a more regular name, something more innocent, something that is going to bring... luck..." Harris says as he scratches his chin.

Then he looks back at Penny with a calculating smile, "I know... Penny!"

She looks at him, and she says, "Penny... Penny..." repeating. She smiles, "It rolls off the tongue easy, but how can I change it? Also, I have a passport with 'Jacqueline' in it, so how do I get back to the States?" she says and for a brief second she had hope, but quickly fell back into a state of defeat.

"Let me worry about that." he rebuts and walks away.

Penny sat in an armchair by the fireplace in Harris's office while listening to the sound of his voice in the hall that was adjacent to the room. It was almost as if she was pushed out of the chair in a bionic fashion and guided to the door where she stopped just off the opening and the conversation became much clearer.

"Hey, it's Benjamin, I need clearance." he says, and continues, "East Lothian. Code; Echo Hotel-4-1".

It's quiet for a moment, then she hears him continue the conversation. "I need an identity change... I need it all, new passport, ID, etc., and the name is Penny Bridge... I will send you a photo, and she's a US citizen, former FBI. Make sure... do not screw this up. Oh, and one more thing, keep this highly classified, this is not temporary, but permanent."

When the call was over Penny stepped out into the hallway and Harris jumped as he wasn't expecting her. The look he gave her she'd never forget, and, at that moment, it was in the open. The statement was made; there were no more secrets between them. He knew that she knew, and he had no other choice but to reveal it all, to tell her everything. That day Penny found out that Harris was not just a 'simple' war correspondent, but so much more, and his connections were running well oiled; he was an MI6 operative.

Penny's thoughts are disrupted by the sound of the landing gear being extended. Moments later the plane touches down on the runway and the breaks are applied. This results in a very loud sound as the 450-ton plane is rapidly decreasing in speed to a much slower taxing speed for use on the tarmac until the Captain parks it at the gate.

The overhead lights shut off and Penny unbuckle herself. She looks around watches other passengers standing up in the plane. She moves over to the seat closest to the aisle and slowly stands up to stretch her body. She opens the overhead bin and pulls out her jacket and bag. At the same time, the man ahead of her stands up and everything goes in slow-motion as she has no chance to avert the situation and accidentally hits him on his head with her bag. The man grabs his head and looks over at Penny, and she can tell he is hurting. "I'm so sorry!" Penny quickly apologizes.

"OK, I'm ok, but you know if you wanted to strike up a conversation, there is another way of doing so," he says with a straight face.

Penny doesn't know what to think and she gets quiet and gives him a look as she was not certain why he would say something like that.

The man starts to laugh, and Penny starts to grin, and reaches out her hand, "My names is Penny." she says as she smiles and is embarrassed at the same time now that she knows he was playing.

He responds back, "Bradford, Seels Bradford." and smiles back at her and continues, "Is this your final stop?" as he pulls out his own bag.

"No, I have a connecting flight. What about you?" she says casually.

"I am making a short stop and I will continue later on." he says as if this was his usual deal.

There's a wait in the aisle as others are getting ready to exit the plane.

As she gets inside the terminal, she realizes that it's too early to call and check up on Damien. Her eyes are searching for a big clock, and she stops at one attached to the wall with roman numerals displaying 11:45 local time. She removes her watch and starts to turn the little wheel on the side to set the correct time. While she's turning the wheel, she can see off to her side a McDonalds, and her stomach starts to growl. She knows it's too early for that as her biological clock had not yet been reset to local time.

She slowly continues to walk through the terminal, and, miraculously, a Starbucks appears. She walks inside to grab something simple to eat as she knew when she was arriving in Geneva that she would have dinner. She grabs her order and starts walking towards the gate for her connecting flight.

She felt a sense of relief that there was only a two-hour flight left on the trip. She needed to stretch her legs from sitting down for so long.

Penny let her eyes wander in a resting mode while walking by the big windows looking out at the airfield as planes were taking off and landing, all while she would occasionally sip on her coffee. In the window she could see the reflection of Bradford, the man from the plane, talking to a Middle Eastern man. She continues to walk toward the gate to where the plane to Geneva was parked. In the distance she could hear someone yelling behind her. "Hey... hey!"

She slowly turns around and she could see Bradford catching up with her. "Hey, wait up for me." he says in between his heavy breathing.

"Wow!" she says and snickers while she waits for him to catch his breath while he is resting his hands on his knees.

"I wanted to know if we could exchange numbers, and when I get back to the States I could call you." he says and gives off a kind and gentle look.

Penny grabs her bag and pulls out a pen and a piece of paper and writes down her number and hands it to him.

He grabs the paper, "Thanks." he says and motions the piece of paper up in air. "I will send you a text so you will have my number too." he says and puts the paper in his pocket.

They continue walking towards Penny's gate, "Will you be ok now?" he asks when she stops.

"What do you mean, why wouldn't I be?" she asks.

"One can never be too protective of a woman travelling alone." he says concerned.

Penny gives up a laugh, "Oh, I think I can handle this, you should just walk a mile in my shoes, then you'd understand." she says as if this was child's play.

He looks at her with an observing look and, on that note, they part ways. As he walks away, he waves back at her with his back toward her, and she looks at him with interest how a simple bump at the airport could turn into a phone number exchange.

Penny finds a spot by the windows and sits down while she waits for the announcement to board the plane. She takes a moment to review the manila envelope with all the instructions. The address for the hotel reservation is jotted down on a stick-it-note and put on the instruction sheet. *Hotel Royal, on Rue De Lausanne. Attorney Office of Shariq Afifi Esq. on Quai du General-Guisan 16, Lausanne, visit the security desk for instructions.'*

Penny continues to look through the envelope and she finds an enclosed box the size of a matchbox. She looks at it and she recognize the type it was. There were instructions to wait to open it until she got to Geneva when she arrived at the attorney's office. She knew better, she had to be a step ahead of the game, so waiting was not an option for her. She looks up and casually surveys the area as she aligns the box with her wrist when it gives off a small click and unlocks.

Penny had a secret that she had shared only with Howard. He had made a universal key out of her. Penny had an implanted RFID transponder and had used her as a Guinea pig to see how long it could stay active or if it would corrode. This had been a project that never took off and it was scrapped by the FBI, but only Penny and Howard knew that she had one of the keys. This secret was now hers alone, and she had kept it from everyone, including Harris. Despite of everything, she had been mostly an open book with him, but this she had kept to herself.

She pushes the inner box out, and inside there was a small piece of paper with a code on it; JO962. It had to be important to have been placed in a box with a such lock. She closes and locks the box and puts it in her pocket. She reaches back into the envelope and pulls out a credit card that has her name on it which she promptly tucks in her back pocket. She folds up the envelop and puts it back in her bag.

She leans back in her chair and reflects on the meeting with Taytum, and the envelope he had given her. He knew what this was all about, more so than he wanted to give the impression of. To elude that this was just a simple courier assignment and think that she was going to just go along with it was a mistake. She had this feeling in the back of her mind that she was going to be in for something more than she had bargained for, but she had been forewarned as her intuitiveness and empath ability was telling her that it wasn't good. Yet, she felt compelled to follow through on it, not out of inquisitiveness, but out of a protective nature.

The announcement goes out that they were ready to start to board the plane. Penny looks at her ticket, she was one of the first in line to get on. She pulls her jacket off her lap and places her bag on her shoulder and gets up to get in line to board the flight.

CHAPTER 8

MARCUS GETS OUT OF THE CAB, he grabs his oversized duffle bag from the backseat, then reaches back into the cab and hands the driver a wadded up 20-dollar bill and shuts the door. The cab drives off, and Marcus lingers by the curb for a bit. He looks up at the sky as if he was looking for help, but not knowing if someone had his back. All that can be seen is a dark painted sky with diamonds twinkling back at him. He looks down at his watch and the time hits 04:00, for some it's early morning, but for him, this was just a routine matter.

He swings his bag up on his shoulder and walks with steady steps through the gate and up to the Hawker 400XP jet that's waiting on the tarmac.

"Welcome back Mr. Weaver, it is all set for you." the concierge greets Marcus as he is walking up the steps.

Marcus smiles, "Thank you John." and hands him the bag as he steps inside and sits down with a big sigh in the oversized leather seat by the window. He takes off his trucker Levi's jacket and throws it on the seat next to him and buckles up.

The door of the jet closes, the engines start to rev up, and the plane slowly moves on to the 2,500 feet runway. In minutes the plane is up in the air, and Marcus kicks off his boots. He looks at his watch and sets the time and it automatically synchronizes it.

John comes by and hands Marcus the schedule for the flight and a bottle of water. "It's been a while since we saw you, Mr. Weaver."

"I know John, maybe things will change... just maybe.". He grabs the itinerary and starts to go through the flight schedule while John walks back and returns with an envelope.

"You already got some information, but this is the last of it from the Major. He made sure that I got it to you, just let us know where you are going to stay, OK..." he asks confirming.

"Ok, I will have it all set by the time we land."

"Very good Sir." John returns to the back of the plane and disappears behind a curtain.

Marcus looks out the window and his eyes are resting on the lights on the ground as they turn color and get smaller as the plane is climbing fast into the sky.

Since he met Penny everything had changed. He thought he had planned his future, but it had come to a shrieking halt. This time taking the jet did not involve any illegal actions; as far as he knew, this was going to be a simple job to extract something. It did however remind him of the time before he went to jail. Just the thought of it jolted his anxiety to kick in.

He grabs his jacket and pulls out a jar of 40 mg Xanax, takes one pill, and opens the bottle of water and lets it go down with a large gulp. He leans back into the seat, takes a deep breath, and rest his eyes on the envelope he was given.

Marcus's past was a dark and sordid one, and it started in early age. He had lived on the other side of the law from the age of 14, when he had been introduced to gang related activities, which later made him very much involved in drug trafficking, firearms violations, and even murder was part of his rap sheet. He had been struggling ever since he came out of jail with the memories of his past that were etched in mind and all over his body, carrying evidence in plain sight of his dark and seedy past, and yet so unfamiliar to the eye of the common man.

In the end, reality caught up with him and the slammer became his place of residence for ten years. The years had changed him as a person. He knew that if he would have a second chance in life, that he needed to start it all over; turn his back to the other side of the law. In his prior life he had been faced with fearless situations, dangerous and challenging matters. He had contemplated many times on how he could use those interpersonal skills. The jail had disciplined him and harden his shell and made it Teflon. He knew he needed to have consistency in his days so there was no other choice, he would enlist in the army.

He had been successful in utilizing his skills and was quick minded, that was until the unfortunate day in Jordan, then it all changed again. Marcus knew that he was still processing that event, and the fact that he had not been able to find Jacqueline. He made the promise to Howard, a code of honor that was unspoken, to take care of her, but had been unsuccessful in tracking her down. For all he knew she could have died, but he didn't want to think like that, and yet she had completely gone ghost on the world.

He looks down upon the envelope and pulls out the piece of information that Major Quentin had sent his way, and an old picture falls out. He leans down and picks it up, then he glances over it before he looks at the note.

"The person is staying at Hotel Royal. We only have a picture of her given to us by the source. The Shariq Afifi's Esq. office on Quai du General-Guisan 16 is the location of where the information is stored. Extract, and send it to me."

He looks at the picture again, it reminded him of Jordan. Although it had been a minute since he had been in those territories, he would never forget Mafraq, never. That was where everything stopped. He puts the picture down and lets it rest in his hand as his eyes are getting sleepy. With the picture etched in his mind as the last thing he had seen, he is now fast asleep.

PENNY'S FLIGHT LANDS 13:30 LOCAL TIME IN GENEVA; the temperature had changed, and it was warmer. Penny tosses her jacket on her shoulder and walks towards the exit in a slow pace. She had arrived, and this was supposed to be the extended vacation she needed, but who was she kidding, she knew better, and all she could think about was to leave. She shakes her head in nuisance and disbelief.

Penny keeps walking until she reaches the right luggage carousel, and she can see the conveyer belt move but no bags had yet arrived. She pulls up her phone and paces slowly back and forth as she texts Harris and waits for the luggage to start dropping out.

"Hi, I'm in Geneva, I will call you when I get situated." and she hesitates before she presses the send button. She knew that he would be surprised, this was her first trip back to Europe since the time she had been in Scotland.

She can see her luggage on the carousel in her peripheral view, and she walks up and grabs it. She looks around to find the exit sign and walks towards it to find a taxi. She'd barely stepped onto the curb when a taxi rolls up. Hotel Royal was located roughly 2 miles away from the airport, she knew, and it was going to be a quick ride, but, with traffic, that wasn't a guarantee.

The taxi ride took her along the streets of Geneva, passed the white contemporary buildings, the Smurf houses and chapels. Penny relaxes as she is taking in the surroundings and, before she knew it, the car pulled up to the curb at the hotel.

The taxi driver turns to address Penny, "We have arrived Madame!" he exclaims.

Penny looks up at the man, "Say again." she says a little startled.

"Hotel Royal." he repeats, and he points at direction of the curb to show that she had arrived.

"Oh, yes, of course." she says and pulls out her cash then hands the driver the money and opens the door.

The man jumps out, opens the trunk, pulls out her bag, and hands it to her.

Penny looks up at the building, the hotel was located on a busy street. The doorman stands by the curb watching her as she walks through the turnstile doors.

Inside the hotel, the lobby was whispering of a business-like elegance, and she scans the area while she walks toward the check-in counter. She observed the hustle and bustle motions; flowers arriving, housekeeping staff conversing with the front desk, and a bellman pushing a luggage cart to the elevators.

As she walks through the lobby, she can hear her shoes hit the marble flooring, and conversations in different languages before she reaches the counter. Her senses were working, the smell, the atmosphere, the international feel the hotel was exuding, this was home for her in a way that was inexplicable. She was not only multilingual, she was one of them, holding Mediterranean roots with Scandinavian upbringing. This was ultimately her playground.

It wasn't hard for her to blend in, she had traveled extensively as a youngster and she knew how to interact with the people, as they were different both in mindset as in the hospitality. This was more relaxing to her, a territory she was familiar with, and yet Penny was damaged by her experiences and she kept her guard up these days. One thing she had quickly learned was to always make sure she knew what was going on within the 360 degrees around her.

Penny gets into her room and she can feel the warm air hit her. She walks up to the window and opens it up to let fresh air in and clear out the warm congested feeling that she walked into. She leans out the window to get a view of what was going on below. The commotion outside was traveling up to her level and she smiles; there was a feeling of being home creeping up in her. She gives the street a last look before she gets back into the room and pulls the sheer drapes to cover the windows before she gets undressed.

CHAPTER 9

BRADFORD IS STANDING BY THE WINDOW and watching the sun set over Lake Geneva. He turns around and picks up the phone and dials. The call is answered quickly, "Bradford here."

"Did she arrive?" the man on the other end says.

"Yes, the front desk called me moments ago."

"OK, we just go forward with the next move?" the man questions.

"She will be here tomorrow and when I am done, I will wire you the funds. Who has the code to open it?" Bradford asks.

"She does, it was part of her package, you'll have to get it from her, it's in a box and the key is part of the USB key."

"What about Neal??

"He doesn't know, and I will have it that way, can't have too many cooks involved in this."
"OK, I hear you, I'll get back to you when I have it." and Bradford disconnects the call.

PENNY WALKS OUT OF THE SHOWER with a towel wrapped around her head and another around her waist. She passes in front of the window where she leans on the ledge and looks out. It was getting a little chilly and Penny takes a deep breath and releases it with a big sigh and gets a little emotional as she had time to think.

Here she was, nestled in the streets of Geneva all alone and with too much time on her hands and too much time to think. There was no Damien that she could reach out to and hug, and no Howard she could lean against and feel completely relaxed and safe with.

The sun had set, and the noise was soaring up from the street, her thoughts are distracted by the honking horns and people talking and laughing. A man looks up at Penny and waves, she smiles and waves back as she pulls herself back inside and closes the window. She walks up to the side table where her laptop was charging. Suddenly there is a knock on the door, she walks over and looks through the cat eye. Room service had arrived with her dinner, she opens the door.

"Bienvenue à tous!" Penny greats the waiter.

"Merci." the waiter responds and pulls the cart inside and places the food tray on top of the coffee table.

"Merci... Bonne nuit." Penny says as she watches the waiter roll out the cart.

"Bonne nuit, Madame." he responds as he rolls the cart out the door and pulls it shut behind him.

Penny grabs the tray and places it on the bed and grabs her laptop. She activates the login by scanning her hand across the side and waits for it to load up. Her laptop had security measures that she had placed on it, and few were privy to the fact that she was a 'jack of all trades', a lone wolf renegade when she had to be. Her tech savvy demeanor had been groomed since early childhood with help from the people from her past.

Penny's closest friend was 'the Owl', someone she trusted unreservedly, and she had known him since as long as she could remember. He was a brilliant code hacker and a protégé computer intelligence, and he had been considered the best kept secret in town. Throughout the years she kept in contact with him, if there was something she needed to have done when she wasn't resourceful enough to handle it herself, she counted on him. She was out and about in the world, and he was in Sweden, and they were working together, but remotely.

The computer pulls up the remote desktop login screen, and Penny enters her credentials. She had only been gone for 12 hours, but there were scores of emails to reply to, and, like she had expected, this "vacation" was just a mere illusion, like she had hinted to Spencer, this was work at the finest.

Between the bites of her dinner Penny works diligently to answer the majority of her emails. She does this for as long as she can keep her eyes open. Penny leans back and grabs her phone and looks for a phone number when she sees that it has already hit midnight.

She had her directives to be in the office the next day, but she also knew she needed her full night sleep. Everything she'd planned to do was being pushed back due to interference by work related matters.

She gets up from the bed and picks up the food tray from the bed and places it on the coffee table.

She pulls the cover aside, removes the towel and lets it drop on the floor. Penny was the one that slept in her birthday suit, she did not believe in sleeping with her clothes on, it was under very special circumstances it would occur, but it was highly uncommon.

She lays down on her left side and she could tell it was still warm outside from as she could hear the air condition unit turn on and off. She leaves the cover off to allow her naked body to be exposed to the air. As she laid there, she was resting her eyes on the white sheer window drapes. The neon lights from the street flickered through the drapes, but Penny's mind was blank; her mind was drained and tired as she'd been going like an Energizer Bunny from a regular day to an unexpected freight train like journey. Her eyes started to feel heavy as if someone was disconnecting her from the energy source that kept her going, and within a few moments the flickering neon lights were dissipating, as she was warped into a deep sleep.

MARCUS JET WAS heading inbound, and about to land. The sound of the wheels hitting the ground and the breaks being applied woke him up from his slumber. It was 00:30, and the tarmac was light up at Jet Aviation airport in Geneva. Marcus looks up a little dazed and sees John sitting down facing him.

"We have arrived." John says factually as he looks at Marcus, it was a look that stated it was time to work.

Marcus grabs his phone, turns off the airplane mode, and within moments the messages started coming in. He scrolls down to review the confirmation for the hotel reservation; he had received.
"I have a booking at the Royal, let him know." he says and looks up at John and receives a nod that it was noted.
John unbuckles himself and proceeds walking up to the cockpit while the plane was slowly taxing into park. Marcus had placed his attention out the window; he realized he had left in the dark and arrived the same way.

John comes back and again sits down in the seat directly in front of Marcus where he leans forward with his hands intertwined and looks up at him. He had a concerned facial expression and with a somber voice he says, "I have a car waiting for you when you get off the plane that will take you to the hotel. You have a few days to get it, then we're taking off. As soon as you're ready, you let me know."

"OK." is all Marcus can say as he knew the look all too well, his task wasn't easy, and John had been around a few times, so he knew what was at stake.

"We'll be here a few days, that's all." John says and hands Marcus a card with coordinates, points at it, and continues, "Use that to contact us through your phone, it's an encrypted code." He looks at Marcus, taps him on the leg, as he gets up from his seat and walks over to the door to get it ready to open it.

Marcus bobs his head forward, "OK, got it." he says to himself as he looks down at the card. As the plane comes to a full stop he grabs his bag as he gets up from his seat. There was a short window of time, he knew, and he had to be quick.

When Marcus exits the door, John pats him on the back, "Be careful out there." he says as comforting as possible. As Marcus takes his last step off the stairs, John pulls the clamshell style door shut.

A car with dark tinted windows was sitting on the tarmac waiting for Marcus. A man dressed in a black suit gets out from the driver side and opens the backseat door.

"Where to?" the man asks with an American accent.

"Hotel Royal." Marcus responds, and that was the only conversation that was needed.

Marcus enters the hotel and walks up to the reception desk.

The night clerk greeted him, "How is your evening going, Sir?" the young man asks with a French accent and measures Marcus as he could tell he wasn't from Europe.

"Oh, better when I get to lay down." Marcus says and gives off a tired grin.

"And what's the name on the reservation?" he continues.

"Weaver, Marcus Weaver." he says as he taps on the countertop with his passport.

The man continues to enter information on the Saber reservation system. "And do you have a credit card for incidentals?" the clerk asks.

Marcus pulls out his wallet, drops the credit card on top of the passport and pushes it towards the clerk.

The man grabs the passport, double checks the reservation, looks up at Marcus and gives him a measuring look. He swipes the credit card and places it back on top of the passport. He gives a few more taps on his keyboard, and then places the key card on top and pushes the bundle back to Marcus. The clerk then points in the direction of the elevators. "The room is on the third floor, enjoy your stay." he says.

Marcus takes his credit card, passport, and room key off the counter, reaches down and grabs his bag, then salutes the clerk with a hand gesture, as he walks away.

He pushes the button to call the elevator and turns around to view the lobby. As he is waiting, he can hear voices in the distance give off a faint echo. He looks over at the turnstile doors and a man enters the hotel and is slowly approaching the reception desk.

Marcus recognizes the outfit he is dressed in; a middle eastern white keffiyeh, with a black Agal, a kurta, and dark shades. Marcus knows this was not the regular middle eastern man and lingers out of curiosity. Suddenly the man removes his shades, but Marcus is too far away to have a good look, and the view from the side made it no easier.

The clerk strikes up a conversation with the man as if he knew him all too well. "Asr bekheir, Khosh amadid, Le Phoque! (Good evening, Welcome Le Phoque!)" the clerk says and continues, "Cheetori?" (How are you?)

"Khoob... Tu Cheetori?" (Good... and you?) the man says.

"Man Khoobam, mersi." (I'm fine, thank you.) the clerk responds.

Marcus is standing by the elevators pondering on his assignment while listening with a half an ear on what was going on at the front desk. He looks over at the two men conversing casually, he was familiar with the language that the clerk was speaking, Farsi, and despite his French not being completely up to par, he knew enough to get by.

"Yek lahzeh lotfan." (One moment please.) the clerk continues, and walks away, at that moment, the bell chimes loud that the elevator has arrived. Marcus looks over at the man in the white keffiyeh one last time before proceeding into the elevator as he is holding his bag with a white-knuckle grip.

He reaches his floor and walks down the hallway; he looks down at the key card, it was room 333. He looks up at the doors as he was passing them by, and finally, he reaches his room.

He sticks the card in the door slot, waits for the click, and then he slowly presses the handle down as he pushes the door inward as he proceeds inside. He us letting the door shut behind him. He hesitates, nothing was simple or safe, so he turns around and locks the top lock of the door. Slowly, he takes one step at a time, first he stops by the bathroom door; he gives it a push and a quick look inside, and then he proceeds into the room and throws his bag on the bed. The drapes were closed covering the windows that faced the street.

He walks up to the window and views the street through the sheer fabric. The signs were flickering as if he had been thrown into some seedy back alley in a red light district, and, yet, he was in the heart of Geneva in a four-star hotel on an assignment for the US Government, and they would not acknowledge this or him if he was caught.

Marcus turns around and momentarily views the room as his thoughts were occupied with the given task. He had to find her, but the photo he was given was dated, and as Q had put it on the note, she was staying at the very same hotel he had checked into. Marcus' strategic plan was to be close, and yet he felt he was still fumbling in the shadows. Marcus' M.O. was clear, there was no such thing as any coincidental matters; he had calculated this. He did need the names of all the individuals staying at this two hundred room hotel. He turns on the tablet, and reaches for his phone and sends a text, *'Q, scramble me the list of the guests at Royal, maquariusw@gmail.com'*

Marcus puts the phone down and gets undressed. He grabs his toiletries and walks into the bathroom, the light in the ceiling flicks on as he enters. He tosses his bag on the counter and reaches into the shower and turns on the hot water. Within minutes the room is filled with steam from the hot water that was coming from the shower.

He needed to wake up, and the flight over had made him a little stiff in the muscles. The injuries he had sustained from his time in the army forced him to constantly be in top physical shape to keep his muscles from deteriorating and causing more pain. The hot water rolling down over his neck was soothing and he started to reminisce of Mafraq. Howard was coming to the forefront. It had been a while since he had crossed his mind, and, thanks to his conversation with Penny before he had left, it was back and fresh. Seels Bradford had been a ghost he had chased, but lost track of, and now the taste of blood in his mount was fresh; he wanted to find him, he was going to find him once his assignment was over, then it was going to be personal, and the past was going to be put to rest.

Marcus gets out of the shower and turns on the lights running along the mirror; it was fogged up. He opens the door to let the steam out and wipes the mirror clean. The reflection was of a man who had a tale to tell, who had hidden messages carved into his flesh along with the scars from battle wounds received through life's unbridled path to the days of combat on battle fields that war had left on him. His tattoos whispered messages from a time when he was on the other side of the law.

Marcus wraps a towel around his waist and grabs his toothbrush from his bag, places a strip of toothpaste on it, and starts his routine task of brushing his teeth all while thoughts were circulating of vivid pictures he had no control over.

106

The phone in the bedroom is going off, and when he comes back out from the bathroom he notices that he has a missed call. He looks over at the phone and views it, "Q.", he says. He sits down on the edge of the bed and returns the call as he watches the flickering neon lights through the sheer window coverings. There are four rings before he hears Q's voice on the other side.

"Good job, you're settled in." he says mission like.

"Did you manage to get me the list?" Marcus responds emotionless.

"I sent you the list." he says and is about to close the call.

"Hold on!" Marcus says quickly, "What am I looking for? Give me some more insight?" he says as he was still stumbling in the dark with only two pieces of information; a dated picture of a contact, a female, and the description of the item, the document, but nothing else.

Q pauses for a second, *"Well, what I know so far is that the information on the document is of a financial nature and belongs to a syndicate of 13 individuals worldwide. I am still working on decoding them. One of the main figures is Victor Afifi."* Q says.

"Victor Afifi? The mercenary, Victor Afifi, with ties to the middle eastern bank Société Générale in Jordan?" Marcus questions.

"Yeah, that's the man, and, as far as I know, he has American ties and was instrumental in providing Seels Bradford his education at Stanford." he says informatively.

"Do we have an idea of Bradford's whereabouts?" Marcus asks and can taste blood in his mouth. His mind starting to form an understanding by making picture frames in his mind of what this was all about.

"No, but he can be anywhere; he has no permanent location, always moving." Q says tiresome, and continues, *"We've lost him countless times."*

"Shariq Afifi, what do you know about him?" Marcus continues with his questions as he was digging for more information.

"Son of Victor Afifi, went to prestigious Oxford university, studied finance and law. He's considered to be shrewd and mastermind-like." Q says.

Marcus knew that he had just enough information to proceed to locate the person. He knew, ultimately, that it was a needle in the haystack he was looking for considering the size of the hotel and all the people who constantly arrived and departed. "OK, thank you, I'll take it from here... Don't call me, I'll call you." and the call is disconnected.

Marcus attaches the phone to the charger and connects the tablet to the WIFI he was tethering from his phone. He loads his email account, and there it was; the guest list was attached in the email from Q. He downloads it and starts to view it by dates, it wasn't going to be quick. The list contained more information than he expected, credit cards, passports information, additional guest in the room, and of course, it was mostly men who had checked in over the past few days. He needed to open each account and investigate all the data for each room to find the person. This was how he was going break down the list, and he was going to start by nationalities.

Time had progressed, and his eyes started to feel heavy and his sharp mind had turned tired; he looks over at the alarm clock, and it had already struck 03:23 in the morning. He knew that he needed a few hours of sleep and a good breakfast before he could absorb the information and continue to sift through the remaining accounts. Who could potentially be the person in the picture he had been given, he was beyond curious.

He looks up at the window; the neon lights were less pronounced now. He gets up and pulls the dark blackout shades together. It was soon going to be daylight, he knew, and he needed complete darkness to be able to fully rest. He was nocturnal by nature, this was the life he had lived for so long, and his pattern, when he was most active.

Marcus pulls the blanket off the bed and drags it to the floor, he stops, his thoughts take him to his own reality, *'Is this my life? Being a glorified cleaner for the government, what future lays in this?'* and he shakes his head as he reaches for the pillows and tosses them on top of the blanket.

Marcus had trouble sleeping on mattresses before he enlisted in the army, but after his return from Jordan he was unable to sleep on beds at all. The added injuries he sustained were the reason, but he knew too that before his stint in jail it was a ruling factor in his habit-forming behaviors. This rolled over to those long nightly surveillance tasks in the army, and they didn't offer hotel beds while waiting, and being the lawless renegade, he had also formed calluses in more places than one.

Marcus lays down and stretches his arms behind his head and gives a blank stare into the ceiling while clearing his mind as he gives off a large yawn. No more thinking, no more concluding, he rolls over to his right side, and he barely shuts his eyes and is fast asleep.

CHAPTER 10

PENNY ROLLS OVER TO THE SIDE to turn off the alarm clock when it goes off, it was already 9 am, but back home it was after midnight. She kicks off the blanket to the side and rolls back over and lays flat on her back.

She had slept all night and tried to get a grip on her jetlag and yet she felt her body was like molasses and moving slow. She tilts her head slightly with the motion of her eyes, as they are wandering throughout the room from right to left until they meet the sheer curtains. She slowly stretches herself, and then pushes herself up by her elbows into a resting position. Today was another day, but it was still work, just in a foreign territory.

Penny rolls out of bed and walks up to the window; she lets her hand slide between the curtains and opens the window ever so slightly. She can feel the warmth of the natural sunlight give her a slight caress through the sheer window coverings. She can sense the fragrant city slicker smell sneak inside in-between the fumes of bakery goods mixed together with other culinary creations. It was clear; the breakfast session was in full mode and the soaring sound on the street was revealing that hotel guest were arriving and departing. She could hear people's conversations travelling upwards, the French and German accents were mixing and now and then she could hear Farsi. It was like she was back to the hustle and bustle she had been accustomed to in Jordan.

Penny continues into the bathroom; it was time to wake up and the water was going to remedy that problem. She turns the handle in the tub and the water flows fast, and before she knows it, the thoughts are sneaking up on her and pictures are forming the chain of the event that had occurred. This unnerving feeling that she was treading dangerous waters wouldn't let go. She would have to call Julia, she needed to get information about Taytum, something wasn't right, she knew, as she replayed the interaction she had had with him, more and more small details crossed her mind.

She gets in the tub and changes it to the shower head mode. This was no vacation and she hurry to get cleaned up all while her mind was laying down her schedule internally.

Penny finishes quickly her shower, and wraps her towel around her body as she walks out to locate the phone, and before she reaches it a call is coming in. She turns around and takes a few quick steps over, and she can see Harris' number display. "Well, Good Morning!", Penny answers happily surprised.

"Good morning to you too..." he pauses, "I thought I'd call you, last time we spoke you were supposed to call me, and I figured you got busy." he continues.

"Yes, things have taken an unsuspected turn, and I left you a message last night." she says with a concerned voice.

"Yeah, I got it. What's going on, and what's in Geneva? Is it business or pleasure?" he asks curiously.

"I don't know. I had taken a day off, and when I got back I was pulled into an unsuspected meeting; that was after I talked to you." She says a bit guilty for not managed to return his call.

"Hmm, interesting, interesting indeed, so, tell me more..." he says as he was naturally curious.

"...it was with people I've never seen before, and they sent me off to pick up a 'package' here in Geneva." she says suspiciously.

"I can tell you are having second thoughts about it, what makes you think it's something else besides a regular job that they trusted you to do?" he asks.

"I have a bad feeling about it." she says and continues, "I need your help."

"OK?" he says as he felt like he was lost. "I actually needed to speak to you about the situation over here." and he gets quiet.

"Should I look over my shoulder?" Penny asks concerned.

"I would, and I really don't know if they have your new information, but I would be careful." he continues, "If they know where I am, they most likely know where you are."

"I doubt they know where I am right now. I would have seen some kind of red flags about it by now, but I haven't seen any yet." she says as she wasn't concerned about it and quiets down.

"You said you needed my help, what is it?" Harris probes.

"I don't know myself; I know what information I have, but don't know how to interpret it. I just get a bad feeling the more I think about it." she says as she was lost herself. Who was the Queen, the culprit, in this game of chess she was thrown into?

"Tell me what you have." Harris says and she could hear him tap in the background.

"First, the name is John Taytum, second I have the place where I need to pick it up; Shariq Afifi's Esq. office on Quai du General-Guisan 16.", she says.

"Shariq Afifi? Are you sure, can you double check?" Harris asks.

"Yes, why?" Penny questions.

"Can you double check? I need for you to be sure." he says and is now being very serious.

"OK, hold on..." Penny says cautiously and walks over to her bag where she pulls out the information and reads it to confirm it for Harris. "OK, I am now reading off the instructions, it is what I just told you, Shariq Afifi's office on Quai du General-Guisan." she says as there was no mistake.

"Penny, do you know who Afifi is?" he says, and his tone had changed.

"No, but I guess my intuition is on par that I have to be careful." she says recognizing the tone in the deliverance of his comment.

"Do you know who you are going to see when you get there?" Harris continues.

"No, just that I am to go there to the security desk, and then continue from there, the instructions are vague, and I only know one step at the time." she responds, and her mind was now churning on the unclear and sparse directions for what she was doing.

"Hmm… let me get you a bit of a background of this man. Victor Afifi was exiled out of Israel to Egypt years ago where he had a carpet shop in Cairo. Yeah, but not Aladdin type…" and before he can continue Penny interrupts him.

"His name is Shariq not Victor.", she says querying as she is correcting him at the same time.

"I know, you said Shariq, but the important part I am telling you, is about Victor. He's the father of Shariq." and Harris gets quiet.

"OK." Penny says acknowledging, "Go on." she says more intrigued as she's now taking mental notes.

"His father sent Shariq to a prestigious school here in the UK, and he has been considered a protégé and a financial genius. Victor is a well-known arms dealer, a mercenary…" and he

pauses as he was thinking of someone she could compare him
to, "Like former Adnan Khashoggi." he says factually. He stops
as he knew this was not what she wanted to hear. "So,
whatever you are picking up, it will have terrorist ties." Harris
continues with a tone of assurance.

"And if I don't show up, then I'll raise questions…" Penny says
hesitantly and stops herself in midsentence.

"Correct. No, you go ahead and pick it up. You don't want to
raise suspicions. Just act like… a dumb blonde." he says as it's
the best way to describe a demeanor that would resonate with
Penny, knowing that would be hard, it was easier for Penny to
be assertive as that was her nature.

"OK, let me get going, and I will get back to you." she says and
wants to get off the phone.

"OK, but hold on a second, there is something you should know
first." he continues, "You recall the war criminal we put away
in Haag?"

"Yes." Penny says as she didn't know where this was heading.

"Afifi was the arms dealer during the Balkan war for the
militia." he says and quiets down.

"Shit!" Penny exclaims as this was the last thing she needed to
hear.

"Just know this, as much as you think this is a coincidence, it
can be equally as much a trap. Know this, nothing is a
coincidence, everything happens is for a reason, the rabbit hole
goes deep." and he stops.

"I hear you; the universe is never that lazy. Let me call you back when I get back into the hotel." Penny says and disconnects the call. She couldn't be sure about anything, not even the phone seemed to be a safe method to communication. She had to digest the information, and she started to roll back her memory; everything had gone so fast and had just been sprung on her; nothing had been optioned to her as a voluntary act. The hotel room was not even in her name, it was in Taytum's name.

Penny knew she had been right, this was no vacation, just like she had told Spencer, it was work, and more so than she bargained for. She grabs a piece of stale bread of the tray from last night's meal, there was no time to waste for a meal.

CHAPTER 11

PENNY'S TAXI DRIVER STOPS OUTSIDE the building, "Madame, Nous sommes ici... Madame, Madame..." the taxi driver calls out to Penny who is deep in her thoughts.

"Oh, thank you." she responds back to him, and hands him the money for the ride.

"No problem... Do you need me to wait for you?" he asks in a broken English.

Penny stops herself in her tracks before she gets out and looks over at the Taxi driver and ponders for a second.

"No problem, I wait for you Madame." the man says as if he could read Penny's mind, and she hands him some extra money.

She exits the car, walks up to entrance door and pushes the heavy doors open. She can hear the sound of her heels echo throughout the lobby with each step as they hit the shiny floor as she walks up to the security desk and then signs her name in the sign-in log.

The security officer looks over the log, "Hold on... there is a package for you." and he hands her an oversized envelope. He makes a few taps on the computer and swipes a card through a slot on the keyboard and hands it to her as he points at the elevators. "Swipe the card on the black box and press the button for the elevator to arrive; you are expected on the 6th floor." he says as it was a well-rehearsed phrase he had to repeat daily.

Penny takes the card and walks over to the elevator where she swipes the badge on the card reader and pushes the button. While waiting for the elevator, she opens the manila envelope; there was a USB key inside and a piece of paper. Penny folds the envelope in half and places it in her tote.

The elevator ride was fast and before she knew it, the ride came to an abrupt halt and the door opens at the office on the 6th floor. She was staring at the front desk person and takes one step out, and she hears the doors shut behind her.

"Bonjour Penny, welcome to Geneva." the clerk says and smiles wide.

It was true, they knew she was there before she arrived, nothing was coincidental. His eyes were hiding behind the typical round banker's glasses, somewhat sophisticated, and still she could sense by his tone and a demeanor he was a 'queen'.

Penny smiles back as she approaches the front desk counter. "Merci, enchanté." she replies, and they were snickering like two 'girls'.

"Please take a seat while I let Monsieur Bradford..."

She stops him in midsentence, "Mr. Bradford!" she exclaimed, "But..." Could this be? Nae, impossible, that was a common name though.

"Mais oui... Monsieur Bradford." he continues as it was correct.

There was no time for questions, she could sense, and she leans over and looks down the hall watching the clerk disappear and enter a door at the very end.

Penny sits down and reclines back, and her thoughts start to think that everything that had happened before she got back to work, the drone, the new acquaintance; was there something there or was her mind just overly sensitive and overly suspicious to everything that had occurred the past few days?

The clerk comes back a few moments later. "He's ready for you, Madame." and points down the hall, where she can see there's light coming from a partially open door that the clerk had entered earlier.

Penny gets up from her seat and walks down the hall, and in an almost slow-motion mode, she can feel as if she was having an outer body experience. This was not her life; this was not Penny's life.

She stops in front of the door, and prepares herself mentally before pushing the door open, and enters. She sees a man standing at the window and taking in the view of the lake with a set of binoculars. Penny isn't sure, is this the same man at the airport, she couldn't be sure, most black men looked the same to her. She makes a sound by clearing her throat.

"You guys have a really nice view from here..." she says to get the man's attention.

He turns around quickly and smiles big at her. "I know." he says and looks down at this desk, fumbling with papers.

Penny is quiet, and all she heard that moment was Harris' voice repeat itself, *"Just know this, as much as you think this is a coincidence, it can be equally as much a trap, know this, nothing is a coincidence, everything happens is for a reason."*. There was an awkward silence from Penny as she realizes that this was the same Bradford she had met and who had been on the same plane from Seattle to London; this was not a coincidence.

"It's crazy... but I couldn't tell you, will you forgive me?" he says with an apologetic smile on his face.

She quietly observes him as she couldn't eradicate what he had said; tell her what? What else was she not privy to, what else had been kept from her? She had her reservations about whether she was going to bring back the information.

"What is it that we need to talk about? I think it is straight forward, Mr. Bradford. I received this envelope from the security downstairs, information and instructions are all in the envelope." she says business like.

"Not so fast..." he says with a bit of hesitance in his voice and he continue looking at the desk as he was sorting through the paperwork.

Penny sensed there was a hint of a southern accent, not too much, just enough that she could hear it. In fact, it wasn't difficult to decipher what he was saying, but he was hiding something, that she knew as much. She wasn't impressed by his salesman pitch demeanor.

"I need to go over the plan with you in case you need to destroy the paperwork, and..." he looks up at her and his eyes were measuring her from head to toe, and then he regains his focus, "... from what I understand, you have a photographic memory, please correct me if I am wrong." he says if he knew a lot more than what he was letting on.

Who was this man, why was he in the know of who she was? She interjects, "No, you are not wrong, and it's actually called an eidetic memory. So, tell me, how do you know that?" She was now on the defense, the blonde act wasn't going to work, she knew that now, she couldn't let her guard down. "I don't even know you from good morning to good night, so please enlighten me." Penny continues. She was a very private person and now someone had been doing a 411 on her, but why?

"Ok... I'll just be straight with you; I think that's for the best." he says as he pauses and looks at Penny. "We just wouldn't let anyone do this kind of trip unless we knew their abilities, you understand that, don't you?" He states with a tone as if he knew everything there was to know. He grabs his reading glasses and looks back down at the paperwork in front of him, and continues, "MBA from Stockholm School of Economics...

you 'interned' at a Swedish Army military base in the administrative office... why?" He asks puzzled and looks at Penny as he knew her personal resume but could not piece together what was going on inside that mind of hers.

Penny stays quiet as she knows that she wasn't going to confirm or deny anything anymore.

"OK," he says and continues, "speaks seven languages and, of course, is proficient in martial art and carries a Colt 1911, hmm... alone with one dog... takes nightly runs and is the AVP for the compliance department at PEGC N.A." he stops and looks at Penny again and is waiting for her to say something, as she was mum through his entire statement, but she was instead waiting, and listening. "Not much of life is it Ms. Jacqueline... or shall I say, former Mrs. Howard Grant... Special Agent Howard D. Grant. You may change your name, but you can't hide from it.", he says concluding and puts down his glasses on the desk and looks over at Penny to see if he had got a reaction from her.

Penny gets up from her seat and grabs her bag. She had enough and hearing her late husband's name was the last straw. Her position had changed, she hadn't signed up for this, that much she knew. "I guess you are aware of my late husband, my name, and my past, so you should also know that I may be a woman with a new identity, but rest assured, you still do not know who I am, and you should not cross me."

He looks at her with a strange expression on his face, almost suspect. The air in the room went from being a light breeze, to intense tension so thick that you could cut it with a knife.

Penny starts walking out the door as she can hear Mr. Bradford talk to her, "Please read through the instructions..." she continues to ignore him, as she continues to walk away and the sound of him becomes just a faint noise.

She stops at the elevator, and while she waits for it she realizes how quiet it is, she could hear a pin drop, and then she can hear Mr. Bradford's loud voice, she could tell he was on the phone.

"...Seels here... yes... she was here, she just left. OK, we just go forward with the next move? When I am done, I will wire you the funds...."

The elevator door opens, and Penny gives one last look over at Mr. Bradford's door, she looks over her shoulder seeing the clerk watching her before proceeding to step inside. She knew it was trouble; the one-sided monolog she overheard told her it was some form of set up, and she had to get out of the place. She needed to hurry back to the hotel to find out what secrets the key held. Never had she been pulled into doing this kind of 'work' before. Something in Penny triggered her cold and callousness-like persona; the dynamics of the situation had changed.

The elevator reaches the lobby and Penny passes the front desk and drops the key card on the counter and continues outside to the waiting taxi driver. The security guard observes her with an interesting and yet perturb look as she doesn't stop but keeps walking.

Penny gets into the waiting taxi, as her mind is occupied with the words ring repeatedly, *MBA from Stockholm School of*

Economics... you 'interned' at a Swedish Army military base in the admin office... why?' How did he know, and who was he really?

"Madame?" the driver says, but Penny is consumed in her thoughts. "Madame?" the driver tries again, and Penny is suddenly aware of the driver wanting her attention.

"Yes?" she says almost childlike and innocently.

"à l'hôtel?" he asks and gestures.

Penny nods, "Oui... s'il vous plait." she says and reclines back into the back seat. Penny's mind ponders on simpler times as she looks out the window at the view of the lake, the water. Yes, the water brought memories back to her while recounting her childhood memories by the ocean in Sweden. She recalls her sisters running around on the beach playing badminton and taking turns, but Penny was only to be found in the water. She was this like a jellyfish who never wanted to leave. She can hear the voices replay in her mind; the calls from her sisters calling her name from the beach as they were leaving, *"Ališia, Ališia"* waving with their hands for her to get out of the water.

Yes, Penny had many names, but she was still one and the same regardless. Penny's secrets were deep rooted inside of her, safeguarded and would only surface when she was cornered in a stressful situation. It was her survival mechanism, find that safe zone within her. Her childhood, her roots would bring that feeling of being cocooned to a place where she could retreat and find her focus.

Penny's real identity was only known by her family; her six sisters and her mother. Yes, her father had passed away, and she knew very little about him, just that he was born right after the end of the Habsburgs Empire. She remembered him as a strong man, but with a devious mind and a killer instinct, that she knew. She had known for some time that she had inherited his warrior ways. For years she had compared herself with the others, and one thing that struck a chord in her that was declared and obvious was that she was the strongest of them all, there was no doubt about that.

She couldn't stop thinking that she had a guardian angel watching out for her all those years she had had with Howard, and she could only think of one, and now they both were up there looking after her.

The time in the taxi going back to the hotel made her lose track of her bearings and her mind went on a trip down memory lane. The taxi pulls up to the curb and stops abruptly. Penny looks up as her thoughts come to a sudden halt with the driver's unexpected stop. She scrambles in her tote for change and is ready to pay the man when he waves at her declining. Penny smiles, and nods in a way that presented a non-verbal appreciation as she exits the car.

Penny walks through the turnstile doors with persistent steps to the elevator, passing the front desk and noticing there is a line. She recognizes a scent that reminded her of Marcus, but that could not be. He was back in the States and he certainly wasn't the only one wearing that cologne. Although she could tell that the smell placed her into a better frame of mind, and a smile slowly spread over her face as she had been occupied with so many things that Marcus had become a faint memory. This was the perfect reminder that she was soon going to be going back home, and very soon. As soon as the smile had crossed her lips, her reality kicked back in.

Penny pushes the button for the elevator and turns around while she waits; this nagging feeling occupied her thoughts that a criminal act that was about to take place, if it had not already. She was not sure the gist of it, and she could not let go of it. She hears the chime of the elevator, and steps inside and her eyes drift over to the front desk as she is pondering. She pushes the button for her floor, and, in that very same moment as the door closes, her eyes catch something. *"No, that was not him, he is not here, it may have been his smell... it couldn't be..."* she says under her breath. She believes her mind is playing tricks on her as so much was going on.

Penny gets into her room, she tosses her tote on the bed, and kicks off her shoes. She needed to get out of these clothes and into something more comfortable, there was no time to waste. She had this gut wrenching feeling that told her that she was about to be set up.

She pulls out her phone and looks over the recent calls, "Harris." she says out loud, and she hits the return call button as she starts to take off her clothes, she can hear the dial tones go through. Suddenly she hears Harris voice.

"Penny, what do you got for us?" he says as he sounded occupied.

"I just got in, but the meeting did not turn out how I expected." she says as she was throwing on a grey t-shirt and a pair of black jeans. She turns on the computer and waits for it to start up.

"What do you mean?" Harris asks and stops what he was doing.

"What I mean is…" and Penny stops herself. She had not entirely digested the whole situation. "Let me tell you, Harris, everything from the beginning." and she recap's what had transpired.

"Do you see what's so strange; Mr. Bradford knows things that no one knows about and shouldn't know about me." Penny says aggravated.

"I get it, but we need now to be a step ahead of him." Harris says, *"Have you checked the USB key yet?"* he continues.

"No, not yet but I am working on it now as we speak." she says as she was listening to him. The PDF file that came up required a code, and Penny remembered the box with the code she had viewed at the airport. She types in the code, and it unlocks the document. "I'm in now." she says victoriously, "It's a PDF file" she continues.

"Ok, I need you to transfer the pdf to a Word document; then encrypt the entire document, then save it again as a PDF file and send me the file." Harris orders Penny.

"OK, got it." and Penny works fast and moments later she says; "I've sent you the file; I'm deleting the coded file and replacing it with the encrypted file."

"OK, that's my girl, you already know what to do." He says relieved.

"Well, I figured as much." she says confident.

He continues, *"Now, I need you to take out the hard drive from the laptop..."* and he runs down the tasks, and list things that needed to be done.

Penny turns over the computer, it has four screws, but she doesn't have a screwdriver. "OK." she says as she continues to listen to Harris while she runs into the bathroom and locates her make-up bag. She rummages through it to find something to use when her eyes catch the cuticle pusher. "I think I found a tool." she calls out, and hurries back to the table.

"What was that again?" Harris says confused.

"I said I found a tool to open the back with." Penny says as she continues to work on unscrewing the screws. After removing all of the screws, she manages to press away the back and remove the cover. Once inside she quickly locates the hard drive and removes it from the computer.

"OK, I got it, now what do you want me to do again?" she asks.

"Send it back to your office, use UPS. I don't want you to have anything on you." he sounded very serious and Penny had seen this before, this was not some trick, this was real. *"This is your leverage to keep yourself alive. You have something they want, when they have it, you are dead weight to them."* Harris orders were carefully measured, and he needed to protect Penny, that went without saying as something in his Leo personality told him that losing a fight wasn't an option.

"Now you need to get out, and I mean get out, you need to leave. They will come back for it; you're just a scapegoat."

Harris says commanding as he was calculating the pattern of the behaviors to be expected. He continues, *"I want you to leave the document and the USB key in the envelope on the table and check out. Any luggage you have, you need to send it back to the US, and use UPS for that too."* he says as this is something he had done before. *"You call me when it's done."* he says and disconnects the call.

Penny looks over at the items sitting on the table and starts putting the pieces together just like Harris had told her to. She continues to pack up her belongings as she is walking back and forth restlessly to get everything into the bag and realizes now what the assignment was about.

Penny worked for PEGC, but she also had a mind of her own. Money wasn't important, but integrity was, and that was all she really had at the end of the day. She was smart, eloquent, and she could run with most people in various circles, but without the integrity everything else meant nothing to her. She couldn't help thinking about the fact that her military information had been brought to light under these circumstances. It was the official version, but it was just a cover up for what she had really been trained to do.

Penny was Jacqueline Grant, but, again, she was also Ališia Lešnik. She was the daughter of a former military officer in the German Army during the second world war who had deserted and fled. Her father had continued disappearing ever so often, her mother had told her; he had an inconsistent presence in the family life. When her mother had asked him what he was doing, she was told to mind her own business. She suspected that he had connection with the UDBA, the secret service organization from the country they had fled from.

Penny remember the stories of people being tracked down and killed outside the communist borders; people who had fled but were still under surveillance. The manhunt had never stopped, and Penny's mother thought they had been spared because her father was involved somehow, and that his way to protect them was to be involved.

Penny was a walking Pandora's box that needed to be kept closed; once this hibernation was awoken, there was no turning back as this smoldering fire could erupt if it was pushed to its limits. She was truly her father's warrior that was hibernating. Ališia Lešnik had become Jacqueline Grant through marriage and her US citizenship. She was the constant chameleon, went through multiple changes as she dodged danger, and bullets. In the middle of her thoughts the hotel phone started to ring, she looks over at the phone, and hesitates for a second, but walks up to it and picks it up.

"Hello." Penny answers with hesitation in her voice. There's silence, "Hello?" she tries again, and then she hears the call disconnect. Penny knows this was just the beginning, she pulls her bag together, drops all her hygiene articles in it, and puts the laptop back together. She stops and thinks for a second if she was going to bring it with her but decides to leave it on the desk. This was just a shell now, all the information she needed was stored on the hard drive.

She sits down on the edge of the bed and grabs her shoes and puts them on, looks over at her phone, grabs it and starts to scroll down the contact list and stops at 'BCE9'. This was something Penny had hoped she would never need to use again. Her finger lingers before she pushes the dial button. She hears two dial tones then a computerized voice.

"Entry Code."

"Bravo-Charlie-Echo-9" Penny responds, then another dial tone goes through.

"Hey Ghost-Rider, that wasn't yesterday, what's the occasion? I never thought I hear from you again." The man says acerbically and laughs as he had been waiting for this day.

"Cut the crap, I know it's been awhile. I need a .45 with 5 clips loaded with hollow points, I need a holster too... something... like a body wrap." she says commanding and with an equally direct mannerism.

"Location?" the man says as he was now back to an accommodating business MO.

"Hotel Royal on Rue de Lausanne..." and before Penny is able to finish, the man exclaims.

"Geneva!? Really? What the hell are you doing in Europe? Last POE was Seattle." He says shockingly and confused as he had not expected her to say that.

"Listen, long story, I didn't expect to need to use this channel, but I have no other option. How quickly can you have this to me?" she says with a tone that she wasn't going to discuss the situation any further.

"Give me eight hours. What room are you in?"

"311."

"I'll text you when it's dropped." he says and ends the call abruptly.

She knew she had to work fast, she looks over at the time, and it's a close to 15:00. She grabs her bag and the hard drive, she looks at the USB key, and she makes her decision and pockets it. There was no time to waste, she had to get to the concierge's desk before UPS arrived. Penny takes the elevator down to the reception desk; the place had quieted down. She could hear the service in the bistro preparing for dinner, and she sees the UPS truck roll up. She had managed to get downstairs in the nick of time.

She fills out the forms for the two packages and the concierge hands Penny a padded package for the hard drive.

"How would you like to pay?" the concierge asks.

"Oh, one second." Penny says as she pulls out her own American Express card and hands it to him. He swipes the card, and hands Penny a pen and the paper slip to sign for it and places the card on the counter.

Penny slide back the signed slip and the pen and grabs her card and puts it back in her wallet. She can see the UPS man going back and forth with packages, she lingers to make sure the packages she was sending was going off without a hitch.

As soon as the truck rolls off the curb, Penny continues into the bistro and sits down at the bar, she started to feel a sigh of relief that she made it so far, then an overwhelming feeling rolled over her, one she had not had for some time. A stress she had let go of, and now it was back. Her blood sugar was low, and she had not had anything to eat all day, but she needed it, she had to feed her grays to stay sharp.

CHAPTER 12

MARCUS WAS WORKING ON THE LEAD he had been given by Quentin. He knew he was looking for a woman, and he had gone over the list and was down to only a few left.

He was certain that one of the names that was on his list was the culprit. So far there were no female names, and he knew that this was a covert situation, so whoever she was, she would not go by a female persona, it was too easy.

Marcus is pulling out the picture again to see if there was something he was missing; at the same time the phone goes off. He reaches out for it as he is looking at the picture with a magnifying glass. "Hello." he says with an occupied tone.

"Busy?" the man says and gives off a laugh.

"Quentin…, yes as a matter of fact I am. You know this is really a riddle…" Marcus says as he was continuing to look over the list as he was listening halfhearted.

"Yes, but you are the man to solve it... that is why you got the job." Q continues.

"So what's going on? I told you I was going to call you and not to call me?" Marcus says as he wasn't expecting his call.

"She has surfaced." he says cryptic, *"And you know who I am talking about."*

Marcus stops what he is doing and puts down the picture, "She..." he says as if he couldn't believe after all this time.

"Yes, she is back on the radar, somewhere in southern Europe. That is all I know." Q says and continues, *"I have my people on it, trying to find out the location, but it's going to be gnarly because she's using Howards connections and you know those guys were loyal to a T."*

"I know, but how?" Marcus asks at the same time sense confusion.

"She used the 'entry code' system. The only reason I can think of is that she is in trouble... but I don't know what it can be after all this time." he says troubled and confused.

"Do you have transcript of the call?" Marcus asks.

"No they used a scrambler... all I can tell is that she is most likely needing something, it can be anything, information, weapon, transportation, you know yourself..." he says to Marcus who had once been a part of that organization, but had left after the Mafraq incident.

"Yeah..." he says pondering, "...thanks for letting me know... I will find out, if I can." he continues.

Marcus closes his phone and the call disconnects. He looks back at the picture and looks closer at the individuals in the picture. He then recognizes that there are some markings on her, it looks as if there could be tattoos on her arm. "She has tattoos!" he says out loud and reclines back in the chair. She was living here at the hotel, and all he needed to do was to blend in and watch people, and that wasn't going to be too hard. The first place to look was the restaurant.

He grabs his phone and gets up from the chair, he was going to get something to eat. It was late afternoon and he had been cooped up all day in the room researching, he needed something to eat.

Marcus steps out of the elevator and looks left and right to locate the bistro he had passed when he walked in.

As Penny orders her food and looks briefly over toward the hotel lobby, she could see a man looking around, and then she turns her attention back to the bartender as her food was arriving.

Marcus walks into the bistro and as he gets closer he can't believe what he is seeing. It couldn't be. Penny? What was she doing here? He walks up to her and taps her on the shoulder. "Hey." he says surprised as he smiles.

"Marcus, what!" she says and smiles back at him, "How did you know where I was, did you follow me?" she says jokingly.

"Well…" what was he going to say, "I was…" and she stops him.

"I don't want to know…" she says as she looks at him with a querying look.

"Relax!" Marcus replies as he was trying to ease the situation.

"Sit down next to me." she says and gives up a fake smile, while she pulls out the bar chair for him.

Marcus sits down and she hands him the menu that she had used, then he calls out to the bartender who is on the opposite end of the bar by waving his arm in the air. Marcus looks at Penny as he had not seen her in a while and suddenly recognizes that she has a tattoo sticking out from under her grey t-shirt. He tries not to stare and starts to read the menu to come up with something quick to order.

"What have you got to eat?" he asks as he is still trying to figure out what he wants.

Penny looks down at her plate, "Croque Madame" she says and looks over at Marcus as she still can't believe he is sitting there and at the same time she thinks *'nothing is a coincident.'*

"OK, I will have a Croque Monsieur" he says.

The bartender arrives and he gives Marcus a look as he is awaiting his order.

"Croque Monsieur, s'il vous plait." Marcus says like a native.

"D'accord." the bartender responds and disappears into the back.

So, it had been him after all who she had seen. What was he
doing here, and in the same hotel and if that wasn't enough he
was also speaking French. She did not expect that of him when
she first met him, he didn't look like a person who was well
rounded like that. Was this just by chance that they were
sitting there together or was it something else? I can't wait to
hear his explanation or, rather, reason to why, Penny thinks to
herself. She's cutting into her sandwich and taking a small
bite, and sips on her water.

"So, what are you doing in Geneva?" Penny says and takes
another bite as she watches Marcus looking over at the menu
yet again, pretending to be occupied as he is waiting for his
sandwich to arrive. She doesn't say anything she just waits,
and he closes it up slowly and his eyes are wandering along the
mirrored wall with all the liquors lined up. Was he thinking of
a credible story to tell, or a modification of the truth, Penny
ponders as she continues to take more bites of her sandwich.

The wait is interrupted by the bartender coming out with
Marcus plate.

"Merci." Marcus let's out. He looks over at Penny, and leans
into her, "I came to see you." he says as he laughs it off and
starts to cut into his sandwich.

Penny stops and turns to him with a questioning look. "So how
did you know where I was?" she says, but now the tone was
more serious, and she wasn't joking anymore.

"Well..." he says and stops as he stares into the mirrored wall
behind the bar, pausing, he puts down the fork and looks at
Penny. "I am still not quite out of the military... this was really

not planned, I can tell you that much, and that's all I can say."
he says.

Penny looks at him straight into his eyes. She could tell they
were different this time, they had almost a darkness spreading
wide and his iris was like a faint blue ring around the pupil. As
she had thought this was no coincidence, was she right? He
had yet to tell her why and just danced around with a few
words and, without saying much, he had given her the clue
that this was not the time or the place.

Marcus turns back his focus on his sandwich, and Penny feels a
sense of being surrounded, she needed to leave as soon as the
shipment had arrived. She continues to eat, as she finishes she
gives out a large sigh of contentment.

"What was that all about? One would think you had not had
anything to eat in a long time." he says and snickers as he is
taking another bite.

She looks over at him as she pushes the plate away from her,
"You are correct, there is nothing like a real Croque Madame
as one you get here in Europe, back in the States this kind of
food is scarce, what I mean is, done the right way." she says
discriminating.

"Maybe you should open your own place." he says indicating.

"Yeah... you may be up to something." she says wondersome as
she stares into the mirrored wall and recognizes that she is
looking at Marcus as he is scarfing down the sandwich, and
behind him, by a window, she could see Bradford. Mr. Bradford
was staring at her. She turns around slowly and she watches

the back of Bradford as he is walking off. She stands up, stretches her arms up in the air and casually walks up to the window and looks out to see if there were more people out there.

Marcus finishes his last bite and grabs a napkin off the counter and wipes his lips as he looks over at Penny; studying her while pondering, *'could it be her, is she the one who is in the picture... nae too easy.'*

"Hey there..." he says to catch her attention, and she turns around and the look on her face was as if she had been in deep thought.

Penny smiles, "Yeah, hey there yourself" she says jokingly as she smiles invitingly. She couldn't let on that something was troubling her, she had to act as if everything was fine.

"What room are you staying in?" he says casually.

Penny blurs out "311."

"What a coincidence, I'm staying on the same floor, 333." he says and gives off boyish laughter.

Penny looks at him; he was still having that inner child and it came out a little after all the hiding from behind that strong façade. Penny's phone goes off on the counter blinking Harris' name, and Marcus looks over at the phone.

"You got a call coming in" he says and then looks at Penny.

She walks up and can see Harris' name all over the screen. "Nae, I'll call him back, it can wait... it's just work." she says as relaxed as she can be without giving off any indication of urgency. Penny grabs the phone and tucks it in her front pocket, and then waves at the bartender. He brings the bill, and Penny signs it off to the room.

"I got to go, I need to rest before I leave tomorrow." and she taps Marcus on the shoulder and walks off with slow steps as time was all she had and, at the same time, her intuition grew stronger and she needed to get back to the room. Harris had called, and she needed to return the call quickly, there was no time waste.

CHAPTER 13

Marcus lingers in the bar as he can't stop to think about what he had seen, he looks over at his phone, and scrolls down to Q's number to send him a text.

'I think I've found her, in room #311"

He knew that he needed to work fast, he didn't have much time before the window of opportunity to get back on the jet waiting was closed; after that he was on his own.

Marcus waves at the bartender, and he brings back the bill as he grabs the plate. Marcus signs it back to his room and gets up from the chair while looking down at his phone viewing the incoming message. He looks up briefly as he catches a view of a man pacing outside the window; Seels Bradford. Could this really be the man who had gone rouge back in Jordan after all these years? The man he and Howard had tracked down? What was he doing here in Geneva?

He looks down on his phone again as he quickly glances over at the man moving out of sight. Marcus slowly moves out of the bistro and walks into the lobby when he sees the man walk inside through the turnstile doors. Marcus stops and turns his back towards the man and sends off a new text to Q, *'Seels Bradford, caught my 12.'*

Marcus slowly walks towards the desk as Bradford is moving away, towards the main restaurant. Marcus stops by the reception desk, and the female clerk approaches him.

"Oui, monsieur?" she says.

"Oh, I don't speak French." he says and gives off a charming smile.

"Oh, that's OK, I understand." she replies in English with a French accent.

"I want to leave a message for Ms. Bridge." he says and awaits the clerk to look her up.

"Ms. Bridge? I do not have a Ms. Bridge here." she says as she scans her computer screen and looks a little confused as she looks up from the screen and continues, "Do you know what room she is in?"

"Oh, yes, 311." Marcus says like it was obvious he knew what room she was staying at.

"Ok, just hold on a second." the clerk continues to look at a different screen, and she turns to Marcus, "Oh, that is Mr. Taytum's room." she says, and she grabs a pen and a piece of paper.

"Thank you... and how do you spell Taytum?" Marcus says and looks down on the paper while writing his message, as it was a purely curious question.

The clerk looks down on the screen while Marcus is writing, "T-A-Y-T-U-M." she says spelling it out innocently.

Marcus folds up the note and hands it over to her, "Thank you." he says as he walks off.

The clerk nods, and watches Marcus while she opens the note and reads it, *'P, I am staying in 333, call me.'* She looks over the counter to check if Marcus had left the lobby. She picks up the phone. "Prix 333 demande 311, Grand, homme, nom Weaver, Marcus Weaver." (*Room 333 is asking for 311, Tall, male, name Weaver, Marcus Weaver*) she can be heard saying. "Bien sûr." (*of course*) and she hangs up the receiver.

Marcus is back in his room as he is looking down at the message he received from the Q.

"John Taytum, x-employee for CNU, now working for PEGC."

"Well, that we know..." he says thinking out loud, as he replies to the message. *"Tell me if you can track down a 'Penny Bridge', I need company name."*

Marcus puts down his phone, and opens his tablet, as he starts to think back on the evening he arrived, the conversation that took place at the receptions desk. "Le Phoque, Le Phoque, what is that again?" he says. He knew French, but this was a word almost like a code, a person's name did not start with a masculine noun. Marcus Google's the name 'phoque', it comes back as 'seal'.

"Seal, what... sealing what?" he says as he gets distracted by an incoming text; "Seal, seal..." he says as he reads the text and stops in the middle of multitasking.

"Penny Bridge, AVP for PEGC"

"FUCK!" Marcus blurts out. He stops his thought process. "Seal..." he says as his mind was working in slow motion, "Seels Bradford?" he says again and pause for a second and continues, "Le Phoque, for seal, the same as Seels!" It was a play on words, and yet two and the same, Marcus realizes. He leans over the tablet and starts to scramble through the list of names that were sent to him, looking for "Le Phoque'. "Nothing, there is nothing on here." he says frustrated as he continues to look over the list. He would need to find out somehow but needed more information. He walks up to the window and pushes the drapes aside, then he presses his hands against the window as he looks out and can see the sun starting to set.

He turns around leans against the ledge and looks over the room as he is pondering. "Seels, Taytum, Penny..." he says out loud. These names all in the same place, why? Marcus ponders to himself. He walks back to the table and sits down. He looks at the screen on his phone and then opens his email account, and sends off an email to Q.

"I need background on all three; Seels Bradford, John Taytum, Penny Bridge." and he sends it off. He grabs the picture of the woman he was looking for and leans back in the chair. He couldn't help pondering if he had been wrong about Penny, but something in him was not letting this rest. He had suspected this was Penny, but he knew nothing about her background, so

there was still a chance he could be wrong. He needed more information and that Seels Bradford was here at the same time was unexpected and a red flag to him.

He pulls up the file and starts to scan the name, Taytum, John Taytum. He opens the account and the additional information was Penny Bridge, and her passport, and credit card.
This had to be it, she had to be the one, and Seels Bradford, where was he staying. He started to go over the file again, reading off the names, and then pondering on the information Q had revealed, The Afifi's.

He gets up from his chair, he needed a shower to clear his mind, he knew a hot shower would allow him to relax and maybe he would be able to see the situation clearer.

PENNY GETS UP FROM THE BED and sits on the edge, resting, as she is looking over at the alarm clock; it was close to midnight. She gets up and walks into the bathroom when the phone goes off, she runs back out and grabs it without looking to see who's calling. "Hello." she says while catching her breath.

"The package has been dropped off." a voice says, and as soon as the call came in, it was gone.

Penny puts the phone down and walks back to the bathroom and opens the toilet lid and sits down as she had barely woken up. This was almost therapeutic, and she was doing a lot of thinking when she would relieve herself. She places her head into a resting position in her palms. She needed to wake up, as she had very little time to waste.

Her delivery had arrived, and she couldn't stay any longer, it was time to get on the move and go dark. Her bag was packed, all she needed was to put on her shoes and leave.

Penny gets up and wipes herself and pulls up her pants, she walks over to the sink and washes her hands and splashes water in her face. She had to wake up and water would bring her out from her dazed state.

She walks over to the phone, looks over the incoming calls, and notices that one says "Harris" and the other one says "Unknown". She had tried to get a hold of Harris earlier, but she must had missed a second call from him when she had fallen asleep. She knew that she was going to have to call him back, but not before she had picked up the package. She walks up to her shoes and sticks her feet in them. She leans over and grabs her backpack, but stops herself in her tracks, and turns around just for a moment; did she have everything? Was there something she'd forgotten? She pats her pocket; the USB key was still there. With those last thoughts she walks out the door and hears it slam shut behind her.

She passes the elevators, and deliberately takes the stairs to the lobby. Once she reaches ground floor, Penny scopes out the area to her left, and then to her right as she approached the front desk. "I am here to pick up a package, room 311." she says to the front desk person who is sitting down behind the counter.

The man gets up quickly as he was startled and had not expected anyone at this hour. "One moment please." he says accommodating and disappears into the back. He brings back a NIKE shoe box and hands it to her.

She looks at it, as she wasn't really expecting this kind of packaging, and looks over at the clerk who was eyeing her. "Thank you." she says as she smiles, and then walks away, but stops sudden, she hesitates, but turns around 180 degrees to the man at the front desk, "Can you call me a taxi please?"

"Yes Madame." he replies.

Penny nods agreeing, as she continues to walk to the ladies' lobby bathroom. She steps inside and stops just inside the door, while waiting for the door to shut completely. She was listening to sounds, assessing the room; was she alone? She stoops down, to double check; the stalls were empty. Penny exhales a sigh of relief, she was getting paranoid, as she didn't feel safe anymore no matter where she was, and a small amount of anxiety was building up within her. She needed to hear a comforting voice, a voice of reason as her sixth sense had given off loud bells within her.

She steps into a stall and closes the lid on the toilet and places her backpack on it. She opens the box slowly; a pair of shoes were staring at her; she pulls them out and drops them next to her. She looks down and grabs the gun she'd asked for, it felt good in her hand, she stretched out her arm taking practicing her aim. She looks back down into the box, the clips were already loaded, and she places them on the top of the toilet tank. On the bottom of the box was a flat, wide-hip corset looking piece of fabric. Penny pulls it out and looks at it; it was a hip hugging gun holster. She pulls it apart and eyes it for a second before lifting her shirt up and wrapping it around her waist.

She grabs the gun and cocks it to check for a bullet in the chamber, it was clear. This was not a Colt, but a Springfield; however, this was better than nothing, she knew, and yet she couldn't help herself from making a face. She couldn't be picky, she realized, she was in Europe after all, and the gun was made in Croatia.

She checks the clips; they were 10 round clips, which gave her 50 rounds. "Ok, I guess this will do." she mutters under her breath. She loads on clip, places the gun in the holster and presses down two clips to the side. She looks over at the other two, she grabs them and looks down at her backpack; she opens the mid pocket, and tucks them in on the inside, and zips it shut.

She is about to leave as she looks down at her shoes, and then at the floor at the Nike's. She grabs one of the shoes and looks over at the size, they were 10, "He remembered." she says as she smiles and takes off her shoes and puts the Nike's on.

Penny gets out of the stall, throws her backpack on her shoulder, and places her own shoes in the box. Right before she exits, she drops the box in the large trashcan and walks out. She walks out into the lobby and towards the turnstile doors, when the front desk man calls out to her, "Madame, Madame your taxi is here!" he calls out to her.

Penny turns to the man and raises her hand to acknowledge him and walks out in the street. It was close to 1 am in the morning; the sky was clear but, pitch black and all she could see were the stars in the sky.

The taxi driver gets out of the car and opens the door for her.

"Merci." Penny says.

"De rein Madame." the man replies. The man gets back into the driver seat and looks into the rear-view mirror as he watches Penny fumble with her backpack. "Where would you like to go Madame?", the driver asks.

"To the train station." Penny says with a tired voice. What she really needed was a bed to get some much-needed sleep, but, ultimately, she knew she could get that on the train. There was only one objective, and that was that she needed to see Harris, he was the voice of reason, the one she trusted.

It didn't take long before the taxi came to a halt at the station. Penny hands the driver a €50 bill and gets out of the car.

"Madame," the driver exclaims, "your change!"

Penny waves at the driver to keep it as she steps up on the curb.

"Merci, merci beaucoup..." the driver replies, and snickers happily to himself as he puts the car in first gear and moves into traffic.

Penny looks up at the big clock facing her on the wall above. It was showing ten to one, she takes one look to her left then to her right, as she continues walking into the train station.

The signs were all in French and she followed the directions to the ticket counter. The interior of the train station was dressed in marble flooring and walls, and as she continued walking, she saw all the closed indoor mom and pop stores.

While resting her eyes on each store she passed, she knew her destination was no longer the US anymore. She was being forced to make a detour, everything had change, her position, and the fact that she still had very little information of who the puppeteer was, or who was pulling the strings; was it Mr. Bradford or Mr. Taytum, and what about Marcus? What was that all about, why was he there?

She had not yet had the chance to read the document that she'd uploaded to her email account and sent off to Harris. There was no other option; she had to travel nap of the earth for a while and ride out the storm somewhere safe. Penny had walked away from the responsibility she had taken on, without knowing the gist of the assignment, but knew enough to save herself before anything else.

Penny steps up to the ticket counter. The man behind the glass looks up. "Un billet pour Londres, s'il vous plait." she says as she rummages through her backpack for her wallet.

"€68." the man says as he is entering the information and printing her ticket.

Penny grabs her wallet, and she looks over her cash. She didn't have enough. "Shit!" she exclaims, she would have to use her credit card, which was something she'd tried to avoid. She slides the card towards the man under the crack of the glass, and within seconds the transaction had been made and she was handed the ticket and her card back. "Merci." she responds and looks down on at the ticket to locate what platform the train was departing from.

CHAPTER 14

"WE HAVE NO TIME TO WASTE" Bradford is saying while staring at the computer at his hotel room.

"I can't do it by myself, I need the documents, without them, it's not going to be easy to track down the people who work for the bank." a man with Middle Eastern accent replies.

"What's the operative plan when it comes to the people who work for the bank? What's the plan to get them to cooperate?" Bradford asks.

"If I can have the names, we can track the families, and you know..." the man says in a little disconcerting and nonchalant way.

"Ok, are there any other options? Money perhaps, or is that not going to be enough? Do you think we need to be life threatening? And then, what do we do?" Bradford says.

"Do you want to keep them alive or just let them go?" the man says.

There's brief silence before Bradford continues, "Once we have revealed ourselves, we need to clean up behind us, we cannot let them know our identities." Bradford says, now almost angry.

"Why are you so worried? Let me handle this on my end." the man continues confident.

"The problem is that I do worry about it, because you are so messy – *Hayawaan...*", Bradford says insulting, and continues, "...look at the last time you and your group screwed up things and here we are now, forced to find a way to transfer money into European banks. We need this to work." Bradford sighs annoyed.

The man was not responding to Bradford's aggravated speech, he knew better to just say nothing and let him vent.

"If we do not have a way of getting funds into US banks via transfer from a European bank; we can't place a satellite cell in the US. Do you understand?" Bradford pauses, "The US banks won't allow transfers from our bank in Jordan; they are blocking our attempt to place money because they know who we are." Bradford says with a more firm, authoritative, and demanding way.

"Ok, Ok, boss." the man says submissively.

"No fuck ups this time!" Bradford says sternly.

"Ok," the man pauses, *"how do we get to the information, where is the person?"* the man says now with a subtle tone.

"She is staying in room number 311, the information is on a USB key, but you just can't take it, she needs to open the file... she is the only one who has the code. So, you need to keep her alive." he says to the man as this was an order.

"Her? It's a woman?" and before the man can continue he gets interrupted by Bradford.

"Don't think it is going to be easy, she is not just anyone, just because she is a woman." he says with a confident tone.

"What's so special, what do you know that we need to know?" the man continues.

"I can't tell you, just listen, she is one who you shouldn't underestimate. Call me back when you have the information." Bradford disconnects the call feeling concerned and then he walks back and forth while nervously biting on his fingers and looking at the computer screen as he was waiting for information to seal the last puzzle piece to his spread sheet.

A knock on the door is interrupting his thoughts. He walks with steady steps and opens it. The room service had arrived, the waiter rolls the table inside.

"Che Khabar?" (*What's new*), Bradford asks quickly.

"Moshekli nist.", (*no problem*), the waiter says almost in code, and continues to place the food on the table, and turns to Bradford, "Mo'afagh bashed..." (*good luck*)

Bradford places some folded paper bills in the waiter's hand, "Mamnoon." (*thank you*), he says with a grateful expression.

The young man gives up a friendly smile, "Khahesh Mikonam." (*You're welcome*) and leaves the suite quickly.

MARCUS GETS OUT OF THE SHOWER; he knows he needs some answers and Penny was the one who was holding them. He looks over at the alarm clock, it was almost 1:30 am, it couldn't be helped, he had limited time, and this couldn't wait.

He pulls out his change of clothes and gets dressed all while he is thinking how he was going to approach her. What her reaction was going to be when he stood there in front of her door. He gives the room one last look before he grabs his hotel key and walks out the door.

As he turns the corner and starts walking towards Penny's room he recognizes a person walking towards him. The hotel was everything but a quiet place, and the closer the individual get to Marcus, he recognizes it's Bradford. There was no time to turn back, and, at this point, it would just look suspect, and Marcus continues in steady pace.

Bradford nods acknowledging, and keeps walking without interruption, and when there is enough distance between them Marcus turns his head slowly to watch him turn the corner. *'So he didn't recognize me...'* Marcus mumbles under his breath as he starts to question why Bradford hadn't recognized him. He scratches his five o'clock shadow chin, and his memories are taking him back in time; digging deep into his past time in Jordan. Why would he not recognize him, he had not changed much, but Bradford had, yet he had a distinct look that was hard to forget.

Marcus starts to relive his everyday routine in Jordan, and suddenly his mind makes an abrupt halt as he vividly sees a bathroom mirror appear in his mind. Yes, that's what it was; his full beard. Bradford didn't recognize him because he wasn't clean shaven when he was in the military. He had been like a chameleon trying to blend in.

He turns around a second time looking in Bradford's direction and grins. He did have the advantage, he knew, but Bradford didn't know.

He reaches Penny's door, gives a slight knock on the door, and without much of a push it slowly opens. He sticks his head inside and gives it a quick look from his position by the entrance and calls out in a soft-spoken tone, "Penny, Penny…" there was no response. He looks around to see if there was anyone else down the hall before he quickly enters the room.

He could see the room had been ransacked, the bed sheets had been ripped up, and the computer was tossed onto the floor and was now resting by the window. He knew this was no coincidence that he met Bradford in the hallway.

"What are you up to Penny?" he says out loud as he was thinking, where could she have gone.

CHAPTER 15

PENNY WAS SPORADICALLY WALKING through the train station as she still had 30 minutes to kill before the train was arriving. She was window shopping at the closed shops and bistro, and she stops in front of the door. It was hours before it would open, and the sound from her stomach growling was getting louder. She knew there was going to be a dining cart on this route, but she would not have much of a choice but to wait until then.

The round white clock was indicating that it was now close to 1:30 am, and the train would be rolling into the station at 2.

MARCUS WALKS UP TO THE concierge in the lobby, "I'd like to leave a message for room 311." he says and leans on the counter.

"One moment." the young man looks over the log in the system and continues, "Oh... Madame has already checked out." he says surprised and in an apologetic manner.

"Checked out?" Marcus says surprised. "I see…" and he pauses, "Do you know where she went?" he continues.

"I believe she got a cab, let me see if I can get a hold of the driver." the concierge says helpfully.

Marcus watches the young man make the call and hears him talk to the driver. He suddenly looks over at Marcus, places the phone to the side, "The driver said he took her to Gare Cornavin."

"Gare Cornavin?" Marcus looks questioning.

"Well, yes, the… train station." the young man looks confused as to why he wouldn't know that.

"Of course." Marcus says and gives up an embarrassed laugh, "OK, thank you." he says and starts to walk off when the young man calls at him.

"Do you need a taxi?" the concierge asks.

It was strange, it was as if he could read his mind. "I will catch one outside." and he raises his hand thanking him. Marcus walks through the turnstile doors and, at the curb, a taxi is waiting.

The driver recognizes Marcus and jumps out, "Where to?" he says excited.

"Gare Cornavin." Marcus gets in the taxi and the ride takes off. The driver is swerving up and down the streets and left and right, like he was driving in a pattern of a maze, and before Marcus knew it he had arrived at his destination. The train station was located a block behind the hotel, but the one-way streets made it impossible to take the straight shot direction. He hands the driver €25.

The driver raises his hand as his way of saying thank you while he throws out "Do you want me to wait for you?"

"Nae, I will get back another way." he says and walks inside the station.

He can hear every step echo as he puts one foot in front of the other. He finds himself walking up the stairs to the platforms, and, when he gets to the top, he looks around. His view catches a person on the other side of the rails walking back and forth as if waiting for something. He hesitates, and then calls out, "Penny?" and suddenly the person turns around, and to his surprise he was staring her in the face.

Penny stops almost shocked; this was unexpected and why was he here. She didn't know what to do or what to say, how should she explain this scenario. Penny cracks a bashful smile, and all she could do was to brace herself for the impact; his million loaded questions and measuring looks.

Marcus makes his way across the rails and jumps up on the platform where she was standing. "What are you doing here, at this time?" he asks inquisitively at the same time with a mixed feeling of being concerned.

What was he really wanting to talk about? She felt as if she was enrobed in all his feelings. He was having this anxious feeling, and a rush as if he was wanting something to be quickly resolved. He was trying to play coy, but she was an empath, nothing escaped her.

"I'm taking the train; we are at a train station... remember?" she says like a comedian with a snarky tone.

"You... you are funny you, that we already know." he says and laughs, and Penny laughs with him to ease the situation. While in the back of her head she had to keep her cool.

"Are you looking for me?" she asks in a confirming way.

"Yes... I was." he says and has more of serious nature, "Why don't you come back to the hotel with me?" he asks.

"Why, what do you mean?" she now takes a step back and is raising her guard. This wasn't good, he was withholding something from her. Penny takes a few steps away, as she wasn't going to go anywhere, especially now and how she felt. She had a feeling that she needed to run, and in the distance she could hear the train rolling into the station. There is this silence that seems to linger in forever, and neither are speaking.

Suddenly he throws out, "I know everything!" and she looks at him almost guilty as if she had been caught.

All she can do is to crack, "That's my ride." and points at the double engine train rolling in. She can see Marcus' lips move, but she can't hear anything as the loud sound from the train is drowning out any possible chance of a conversation. Penny turns around and keeps walking with fast and steady steps, she knew the train wasn't going to stay for long. She watches the conductor lean out on the step with a whistle in his mouth, the train was about to departure almost as fast it arrived.

She keeps walking faster and has eyed a set of doors, while Marcus moves closer towards Penny, and, without a moment's notice, she jumps inside a car and pushes the button to shut the doors.

The conductor let his whistle blow loud and makes the final decision to close the remaining open doors simultaneously, and with a jerking motion the train is moving.

As the train rolls out of the station, she sees Marcus' disappointed face, and she knew that this was just temporary, he wanted something and he said he knew, and yet she could only speculate. Did he know who she really was, or what kind of business she was conducting? She didn't know what it was, not yet anyway.

Marcus watches the train leave, and he knew that he was not going to conveniently fly home in the jet with his assignment finished any time soon. "OK, I guess it's time to do some real work." he says with a sigh with a feeling of frustration of why it had to be so hard to get some straight answers from her. Then he was reminded that it was Penny he was talking to; she was ultimately a woman.

All he could do was to shake his head and walk down the stairs, he was going to have to find out where the train was going. He was going, where she was, that was without a doubt his next destination.

He walks up to the counter and stops and just stares at the man behind the ticket counter. His PTSD was quickly surfacing without any control of stopping it. He was about to lose control over his emotions and that was making him tongue tide, and all he could feel was stress and uncontrollable rage. The sweat started to accumulate on his forehead like beads, and they were starting to roll of down his temple. Softly he starts to count, as the man is watching him, and his lips move.

"Qui?" the man says questioning and waits for Marcus to stop the countless counting to say something. "Are you ok? You don't speak French? Well... OK." the man says apologetic, and almost with a distaste in his mouth.

Marcus could feel he wasn't welcome, but he couldn't let himself act on it. He was almost frozen in his position and then the man grabs his attention.

"You just missed the train to London, are you going to London?" the man asks.

"No... but thank you." he mumbles and moves away from the counter in an artificial manner. "London, what was in London?" he questions out loud.

"Monsieur, do you need a ticket to London?" the man asks as he leans forward inside his cubicle behind the glass counter.

Marcus doesn't react to the man's question and just keeps walking through the train station in a trance, and out in to the street while his mind was making a blue print schedule of how he was going to get there before she arrived.

He looks over his phone and he remembered, the card, the coordinates, he needed to call John. The flight plan was going to change, that was all there was to it. Marcus sticks his hand in his pocket, and he pulls out the card, and with shaky fingers he enters the numbers. The phone is ringing, and he can hear John's voice on the other end answer.

"John, make the plane ready, we are taking off tonight." Marcus says.

"OK, you got the package?" he says confirming.

"No, its on the move, and we are going to head to the destination, before it arrives."

"What's the destination?"

"Latitude 51.5081 - Longitude -.128"

"OK, we'll be ready." and the call is disconnected.

Marcus looks up and views the empty street and can see in the distance a taxi, he waves it down as it is passing by, and the vehicle makes an immediate u-turn, and pulls up to the curb.

JOHN IS WALKING up to the pilots and he hands them the flight schedule, "Get it ready to departure in an hour." he says factually.

The pilots are looking at the coordinates, and at each other with a confused look.

"Don't ask, just get it lined up, I'm just the messenger." he says and throws up his hands in the air as he has no better answer and walks to the back of the plane.

MARCUS WALKS INTO HIS ROOM, he needed to get to his Xanax, his body was tingling and sweating. He grabs his bag and locates the jar on the bottom, and all while his hands are shaking as he manages to get two small pills in his mouth. He swallows them without any water and with a relieved feeling he leans tiresome his behind on the cabinet as he is waiting for it to take effect, and start to feel his pulse slow down and his hands stop shaking.

It was obvious, he wasn't able to think clearly without them. The confrontation with Penny had triggered the feelings and he grab a towel that was resting on the bed and wipes the sweat from his forehead.

He looks around and tries to focus as he pulls his paperwork and tablet together. He packs it all up and clears anything that could be compromising. He gives the room one last look as he grabs his hotel key and exits the room.

He had a cab waiting by the curb, and the man gets out and walks up to Marcus, then he grabs Marcus' bag and places it in the trunk.

Marcus' mind was miles away as he was now churning over the assignment. Just like he had thought, it sounded too easy, and it was. He leans over to the driver and hands him two wadded 20-euro bills and tells him to head to the Cointrin airport.

The driver acknowledges the order and rolls away from the curb as Marcus leans back in the seat and falls back into his analytical thoughts in regard to who Penny really was.

Now he needed to know more, whatever was thrown his way, nothing could be a surprise. He knew that he could expected the worse but hope for the best. Something told him that Penny was not as simple as it had seemed, she was more complex, and that was one of the reasons he wasn't going to give up.

PENNY WAS sitting by the window watching the landscape pass by as she was still agitated and upset over the situation at the station. She couldn't let go of what he had said, and she sat there by herself mulling it over. What she really wanted to know was what he wanted. She looks at her phone and she knew she had to call him. She pushes his name in her contact list and waits for the tone, but instead she receives a message, *"The subscriber is out of the coverage area."*

She disconnects the call and puts the phone on her lap, and then leans back into the seat and reclines it a little. It was going to be a good 8 hours before she would reach London, and, of course, she would have to change trains in Paris. She needed to get a message, a covert message, over to the Harris in Scotland. She looks back down at her phone and thinks of something that would seem obvious and yet simple and innocent. Penny picks up her phone types in a quick text message, "8 hr - Mr. Paddington Bear", sends it off to Harris and puts the phone in her pocket.

The train is flying through the open landscape in the dark of night, while Penny is sound asleep. The time ticks closer to dawn as dawn is rapidly approaching and the sun is rising on the horizon.

Marcus is slowly waking up in his seat as the plane is flying over the Thames.

John walks over to Marcus, "We will be landing at Stansted shortly, give or take 35 minutes." he says as he pats him on the shoulder.

The train was steadily moving and was set to arrive at Paddington station in a couple of hours and Marcus knew that he had to be there before she arrived; he knew she did not expect him there. A feeling of being a step ahead was not surfacing, in fact it was the opposite, a feeling of uncertainty had crawled under his skin, and that more surprises were to be expected.

CHAPTER 16

HARRIS PULLS UP TO Hotel Hilton Paddington, he gets out and grabs his walking stick. The valet comes over, "Any luggage sir?"

"Yes, I have a bag in the back." he says as he takes a step back to allow the valet to pull out the bag from his back seat.

The top-hated Doorman with white gloves waves at the bellboy by gesturing with his hands to handle the luggage. The bellboy comes running, grabs the bag, and brings it inside while Harris lingers on the sidewalk and watches the valet drive off. He casually looks over at the entrance to Paddington Station and lets his eyes take a wandering look to his left, and then to his right. He knew that he couldn't leave anything to chance, too much had happened, and he had to check his 360 to make sure the coast was clear.

He turns towards the hotel entrance and walks up the steps to the turnstile doors and pushes at it as he steps inside the lobby. In the distance he can see James, the General Manager for the hotel lingering about keeping a watchful eye on everything. James casually looks up and their eyes meet. Harris watches him make his way towards him and can see his smiling face light up the lobby.

"Ah, you are back Ben, that wasn't yesterday." he says as he is approaching Harris.

"That's right James, I am picking someone up." and Harris grins with a face that was telling.

"OK, well, lets get the best for you then." James continues and walks him over to the concierge counter where he gestures to the clerk who hands him a key. The bellboy walks up to the concierge desk and James shows him the room number. The bellboy disappears with the luggage.

James turns to Harris, "This isn't business, is it?" he says as they are walking towards the elevators.

Harris pushes the button for the elevator and the door opens up. "Not this time." he says and grabs the key from James' hand then walks into the elevator.

James watches with a puzzled look on his face as Harris disappears behind the closing elevator doors, and then he shakes his head in confusion as he makes his way back to the lobby. He knows all too well that the last time Harris had stayed there it had turned out to be an expensive situation that his department had paid handsomely for.

Harris has arrived at his room and pushes the keycard into the door, it unlocks, and he steps inside; his eyes sees his luggage that was placed by the desk. He places his walking stick by the door and shuts it closed.

The room was exquisitely decorated in art deco style, by the end of the bed a lounging couch was placed. He removes his jacket and throws it on the bed, and then the gun holster and places it on the bed, and he walks into the bathroom. It had white tiled walls, and a deep bathtub, the counter to the sunk-in white sink was in black granite.

He takes off his glasses and places them carefully next to him on the sink, then he grabs a towel. He looks into the mirror while washing his face, he had a lot on his mind and in the midst of it all his thoughts were impeded by Penny. She was soon arriving, and he needed to be there before the train hit the station. It was his way of scoping out every entrance and exit to make sure that he had a plan B if anything was about to go wrong, and he was used to things going wrong.

He was not the ordinary Scottish chap with an estate on the countryside; he was a true mole and had even thought about the hotel. It was conveniently placed just across the street from the station were there were enough distractions to easily disappear in, and that made it the perfect location.

During his governmental work he had learned to keep people close, let them feel they were important. Harris knew how to rub egos the right way and, in the interim, it had brought him valuable benefits and, not to forget, the connections he had made; they would last him a lifetime, and they were indispensable, just like James.

He had left Penny a message, to expect him to pick up her up, it was safer that way. He knew she didn't need anyone to help her, but he felt that times had changed, and no one was safe anymore, not even him.

He dries his hands and puts the glasses back on. He walks up to the bed and reaches for the gun holster and straps it on. He stops for a second to take a deep breath and lets his eyes rest on the view through the window. It had been a minute since he had seen her, and it was not under great circumstances then, and neither was it today.

Harris leans over and grabs the gun and situates it comfortably in the holster, and then he puts on his green tweed shooting jacket. It did a nice job of covering his firearm. He walks up to the table and reaches for the keycard as he continues towards the door and grabs his walking stick, then he places the keycard in his pocket. He feels his flat cap tucked inside the jacket, pulls it out, and puts it on. He makes a quick stop at the mirror and gives himself a last look; *'like an ordinary British countryman who is minding his own business'*, he thought to himself and grinned.

While Harris is walking out the door, Marcus' jet is touching down at Stansted.

John comes by as the plane is almost coming to a halt. "Where are you heading next? Do you need some currency?" he asks as he looks at Marcus.

"I need to get to Paddington." he says as sure as he could be.

"OK, you'll need to get on the express to London, that is the fastest way." he says and sits down. He was the man who stored information in his head like a walking Wikipedia. "You'll need this…" he says as he hands him a couple hundred pounds in small change, "…that is all I had available." he continues.

Marcus looks at the money and back at John, "Thanks, I owe you.", he says with gratitude in his voice.

"Don't thank me yet." he says and gives him a concerned look, and continues, "Listen, when you get to London, the express' first stop will be at Victoria Station, then you need to grab the Underground, yellow Circle line, that will get you straight to Paddington." John says, and stands up while continuing to look at Marcus and continues, "We all good?"

"Yes, all is good… and noted." Marcus says and stands up and follows John to the door.

"We're a phone call away… know that." John looks over at the cockpit and back at Marcus, "Give us a few hours heads up, you never know where we are at." he says and then proceeds to open the plane's door for him.

Marcus walks down the steps and disappears into the terminal, and as he walks in the jet is taxing back out; almost as soon as it had landed it was back in the air.

HARRIS WALKS down the steps into the Paddington Station, as he can hear the announcements rapidly release one after another, and then, *"Train from Paris on inbound, arriving at platform 14."*

He keeps walking with steady steps and adjusts his cap as he was taking a surveying look around, and then continues to walk towards platform 14.

The station is busy this time of day, and that was good in Harris' way of looking at things, as crowds were perfect places to hide in plain sight. He walks halfway onto the platform and steps to the side then leans again a brick wall to rest.

The train rolls into the station and its breaks are screeching loudly. The conductor is leaning out through one of the first doors as the train is slowing down and coming to a complete stop. The doors open up and people are exiting the train fast, almost falling onto the platform like wild animals being released.

Harris is keeping a watchful eye on the people passing by, he had not seen Penny for a while, but she had a distinct way of carrying herself, so it wasn't going to be too difficult. Women and men who were passing by looked like they were from all continents of the world. Then... there, suddenly something of an anomaly appeared, and there she was, but she was walking with firm steps as if she was on a mission. Her hands were firmly gripping the latches on her backpack.

Harris follows her, and watches her closely, and so it seems that others have too caught an interest in her he realizes quickly. He recognizes that a few middle eastern men are following Penny a bit too close, and as they are getting closer and the crowd is getting thicker around her, he hears *"Watakhudh laha!" (Take her!)* and they grab her without a moment's notice.

Harris pushes himself through the crowd and, as he is about lose sight of them, they suddenly all disappear up the stairs to street level. As they are pushing Penny up the stairs, Marcus has made his way to the steps going down to the train station, and he is walking slowly down. He sporadically looks up and gives off a confused expression when his eyes meet Penny's, but she is more confused of how he got there. She turns her head around, and gives him a serious look, he knows, her situation is not by choice.

Penny is putting up a fight at that moment and is trying to get out of their grip. *"Ajaleh kon!"* (*Hurry up!*) Penny yells.

Marcus reacts to the command, then he stops and looks up, "Ant!" (You!). The men look back at Marcus and he continues, "Nem ant!" (Yes, you!) he yells out loud at them.

The three men make a complete stop in their tracks, and they are all looking back at Marcus. They watch as this blond man just stares at them and communicates in their language, and they look back at each other puzzled. He was the only man who was on the stairs besides them.

"Taeal wahsul ealayh min lay!" (Come and get it from me!) Marcus continues.

"Don't Marcus, stay out of this!" Penny says as one man is holding her while the other two are approaching Marcus.

"Big mistake." Marcus says under his breath.

Then, suddenly, an old gentleman appears and is slowly walking up the stairs with a stick. He is dressed in a green tweed shooting jacket and a cap, and as he is getting closer

Penny starts to wonder if she had not seen this man before. The man passes Penny and gives her a quick look, and he turns his look back down at the steps. The man holding Penny gives Harris a uninterested look and turns his attention towards his two other accomplices.

In a snap moment, Harris swings his stick at the man, and the man loses his balance and falls backwards. At the same moment, Harris grabs Penny and they make a run up the stairs as fast as their legs can carry them. Harris steps out in the street and stops the cars, and then pulls Penny across the street and into the hotel.

Penny is catching her breath as they are standing in the lobby waiting at the elevator, and it doesn't take long before the elevator doors are opening, and they are safely inside. Harris pushes the button for his floor and the elevator starts to move upward. There is this odd silence, and the only sound heard is that of two people breathing heavily while a nervous, heart pounding feeling is filling up the volume of the elevator.

The ride stops and the doors open up to a carpeted hallway, and Harris says nothing as he steps out of the elevator and into the hallway while holding out his hand to stop Penny from taking a step forward while he gives a quick look to his left and to his right. Then, with only sign language he is clearing the path for her, and she follows his lead without a word spoken.

CHAPTER 17

BRADFORD IS LOOKING out the window, he was alone, he had no one. His life had been dedicated to one thing, and that was to himself. He had no family of his own, only his extended family, and he had protected them by staying away. The line of business he had chosen was laced with punishments, it was not just him who was going to die if he stepped out of line, but his entire bloodline, and that meant every single innocent person he was closely related to. Yes, he had traded a normal life for what he desired mostly; money and power.

The phone rings and interrupts his solitude. He reaches out for it and grabs it from the nightstand, and with a tired raspy voice he gives off a deep "Hello."

"Sobh Be Kheyr." the man says with a thick middle eastern accent.

"Sobh Be Kheyr." *(Good morning)* Bradford says tired while he was clearly still not awake and ready to hold a conversation in Farsi.

"We found her... Oo, Shoma refigh" (*Her, your friend*) he says to remind him that they had tracked her down.

"Mish tekrar konid?" (Can you say that again?) Bradford starts to wake up.

"We found her, she's in London..." the man continues.

Bradford sits up, "Is she with you?"

"We lost her, there was an interception" he says disappointed.

"What do you mean?"

"Some guy picked a fight with us and two of our guys are in real bad shape, and then there was this old man, I don't know if he was with her, it went so fast and I..." the man says and gets interrupted by Bradford as he didn't want to hear more, excuses were for kids and these were soldiers.

"Where are you?" Bradford asks now annoyed.

"Paddington Station."

"I'm on my way." he says and hangs up. Bradford looks down at the phone, scrolls over his numbers and selects one. He puts the phone to his ear, "Make the plane ready... destination... London... give me 45 minutes."

MARCUS IS IN the bathroom at the train station, he looks down at the sink and starts to sniff, there was a strong smell of sewage that snuck up into his nostrils and it clung on to his nose hairs like a clear film that would not release itself. He had visited better toilets in the middle east and that was not much to cheer for, but the strong sewage smell he was exposed to in this small underground toilet was nauseating. He turns on the water by turning the elegant knob shaped handles. The beautiful engraved letters on each knob indicating hot or cold water were no match for the brown rusty water that poured into the sink.

Marcus leans his hands on the sink so he could take a closer look at his bruised face in the mirror. He couldn't help but notice the random black spots all over the mirror as it was quite old and worn. He looks down to see if the brown colored water had turned clear, but the dim flickering light made it difficult to figure it out. He looks back up at the mirror to assess the damage he had sustained in the altercation with the three men. All he could do was to grab a paper towel from the metal box that was stuck to the wall and wet it so he could at least try to clean up his wounds.

So many thoughts were circling in his mind, he had to track Penny down, but how? And who was the man in the green coat? How convenient that he was there. What was so special about this information, and, more so, why did the US Government want it? He knew that he had to reach out to Q, he had some explaining to do, and there was no time for any games, he needed to know everything.

Marcus leaves the bathroom and makes his way back up to street level and on to Praed Street. He was facing Hilton Paddington Hotel. The grand Victorian style hotel was stretching all the way up to London Street. He looked left and then right, this was unfamiliar territory and he wasn't sure where to look. Where could she have gone? He starts to walk towards London Street, he was a little lost as he had never been to London before. He looks down the street both ways, and he knew there was nothing there that drew him. He turns around and walks back to the point where he lost her, and he stops at the other cross street, Eastbourne Terrace the sign said, he scratched his head and turned back around, and he was again facing the hotel.

Nae, it seems too easy, he thinks, but what did he have to lose, he had to start somewhere. Marcus crosses the street at the crosswalk and walks along the cast-iron fence that was decorating the sidewalk and whispered a tale of grander days. He stops at the entrance for a moment before he walks up to the red carpet dressed steps. The doors were heavy wooden turnstile doors and had a solid wood exterior; things seemed to have stood still just for a minute in this building, it told a tale of history without reservations.

He walks through the doors and inside to the lobby; he can see people to his right checking in at the reception desk. He watches the concierge to his left walking back and forth behind his desk. Uniformed staff were busy crossing the marble pattern floor, and despite of it all, it was rather quiet. He suddenly hears someone clearing their throat behind him, he turns around and jumps where he stands.

"May I help you?" the suit dressed man asks in the Queen's English replete with a posh accent.

Marcus is little taken aback by his accent and says nothing, but instead gives the man a measuring look; he recognizes the

Hilton emblem on his breast pocket and realizes that he is working there.

"Are you checking in today, sir?" the man continues.

"Oh, no, I was..." and Marcus stops himself, takes a quick look around and sees the restaurant, "...going to have a bite to eat." he says recovering his statement from the pause.

"A bite?" the man says and frowns a little, "Will you need a moment...." and he stops while he is returning Marcus' measuring look, "Well, I mean, do you need to wash up before the dinner is served?" he says as he clearly demonstrates that he waits for an answer.

"Oh." and Marcus gives up a laugh, "Yes, of course."

The man starts to walk off then suddenly stops and turns back around to Marcus, "Well... this way." he says and proceeds to walk into the back. They walk past the kitchen area, "Since you are not staying here, I suggest you wash up here." and points at the employee bathroom.

Marcus nods and walks inside; the bathroom was exceptionally clean, and you could almost eat off the floor. It sure was strange, the entire situation was strange, too many oddities were constantly surfacing, and suddenly he remembers. He pulls up his phone and he sends off a text to Q, *"Inside the Hilton Paddington, meet me in the lounge."* and sends it off. He finally had a proper light and was able to look at his face. It wasn't pretty, and he now understood why the man had asked him if he needed to clean up. His face had bloodied bruises and definitely needed a lot more attention than he got from the paper towel.

Marcus turns on the water and it's running clear, and the towel hanging on the rod next to the sink was folded in hotel fashion. Despite the situation, he was, after all, grateful for this gracious act.

PENNY IS SITTING down by the end of the bed on the lounging couch waiting for Harris to come back out from the bathroom. She was leaning forward with her hands intertwined and shaking her head in disbelief. Her thoughts were going back in time, and the feeling of stress was creeping back up inside her. She gets up from the couch and starts to pace back and forth, and as she is mulling over all that had happened, and why. Who was out to get her and why? She didn't want to believe that it was all in correlation with the documents she had been sent to get.

The door to the bathroom opens, and Harris is standing in the doorway watching Penny pacing, and he can tell she is starting to get into a manic state; he could tell by her behaviors that the shock was surfacing.

He walks towards her and stops her in her tracks; she looks up and he can tell by her empty look that she is somewhere else. Harris pulls her closer and hugs her, and Penny leans into his shoulder. She could feel the warmth and in the next moment tears were rolling down her cheeks. It was her release and purge to finally relax and feel that someone was catching her emotionally.

He looks down at Penny while comforting her by stroking her hair. "It's going to be ok, I promise..." he says whispering. Harris is looking over at the alarm clock by the bedside, it was already in the afternoon. Time had escaped him and he pushes Penny off his shoulder slowly and looks at her, "How about something to eat?" he asks her like a concerned father figure. Penny nods agreeing as she is wiping her tears off her cheeks. "Go ahead and use the bathroom and get cleaned up, you'll feel better, I promise" he says reassuring.

Penny grabs her backpack, disappears into the bathroom, and closes the door. Harris is standing by the window looking out with his arms crossed, waiting for Penny, and thinking about what was coming next. He had a feeling that something was brewing, he was intuitive like that. In the midst of his thoughts he could hear a buzzing sound inside the room, he turns around looking to see what it was. He slowly surveys the room and tries to figure out where it is coming from, suddenly it stops.

He could hear water running from the faucet in the bathroom, and in the next moment that stopped too. He was waiting eagerly for Penny to come through the door any second now, and then, the door slowly opens and there she was and it was an awkward silent minute before Harris breaks it, "Let's go down to the bistro and get something to eat..." he pauses and waits for acknowledgement before he continues, "We need to eat and then we can talk, ok?" he says assuring.

"Yes, you are right. I feel I need something to eat." Penny says agreeing.

Harris grabs his coat and Penny grabs her phone that is underneath her jacket. She looks down at it and she can see that she missed a call and that there was a voicemail. "Hold on, I missed a call." she calls out to Harris who is already standing with the door open and ready to leave. She places the phone to her ear, and her face is changing from being ok to a concerned look, and at the same time she is looking at Harris. "We need to talk." she says.

Harris closes the door, "Here? Now or over dinner?" he says and is now paying close attention to what's coming next.

"I am concerned..." she pauses, "I think that I am in over my head." she says and gets quiet as she looks at Harris and her mind goes back to the airport moment she had with Bradford.

"Who was that on the voicemail?" he asks and interrupts the silence.

She sits down on the bed, "You know the documents I sent you... did you get the chance to look at them?" she asks and gives him a defeated look.

"Yes, and that is what I wanted to talk to you about... did you?" he says and his tone changes, he was in an analytical stage.

"No, and I can already tell its bad news." Penny looks down at her phone and shakes her head.

"I can tell you it's not good, we can just as well deal with it now as I suspect that the voicemail is about that. Correct me if I am wrong." he says and walks up to the desk and reaches into his bag and pulls out his laptop. He opens it up and turns it on. "I believe you are right... that you are in over your head and I will explain why." Harris says as a matter of fact.

Penny turns around and looks at him with a serious set of eyes, "How bad is it?" she says, and now she wanted to know what it was all about.

"I've looked at the documents you sent over…" he says while being occupied by looking at the computer screen.

"And…?" she asks impatiently.

"I told you that Shariq Afifi was the son of Victor Afifi, from the office you visited." and he looks at Penny, "And what I can see is that this financial plan, or should I say plot, was put together by him."

"Financial plot?" she utters surprised, "He would have needed information to pull this together because…"

Harris interrupts and can already sense what's next to come, "And who was the individual who assisted him in that?" Harris gives Penny a questioning expression.

Penny thinks, and mumbles to herself, and goes back to how it all began, "Taytum, Neal, and who else…?" she says.

"Who's Taytum? Who's Neal?" he asks as if he was missing something.

"I am thinking… how it all started."

"Your office sent you to pick this up, and then you met with someone at Afifi's office… correct?" he states and asks at the same time.

"Yes!" she says with a firm tone, "And he called me and left me a message, Bradford left me a message."

"Bradford?" and Harris is now confused, "Who is Bradford? Is that his first name?"

"No, that is his last name, Seels Bradford is his full name."

Harris sits down on the chair at the desk and pulls up the PDF file and enters the code JO962, and the 10-page document opens up. "Bradford, how do you spell his first name?" Harris asks.

"Sierra-Echo-Echo-Lima-Sierra." Penny spells it out and moves closer to watch him search in a system she was not familiar with. "What system is that?" she asks.

"This..." and he looks over at her while pointing at the computer screen. "This is the opening to the rabbit hole, and it goes deep." he says and turns back around facing the screen. "OK, so you went to the Afifi's office and Bradford was the one who handed you the document... hmm... and... let's see what's the connection between the two of them." he says calculating.

"I tell you it is something I have never seen before or even thought was plausible, or even that someone would think of." Harris says as he is searching for Bradford.

"What is?" Penny asks and pays close attention to Harris as he's busy searching for Bradford.
"The plot." he says as he is deeply involved in his multiple window changes and jumping from text pages to highlighted hyperlinks with pages that has pictures.

Penny suddenly sees a picture of Bradford. "STOP!" she exclaims.

Harris looks over at Penny, "Stop?" he says questioning.

"Bradford, I saw a picture of Bradford." she says excitedly.

Harris goes back and there he was, a picture from a meeting that Harris had taken at a restaurant somewhere in the middle east. "You are sure?" he asks and wants confirmation. What he knew about the man on the picture was everything but good.

"Yes, I am certain." she says and stresses on the facts as she knew them. There he was without any doubts, she wasn't someone who forgot, she had eidetic memory.

He looks back at the computer screen with the photograph staring him in the face, a man in a middle eastern outfit. He leans back in the chair with his hands resting at the back of his head. "You know, Penny... he is a middleman handler for the banks in the Middle East?" Harris says and looks over at her waiting for a reaction and there is none, and he continues, "He is considered the golden child, with an MBA from a highly accredited University in the States, which was paid for by a financial group in Jordan. There is a chance that Victor Afifi paid for it, but no one knows for sure."

Penny is listening but not saying much, just nodding and listening attentively.

"If this was not enough, he's also a weapons expert; he was in the US Army, since 1991 he has been an operative in Europe and has a few places in the world where he stays." Harris pauses. Penny is just listening to Harris as he continues

breaking down the facts of acts and accolades that were
nothing to be proud of, or something one could put on a resume.
"He is the one who handles finances and the purchasing of
weapons for a terrorist cell that is operating in Europe at this
present time."

"This is not good... and I don't know what the connection he
has in regards to Taytum, but if this is what you know, then
it's not good." she says and ridges are beginning to appear on
the forehead as she is thinking. She also feels equally surprised
by how he had managed to dodge the bullets.

Harris has been focusing on the computer applications and
then he gets interrupted by Penny. "You looked at the PDF file,
tell me, what are we dealing with here?" she says demanding
while at the same time she wanted his summary.

"Have you heard the term 'financial terrorism'?" Harris asks.

"Yes and no. It can have multiple avenues and it depends on
the situation... is that your take on it since you asked?" she
says as she could read between the lines fairly easily.

"The documents show me that they are well put together and
organized. This could be a financial shock to the system and
who knows in what way this would go; there are several
avenues where this could end."

Both of them are just looking at each other, words were
overstated at this point; what else could be said? This was a
moot point, and what Harris knew corroborated with the file
Penny had sent him. The information painted a grim picture of

what extent some were willing to go to make their point, that was evident.

"So, this whole plot is going to bring down banks that are currently in good standing, that are vulnerable to larger institutions, but, by all means, are not desperate to merge. They plan to come up behind these institutions and cut them off at the knees. It is going to result in them completely monopolizing the market." She says and breaks the long silence.

Harris sits there for a moment then changes position and has both his hands attached to his face in a pondering way, and then he turns to Penny, "What do you know about this man?" he asks.

"Just that he is the one who I picked up the documents from." she says unimpressed.

"He went to Stanford, speaks Farsi and French, besides English. He is working with a group of banks that endorse terrorism, but the problem is that this terrorism was mostly conducted in the Middle East and is now overflowing into Europe. To finance this, there must be money, and with no banks that will allow certain entities to deposit funds in banks in Europe and the United States, they need to find a bank they can control and flood money into... in the money laundering aspect. Do you follow?" Harris says with a very calm and collected manner.

"So let me understand this, Bradford is a terrorist, American born, working for a bank under a veil of being someone he is not, assisting terrorism by helping to funnel money to banks that are used for terrorism, to be able to supply whatever the terrorists need when they are in the western territories?" she says in disbelief and continues, "Now I know why he wanted to have a meeting." she says under her breath.

"Say again... Did you just say that he wanted a meeting?" Harris asks as if he misheard.

"Yes." she replies while looking down on the phone and then back at Harris as they both thought the same.

"In a nutshell, we are dealing with a terrorist." Harris says, "But... it is much more complicated than that." and he stops because he wants to mull on how to break down the explanation to Penny in a way that she could paint the picture in her mind.

"You have a bank in the US that wants to monopolize the banking world, be big and powerful. You have Bradford who is acting as a liaison and middleman with terrorists, and who should be considered a terrorist because he is enabling them to do whatever they want to do. The reason I see Bradford wanting to meet with you is that he wants these documents because they contain the contact names that he needs. This is so he can engage with them directly, either to recruit, persuade, or even threaten them..." he pauses, "...and with that said, the individual's entire family is at risk."

Penny listens intently, and she is now seeing a clearer picture of the plot.

"Eventually they take over the bank by merging or by offering pennies on the dollar for the bank, and then, by being in control of the bank, they can also control how the money is laundered in Europe. Terrorists will do anything to reach their goal, you know that. This is the new way of war; financial terrorism. It is effective and unpredictable and will come out of left field. The effects are not just immediate, but long term and lasting." he says.

Penny is now contemplating on Harris' words, 'a new way of war', and she gets up from the bed and walks slowly up to the window. Her eyes are wandering from left to right, and she is watching the movement on the street below, and the further her eyes wander to the right she can see London Street and cars passing by. She can't stop thinking about the consequences this could have globally, and she says wonder some, "This can cause a new type of war..." She turns around and leans against the windowpane.

"You know what war does?" Harris says and looks at Penny. "You have been in that position before; remember years ago, you and I, Penny, where we were? If it wasn't for you, I would not be sitting here, and neither would you. This is different, it is more sophisticated and so underhanded that once it is all said and done, it will be hard to unwind." Harris knew what he was talking about; he had seen enough and investigated people in the underworld.

"Let's figure out a plan to expose this, but we need to start by cutting off the first culprit." Harris says and pulls out his paper pad, "I need names and everything you can remember, in the smallest detail as possible." he continues.

Penny's mind starts to go back to the first time she met Taytum and Neal, and about Marcus, who she had met back in

Seattle, and how he suddenly showed up in Geneva and at the same hotel. She didn't know if that was a coincident or planned. She was clear about one thing, Bradford was not a coincidence, she could see that he had been escorting her to London, to make sure she was alone.

"OK..." he says and pauses, "You know that the three wise men at the train station were waiting for the right moment... before they tried to catch you."

Penny looks at him, this was unusual, "I wonder how they knew Harris..."

"The hotel that you stayed at, what was the name?"

"Hotel Royal" Penny says innocently.

"And this was set up by the company?"

"Yes, Taytum, to be exact." and she is a little surprised about the questions regarding her accommodations, "Why the interest in where I was staying?"

"You see, Geneva is a hold up for businessmen and... terrorism and visits from the middle east, but clearly done all under the radar." he says and looks up from his computer screen, and turns to her, "Have you heard of 'the Seal'?" he asks casually.

"Should I? No, I haven't."

"The Seal, is a group that Bradford reigns over. Now, you said that you stayed at the Hotel Royal, so let's send out a request to see if he stayed there. You'd be surprise how people hide in plain sight." and Harris starts to type an email, and all she can see was encrypted language. Harris closes the program down, and he gets up from the chair.

"Let's go now and have that meal, I am starving, work gives me an appetite." he says and closes the lid on the laptop.

Penny felt like someone had punch her in the stomach, and food was really not on her agenda, but she couldn't think clear with no sugar, and she needed to get her blood sugar back up.

CHAPTER 18

PENNY AND HARRIS WALK INTO the bistro; they are approached by a waiter, and before he has a chance to say a word, Harris takes charge, "Can we get a table with privacy?".

The waiter turns around to view the layout, "I know exactly what you are looking for." and he escorts them to a table that is situated close to the kitchen entrance. It has a wall that blocks the view from people as they enter the restaurant.

"Perfect!" Harris exclaims, and sits down.

Penny takes a seat on a couch that was pinned to the wall, her view was of the free-standing tables. She never sat with her back to the door, she needed to view what was coming, it was ritualistic for her.

Harris is sitting right across from her, and she can see his eyes looking up at the large mirror that was right behind her, it showed him his 6 o'clock. It was all about being protective, and without making too many waves, he was certainly observant, and sly that male Leo.

Penny is going over the menu and turning over the folder. She glances over the dessert menu, and back at Harris with studying eyes; how old was he? It had never been discussed, but she knew his birthday was a few months away, to be exact July 22nd.

"A penny for your thoughts?" he says and looks up from the menu and smiles.

"Well, that's my name." she says and returns a smirk, "I'll be honest with you, on a serious note, I was thinking whether or not I would make it to your birthday..." she pauses, and Harris looks up, directly at her, and gives her a disagreeing glare. Penny continues, "Well, considering all the stuff that happened over the past few hours, it should be a good indicator that I have a target on my back... I'm being realistic now." she says and dives down into the menu just as the waiter comes back to the table.

"Are we ready?" he asks.

Before Harris can intervene Penny chimes in, "I am... I'll have the sea bass." she says and looks over at Harris and gives him a smile.

He gives her a look that he wanted more time, "I'll have what she's getting." as he points his finger in Penny's direction, and then folds the menu closed and hands it to the waiter.

J.D. Bridgeford

"Would you like to look over the wine menu?" he asks as he looks at both of them, and they both shakes their head as in a 'no'.

Harris waits for the waiter to walk off; he observes him grabbing the empty wine glasses and the menus, and then he disappears around the corner.

"Let's get a little serious here..." he says and leans into the table as his words matched the grave feeling he was giving off, "...you need to set up the meeting with Bradford."

"I don't even know where he is." Penny says defeated.

"He called you and left you a message; you call the shots... if he wants to meet you, then you are in control." Harris says and casually leans back in his chair and places his right leg over his left leg.

Penny looks at him, she could see where he was coming from. "Ok, I'll call." she says confidently and after enough deliberation on the task at hand, "Where should I set up the meeting?" she continues.

Harris has a pondering look on this face as he was thinking. "The blue ginger, on Harrow road." he says after a long pause.

"What is that?" Penny asks.

"An Indian restaurant..." he looks at her and can see she is still not sure she understood, "...you know, dot, not feather." he says as he puts his index finger to his forehead and chuckles.

196

Penny smiles as she loves the silly side of him. He could ease any situation with his sense of humor, typically dry, yet light-hearted. She looks down at the phone and presses on the incoming phone number, she puts the phone to her ear and listens to the call ringing, and, on the third ring, she hears a voice on the other end.

"What took you so long?" Bradford says. His voice was loud and abrasive, and firm at the same time.

Penny could hear loud noises in the background. "Listen, you called me. Don't turn this on me. What do you want by the way?" It's quiet and she continues, "Where are you? I can barely hear you. What is that background noise?" she says annoyed.

"I am at Stansted. Listen..." he says, and then changes his approach by adding a thick layer of charm, *"You know what I want... we can make it easy and you can move on with your little life in Seattle."* he says and waits for Penny's response.

"Stansted? I see." she pauses and looks up at Harris and signals with her finger by pointing it downward and mimicking with her lips '*he is here*', and continues, "OK, meet me at the Blue Ginger on Harrow Road..." she says and waits for his response.

"OK, what time?"

"Noon, tomorrow." and she disconnects the call. Penny and Harris sit quietly after the call, just watching each other and sipping on their water as they waited for their meal.

Soon enough, the waiter arrives, and their food is placed in front of them. "Is there anything else I can get for you?" the waiter expresses, and then he looks first at Penny, then at Harris.

"No, not a thing." she says while she looks at Harris and gives off a smile like the cat who swallowed the canary. The waiter nods understanding as he gets the queue and leaves.

"So?" Harris asks as he takes his first bite.

"He's here..." she says and reads his mind, as she knows what he was asking about, "...must have just got off the plane in Stansted." and she sticks her fork into the seabass.

Harris looks up, finishes chewing, and queries, "What makes you say that?" while taking another bite.

"I could hear jet engines in the background." and she takes a second bite of her food.

"Hmm, I wonder how he knows where you are..." and he gives her a measuring look, and is thinking as he is circling his knife in the air, "What did you carry with you... I mean what belongings?" and he stops.

Penny looks confused, "What do you mean? I just had the backpack with my hygiene articles and change of clothes... and the phone." she states innocently as she is not understanding.

"You are here, and he is getting off the plane in Stansted... how did he know you were in London?"

She looks up and stops in her tracks, then she wipes her mouth with the white linen napkin, and takes a sip of her water, "That is a good question, almost too good to be true for being coincidental, but, then again, Bradford has been the one that I consider to be the least coincidental person in all this... more consistent and almost like a jack-in-the-box when I least expected, but it was always him." she says and looks down at her food poking at it while thinking.

"I think he is the one who sent those camel jockeys for you, something just tells me that." and Harris grabs his glass of water. "I think I need something stronger... I think it's time to put on my thinking cap." he says and waves at the waiter to come.

"Can I have a double shot of Glenfiddich India Pale?" he says to the waiter, and he watches the waiter write it down in his black folding book then place it in the front pocket of his apron before he walks off.

Penny continues to eat and watch the situation unfold while she surveys her surroundings casually.

"I need to feed these grays as I think we are going to corner one of the pieces of this puzzle." Harris says and continues to work on his plate.

BRADFORD IS in the car thinking of Penny. He was pondering on the meeting that was set, and then in midst of his thoughts the phone started ringing and interrupted his train of thought. "Yes?" he says as he expected Penny to call back, but instead he heard an unexpected voice.

"Seels... I need you to come and see me, I need your help." the man says in broken English and with urgency.

"Afifi, what can I do for you my dear friend?" Bradford says very caring.

"I have problem, but I don't trust these phones, just come and see me." he continues.

"I just landed in Stansted and am on my way into London, I can stop by."

"Very good, I'll see you shortly and we'll have tea." he says, and the call is disconnected.

Bradford knocks on the glass for the driver's attention, and the driver pushes the glass window open, "Yes, sir?" the driver says as he is acknowledging Bradford's tapping.

"Let's change our route, take us to Hyde Gate Park by Albert Hall, Afifi's house please." he says directing.

"Yes, sir." and the driver shuts the window closed.

Bradford rest his arm on the ledge of the window as he looks out. His mind is distracted by multiple things and he can sense that the car is speeding faster on the highway. He had made the trip to track Penny down, and now he was called in by Afifi, and it wasn't sounding too good. He wasn't aware that he had caught wind of his own ongoing operation, or had he? He started to feel uneasy that there was something he wasn't privy to. Afifi had briefed him about everything in the operation that was in the works, but this situation he had not been made aware of.

MARCUS IS IN THE BAR WAITING for Q, and he is about to send off another text when he feels a tap on his shoulder and turns around.

"Good to see you Weaver... I wish the circumstances were different." Q says and shakes his hand as he scopes out the lounge area. "What are you having?" he asks Marcus.

"Scotch on ice."

Q waves at the bartender.

"Yes, sir?" the bartender responds.

"Give me a double scotch, hold the ice."

"Yes, sir." the bartender turns around quickly and starts to fill the glass, and Q looks at Marcus with an analyzing eye. The bartender distracts him as he places the drink on a cocktail napkin.

Q grabs his drink and takes one sip; it goes down strong and much needed. "Let's walk over here where there's more privacy." he says to Marcus, taps him on the arm, and walks off.

Marcus grabs his drink, follows Q's lead, and sits down in the low couch seats.

"So, what's going on?" Q says and takes another sip on his drink and reclines back with his hands on the couch's arm rests.

"I need to know the whole story, not just what I was told...." Marcus pauses and watches Q, "I have followed the lead for the 'package' here..." and he points with his index finger down to indicate here in London, "...the package that you asked me to retrieve... but... unless..." and he pauses as he felt that it was time to change the odds and put pressure on Q. He wasn't willing, anymore, to accept the terms he had initially signed up for, as the middle eastern men had become a problem and the fact that Penny was his prime suspect, but, yet, could not confirm it as she had managed to evade him.

"What information are you expecting to get?" Q says and wants to play difficult and see how far he could push back.

"OK, let me put it this way." he stops and gives Q the eye, "I believe with 99% certainty who this woman is... and when I track her down, I will then contemplate what the terms will be to hand her over..." He pauses and watches Q squirm in the seat and continues, "...it's no longer about the money, it's about integrity. You want me to retrieve it, then you will need to tell me the truth." he stops and looks at Q as the ball was now in his court. Marcus was no low life jockey who Q was dealing with, he was a well-seasoned military operative and there was no fooling him.

Q sits straight up and holds his drink with both his hands, cupping it, and he leans forward. "OK... but what I tell you, stays between us, and if I catch wind that you spilled the beans, I will deny any of it." and he leans back in his chair as he is waiting for Marcus to confirm his discretion.

Marcus looks at Q, he was pondering on how much he could trust his word as it had not been worth much. He felt he had not much of a choice as he was stuck between a rock and hard place. "Go ahead, I am all ears." he says.

"Do you recall Mafraq?" he says and Marcus nods agreeing, "The assignment you had with Howard was to locate the rouge troop and you guys did, Bradford." Q quiets down and takes a sip on his drink.

Marcus sits back and looks at Q with a blank stare as his attention had warped sped back in time.

"I know who he is now, thank you Weaver, I owe you big time." *Howard says.*

"No, we did what we had to do, I would do it all over again" *Marcus says.*

"You'll have to come and visit me and Jackie on the west coast when you get back home." Howard encourages him.

"Yea, where is she, your woman? I haven't met her yet."

"You will, believe me you will, she is something else Weaver." Howard pauses as he looks pondering at Marcus. "Promise me that if something would happen to me..." he says concerned.

"Nothing will happen to you, stop talking shit Howard." Marcus says assured.

That was the last conversation the two men had had. Marcus snaps out of his thoughts and looks at Q, "I remember what happened" he says tiresome.

"I have worked on a case to get Bradford to come in, we know that he was behind the bomb that killed Howard." Q says and lets his eyes wander toward the exit. "We know that he has ties to Afifi, the mercenary. His son is part of his organization and does all the financial planning and that is what the packages is all about." he finishes.

Marcus still feels that there is something missing, "So, the package is about Afifi's financial records? I am lost here?"

"No, the package contains a financial plot, a plot that will bring the financial institutions down to their knees, and Bradford has been working with someone in US, and we are observing it all, but we need the evidence to stop it all." Q says and is showing a stone face and his tone is very serious.

Marcus knows now that this was bigger than just a simple transaction, and the middle eastern men made sense now. They wanted what Penny had, and he knew now for certain she was the woman on the picture. "Let me ask you, the picture, where did you get that from?" Marcus asks curiously.

"That's a picture from Mafraq, we got a tip after we tapped Bradford's phone. He gave us the details of the picture, and he must have known it existed."

"Mafraq?" Marcus says surprised and yet he had already figured out that it was in the middle east, but didn't think it was in Mafraq, and continues, "It makes sense now." and he takes a sip on his drink.

"What does...?" Q says confused.

"I know who she is, it's Penny... yes, *that* Penny Bridge, the AVP." he says and looks at Q to see what his reaction was, and he is not reacting. "Did you know it was Penny Bridge?" Marcus continues as he can see that Q is almost a bit uncomfortable.

"We knew, but we have nothing else, she is an anomaly. We've tried to find out more, but since she shot down one of our drones, we backed off." he says defeated.

"So... you found out that she was going on this trip because..." Marcus stops himself, "...the conversation you got from Bradford's tapped phone." he says with confidence and looks at Q for confirmation, even though he knew that's what it was for certain.

"Yes..." Q says and continues, "...but we need the document so we can push the trigger on our operation 'SEALJO962'." he says adamantly.

"'SEALJO962'? You already have an operative?"

"Yes, we have worked on one for the past 8 months... you asked me about Taytum... he is the one who sent her to pick it up. For what we know, well, Taytum and Bradford, they went to school together. Taytum was the bright one, and Bradford... well, not so much." he says and fills in the blanks for Marcus. Q continues, "They both went to Stanford, and Bradford's tuition was paid by the Société Générale DE Banque in Amman."

"Who are we? And Amman, Jordan? What's the chance that Afifi is involved in this contribution?" Marcus says questioning and analytically.

Q says nothing, his facial expression is speaking for itself, then he stands up and cracks his neck as he looks at Marcus, "FBI is involved in this, that's all I can say... find her for me, and get the information so we can put a lid on it." he says and empties his glass and puts it back down on the table.

CHAPTER 19

BRADFORD ARRIVES AT AFIFI'S HOUSE, the driver gets out and opens the door. The townhome had this whitewashed exterior with a black wrought iron gate. It was a modest looking house, but the exterior fooled the best, as the interior has a palatial like feel to it. Bradford gets out and walks up the stairs to the door where he grabs the brass horseshoe handle and lets is fall onto the strike plate, and it gives off a loud knock on the black door.

The door opens and a penguin-like dressed house butler shows Bradford in. He stops in the large circular entrance and looks up, admiring the ceiling, and, without forewarning, the sound of the heavy door closing gives off an echoing sound that causes Bradford to jump in his skin.

"This way please." the man says. The butler's shoes give off a loud sound with each step he takes across the marble floor until he steps into the carpeted hallway.

Bradford carefully keeps his senses alerted as he did not know what to expect, he was treading in dangerous territory. A middle eastern man was, after all, a middle eastern man, and a man in his position and power from that side of the world was not someone you wanted to cross.

Bradford follows the man down the long hallway, and at the end of the hall a large room opens up. The man turns around and looks at Bradford, but says nothing, and walks off. Afifi is standing with his back to Bradford and is rummaging through papers at the table.

"Afifi." Bradford says to get his attention. He turns around swiftly.

"Seels." he says with a tiresome voice and walks up to him and embraces him like he was a 'family member'.
"We have a problem with one of our targets." he continues as he walks Bradford over to the seating area.

"Who are you talking about... and why are you so upset?" Bradford asks as he was unaware that Afifi had problems.

"The Englishman, I've tried to take care of it, but he is a slippery one." Afifi says discouraged.

"Where is he? Is this the reason you asked me to stop by?"

Afifi gives him a look of pleading for help without saying it.

"OK." Bradford acknowledges tired, "What can I do to help you?" and he rests leaning forward in his chair with his hands crossed.

"I was going to call you much earlier, but I thought my men could handle it... I have not heard from them. I got a feeling it is not good." Afifi says and thrusts his hands into the air as he was frustrated and had loss for words. He shakes his head while he walks back to the table.

Bradford could tell this was serious, "So, where are your men now... or should I ask where you sent them?"

Afifi's frustration has impacted his attention span, and he is only listening with half an ear as he is treading back and forth across the carpeted floor by a large window. "I have not heard from them, so I suspect the worst. Last time we had a location, it was in East Lothian, somewhere up in the North." he says and gestures upwards with his hands.

"East Lothian, as in Scotland?" Bradford asks and confirms at the same time.

"Are you familiar with the area?" Afifi says as his turns around and looks at him as this came as a surprise.

"Not really... What's his name?"

"Let me look..." he walks over to the table and searches through the papers that are scattered across his table, "...he goes by Benjamin..." he pauses and sighs wonder some, "...I need to tell you he's MI6 intel."

"OK." Bradford responds as if that meant nothing to him.

"Aya mitavanid be man komak konid?" (Can you help me?) Afifi asks and continues with, "Jedi migooyam" (I'm serious.) he is pleading with Bradford and has a serious tone in his voice.

It wasn't often Bradford had to help Afifi, as he was well connected in the world and this seemed to be something simple enough. "Yes of course." he says and feels reluctant, "Do you want me to smoke him out for you?" he was confirming what he already suspected.

Afifi looks at him, it was a given, and not much needed to be said. "I have old picture, not sure if that will help, and I have the address." Afifi hands Bradford the address and the picture.

"Is he an aristocrat?" he asks when he reads the address.

"What you mean?" Afifi asks, he wasn't sure what he had missed.

"The address is associated with aristocratic ties... the Balfour family." he says, and it was obvious and not surprising, but Bradford looked at Afifi as how he could not have known.

"I'm not familiar with that, I just know he..." and he points at the information that was in Bradford's hand, "...and a woman created problems back in the day, and they are still being a problem today... and he's still active..." he quiets down and looks out into thin air as he was contemplating, "...her, I do not know where she is... she's gone, like a... like a ghost!" and he gestures again with his right hand.

"I didn't know you were also looking for a woman, what do you know about her?"

"Nothing." he says discouraged.

"I understand..." Bradford says while recapping in his mind what he had told him. "He lives in Haddington... hmm, Edinburgh."

Afifi turns around, "You will go?" he says excited and his demeanor changed from giving off a feeling of defeat to a hopeful smile spreading all over his face.

"I will go and see this Englishman you are referring to and maybe I will find your men too." he says.

"You keep me informed what is happening, right!" he says to Bradford as he watches him look over the address he was holding in his hand.

"Yes, I'll keep you posted." With those words he folds the piece of paper then grabs Afifi by the shoulders, and nothing else needed to be said. He had his back and he was going to take care of it, as he always had.

Afifi watches him walk out of the room, down the hall, and back out the front door.

Bradford stops outside with the heavy door slamming shut behind him. He looks out into thin air, he contemplates on where he was; a stone's throw away from Albert Hall, and Kensington High Street was just around the corner. He walks down the steps to the street and pulls the jacket closer as there was a damp feeling in the air. It had rained as the street was whispering wet. He wasn't far away from the hotel, and he had two things to do now, because when problems appear they seldom came alone. It was like this feeling that when it rained, it poured.

MARCUS FINISHES his drink and puts it down on the table in front of him. He leans back in the chair and lets his eyes rest on bar, the drink had made him sleepy and his eyes were getting heavier. He pushed himself up from his seat, then he stands up and stretches. He walks by the bartender who was steadily cleaning up the bar and packing it up for the night and pushes the door open into the lobby. He looks over at the receptions desk, it was empty, besides the clerk behind the counter. He walks up, and the man quickly recognizes him.

"Yes, Sir." he said and waited for Marcus to respond.

"I wonder... do you have a vacant room by chance?" he says as he knew that a reservation was needed.

"Just a second..." the man says as he points with his index finger straight up into the air, "Ah, I do have a vacant room." and he looks at Marcus for confirmation.

"Gotcha." Marcus says in an American accent.

"And how are we paying for the room?" the man asks, and Marcus pulls up his credit card and hands it to him. The man takes the card and types in Marcus' name from the card, then looks up and addresses Marcus, "Mr. Weaver... identification please." Marcus hands him his passport, and, at the same time, Harris and Penny exit the restaurant and walk over to the elevator.

Marcus looks around as he is waiting for the front desk to finish entering the information and glances over at the elevator where he sees someone looking like Penny and the man from the train station disappearing off into the distance. He looks back at the clerk, "Did you see the two individuals at the elevator?" he asks.

The clerk is creating the key and not looking at Marcus, "Oh... you mean Mr. Benjamin..." he says as if he had eyes in the back of his head.

"Yes." Marcus says with no idea who Mr. Benjamin was, "What room does he stay in?" he continues.

The clerk looks up suspiciously, and hands Marcus the key card, "I can't tell you sir, but you room is 444." and hands him back his credit card and passport. Marcus nods agreeing and acts ignorant about it. He walks up to the elevator, and looks up at the display above, it had stopped on the 5th floor. Marcus pushes the button and the elevator proceeds going down.

HARRIS PUTS THE KEY CARD into the lock, and there is a click and he pushes the door open. He holds the door open for Penny, then he steps into the room, removes his coat, and places it on a nearby chair.

Penny is walking into the bathroom as the phone rings, she looks over at the side table by the bed, and back at Harris. "Are you expecting a call?" she asks and looks uncomfortable about it.

Harris reaches over and grabs the receiver, "Ben, speaking." he says very assertive.

"It's the front desk, sir." the man says.

"Yes, go on..."

"Do you know a Marcus Weaver, American..." the man continues.

"I don't recall that name... hold on...", Harris says and turns toward Penny, "Penny, Penny..." he calls out.

She emerges from the bathroom, "Yes, what's going on?" she says and still has soap on her face.

"Do you know a Marcus Weaver?" he asks.

"Marcus Weaver... no." she says naively and gets back into the bathroom and finishes rinsing her face. She grabs a towel that is resting next to her on the sink and pats her face dry while she is looking at herself in the mirror. "Marcus... Weaver... no, his name was Scott." she says to herself and shakes her head regarding her thoughts.

She walks back out to the bedroom, and Harris is sitting on the bed. "Why the long face?" she asks. "Did I miss something?"

"Someone is asking about me..." he says as he his mind was churning on what it could pertain to since he knew that no one knew he was staying at the hotel. "You are sure no one knows where you are?" he looks at Penny.

"I'm certain of it." she says and in the back of her mind she couldn't forget Marcus walking passed her at the train station.

Harris gets up from the bed and walks over to the table and turns his computer back on.

"Harris." Penny says and her tone was ever so gentle.

He looks over at her while being hunched over and keeping an eye on the screen, "Yes?" he says acknowledging.

"There is something I have not told you..." and she stops herself.

Harris stands straight up with his back towards her, and slowly turns around.

"I know a Marcus, but his name is Scott... not Weaver." she says with a lack of confidence, and behind those words Harris could sense a fear that she may have been wrong.

"Penny, you don't need to convince me, I have doubts too, not just you. You have your own reasons to feel that you are not sure, and I have to do what I have to do to make sure we are safe." he says and she knew there and then that she was not alone in feeling that something was off.

Harris was a number 33, in the numerology world that was a highly intuitive individual with a devious mind, and Penny was a number 1 personality; they were compatible and both very passionate individuals.

Harris had sat down and was tapping on the computer when Penny walks up to the desk and leans over and watches him access the hotel's computer system. He had some ways to access a lot of things, but she wasn't sure how legit it all was, and, at this point, the situation outweighed the necessity of being held to the highest level of integrity.

"I know that we are having a meeting tomorrow, but something tells me that we need to flush out who is asking for me and why, since the front desk person said he lives here at the hotel." and Harris types in the name.

The computer was slowly pulling up names and Marcus Weaver finally comes up. Harris clicks on the name and there it was, his passport had been scanned into the system and a picture was slowly forming.

Penny takes a step back and sits down on the bed, and Harris asks out loud, "Do you know him?" and he turns around and she looks alarmed. "What... do you know him?" he asks again as he taps on her leg to get her attention to look at him.

"That..." and she points at the screen, "... that is Marcus Scott."

Harris says nothing, then gets up from the chair and walks over to the phone and picks up the receiver. "Ben here... tell me what room Weaver stays in?" he asks and there is a pause. Harris hangs up the receiver, walks over to the desk and grabs his jacket. "Get your shoes on, we are going to make a visit." he says to Penny.

She grabs her shoes, and, as she is watching Harris searching his pockets, she sees him pull out his gun and ejected the clip, he checks it, and puts it back in. "What room is he staying in?" she asks as she knew that this was a visit she wanted to have avoided.

Harris says nothing, just keeps walking towards the door, and she follows quickly behind him and hears the door slam shut behind her. He was in his own world now, she could tell.

When Harris was in a situation, he would first go quiet before he would say anything; this was a coping mechanism and mental preparedness.

Harris walks with steady pace towards the door to the stairs and pushes it open, then he starts to walk down quickly. He stops at the 4th floor door and waits for Penny to catch up. He looks at her, "When we get to his door, I want you to hold your distance, we don't know which way this will go... OK?" he says a little controlling and wants assurance from Penny. She nods acknowledging. This was the way it was going to be without any questions asked, that was how he operated at times.

He pulls the door open and with soft steps he walks down the hall, looking at the doors on his left and his right as he passed them. Then he stops and holds out his hands as a signal for Penny to halt. He gives her a look that he was at the right place.

Harris knocks on the door and waits. Then the door slowly opens, and she can hear words being exchanged, but is not able to figure out what is being said. Harris looks back toward Penny and points at her then looks back at the person in the doorway who she can't see. Then the person emerges from the room for her to see, it was Marcus, but what was the question.

Harris waves at Penny to come his way, and she walks up to the them. "He says that he has to talk to you." Harris says as he looks at Penny and then back at Marcus.

"Why are you following me?" Penny says annoyed as she could tell that he was not an illusion that she had seen at the train station.

"I think you both need to come inside." he says seriously and sincere.

Penny looks at Harris, "Go on, I got you." he says to her and she knew what he meant.

Penny walks inside and Marcus follows. Harris gives the hallway a last quick glance before he proceeds to walk inside and close the door behind him.

CHAPTER 20

MARCUS IS SITTING DOWN in a chair by the window, spreading his legs and holding his hands together as he wasn't sure how to convey what he knew. He had lied to Penny from the beginning, he had some explaining to do.

Penny watches Marcus and she feels that she needs to break the ice somehow; whatever conversation that needed to be had, it had to start from a point of honesty. "Listen... Marcus... Weaver?" she says and looks at him with a confused expression on her face, and then she rolls her eyes while shaking her head as she wasn't sure what to believe anymore. "You told me your name was Scott, what else is there that I don't know? Now is the time to break out all your cards and put them on the table!" she says with a no-nonsense attitude.

"I..." and he stops and looks over at Harris who is standing in a resting position holding his arms crossed close to his chest. He continues and points at Penny, "...you know the information you are bringing back to the states... umm... the government wants it, the FBI wants it." he says and gives off a bashful look as he clenches his teeth together.

"What are you talking about?" Penny says conceitedly assertive.

"F.B.I.... hmm..." Harris says and both Penny and Marcus are looking at him. "If that was the case, why did they not snatch this up already?" he continues.

"I am telling you what I know, and what I found out today." Marcus says firmly as his index finger is pointing downwards.

"OK, so if you say this is true, who was your source?" Harris asks demanding as there was no room to hold back or dance around the topic.

There's a moment of silence and then a moment truth, "Captain Quentin." he says surrendering.

"Quentin... Captain? Who is that person and why is the military involved in this?" Penny says annoyed as she had tried to move forward with her life and now it was all back again; this situation with her husband and the military. It was a wound that had never healed, and it was now completely ripped up. She had lived quietly, she thought, to keep it covered with her new identity and somewhere in the back of her mind she knew this would all resurface again.

"OK, so you are telling us that the military and FBI are working together, and the purpose of that is...?" Harris questions with doubts.

Marcus looks at Penny, "The documents you are in possession of detail an elaborate financial plot, tell me if I am wrong." and he looks back at Harris with a look that he wasn't playing any games.

"OK, so you know the context…" Penny begins.

Marcus interrupts Penny, "And the middle eastern men in the train station, do you think that was a coincidence?"

Penny looks over at Harris, "What do you think?" she continues and looks back at Marcus.

"Let's play with open cards." Harris responds, and continues to look at Marcus, "You tell us what you know, and we will tell you what we know." he extends a bargaining chip.

"Fair enough." Marcus responds, and he looks over at the time, "This will take a minute to go over."

Penny looks at the time, "Well, time is all I have now."

Marcus starts to relay the information that was given to him by Q, and both Penny and Harris are intently listening to what he is saying.

"I don't know what to say…" she says shocked and speechless. She was a hard-working person and she had been used to participate in something that was not in her character to do. She consistently worked to hold herself to the highest integrity, and now she knew that she had been conversing with someone at her bank who walked with none. Penny starts to pace back and forth as she was thinking how she could get a hold of more factual information, and not only stop this but have the right people going down with it. "Edwin." she says as she had an idea.

Harris and Marcus looked at her as they had no idea what or who she was talking about.

"OK, so Taytum and Neal were the two who gave me the assignment, and if I can have access to the system, I can see what they did." she say cryptic.

"Taytum and Neal?" Marcus asks and looks confused, and continues, "Taytum is a good friend of Bradford."

Penny looks at Marcus and wondered how he knew the name of the man who had given her the information. "What do you know about Bradford?" she says and stops her enthusiasm in its tracks.

"Bradford was a troop who went rogue in the middle east where I was stationed, a friend of mine lost his life trying to catch him, but Bradford disappeared after his death and went into the terrorist business. I saw him back in Geneva." Marcus says in an unofficial, informative way, "...And why are you asking about him like that?" he says, and Penny gets quiet.

"OK if we are to hold open cards on the table, that goes both ways, not just from me" Marcus says and is not happy about the exchange.

She looks at Marcus, "Bradford was the one who handed me the information."

"And who is Edwin?" Harris asks as he looks over at Penny with his hands stretched out indicating that he was lost too.

"Edwin is in the IT department, and if I need access to the system, he is the one who can help. I can call and get remote access to the system, but we need to do it now as..." and she stops and looks over at the time and she quickly calculated the time difference, "...we have to get in before the everyone is back in the office." and she pulls up her phone.

"I wish we could see back in time and find a way to see how this all started." Harris says as he was thinking out loud.

"There may be a way, but it may be a long shot." she says and looks at her phone.

"We can?" Marcus asked and is surprised by her statement.

"There may be a way... I mean we can check the surveillance records for the bank, they are supposed to hold these recordings for six months before they record over them." she says as if she knew more about it than she was ready to reveal. Penny taps on her phone and she puts it to her ear, "Edwin... It's Penny."

Edwin is barely awake as he answers the phone on autopilot with his eyes remaining closed. *"Penny... do you know what time it is?"* he says as he was still holding his head to the pillow and thinking it was just a dream.

"I know it's too early for you, but I need your help." she says with desperation.

He looks over at the alarm clock on the nightstand. *"Can't it wait until later on today?"* he says sleepy.

"If I could... I would, so, no... are you awake?" she is now getting frustrated as she wasn't sure he understood her.

He sighs loud and sits up in the bed and lets his legs rest on the edge, then with one hand pressed against his cheek he gives himself a moment to wake up. *"OK, I am awake. What do you need?"* and he shuffles himself to his desk.

"I need access to the surveillance system; I am looking for someone."

"Listen Penny, I don't want any problems, I have enough heat around me with two guys prancing around in the office, and I hear your name being used repeatedly." he says as he wasn't feeling it anymore.

"Was it Taytum and Neal?" she throws out at him.

"I don't know their names, but I haven't seen them before, possibly corporate rats. What's going on Penn?"

"Edwin, I can't say anything right now, but I will fill you in when I get back."

"OK, but I don't want to be in trouble or get my ass fired for this."

"If you don't help me you may have to look for another job anyway, not because of me, but because of other factors." she says as it was inevitable.

"Well then, fuck, what do you need?" he responds ready to help. What did he have to lose, it was a catch 22.

"I need access to the internal system; can you do that for me?" he can hear her speak with conviction.

"Well, shit, that alone can get me fired!" he says as he shakes his head and gets into the system as he listens to Penny.

"Shut it down for maintenance and get me access for a few hours."

"We're not even scheduled for that... but what the hell."

"Then you're scheduled now..."

Edwin interrupts her, *"I figured you'd say that. Man... Penny, what the hell have you got yourself into?"* Edwin says with a defeated tone.

"I can't talk about it yet. What do I need to get in?"

"Dang, you owe me one for this shit." he says as he is typing while listening to her, *"Let me finish this and I'll send you an encrypted code."*

"OK, I'll be waiting... Oh, Edwin, thanks, I promise you won't regret this."

"Um, yeah... I already do."

"Thank you!" she finishes and disconnects the call.

"You're welcome..." he says out loud to himself as he is working on the encryption code.

"OK, Harris, I have an encrypted code being generated by my IT guy back in the States, he will email it to me, and that will give us access to my office and the corporate office where Neal and Taytum are located." she looks at Marcus and Harris waiting to hear their response to the situation.

"So, when we have the code, we are going to check everything that has Neal and Taytum's fingerprints on it." Harris repeats as it was confirmed what needed to be done.

"So, let's stay low until that comes through. We have about 3 hours to find what we are looking for." she says as this was the best she could do.

"I tell you; you never cease to surprise me!" Harris continues, and smiles as he is in disbelief, and, yet, he was expecting nothing less.

"So, what is the plan now?" Penny asks and then she looks at Marcus with a questioning look.

He has been listening to the conversation quietly and observed the dialog between Penny and Harris intently, he knows that he will be given his marching orders and is just waiting for them.

Penny looks over at Marcus, "I am going to go back and retrieve the computer and then we can get cracking on it." she says and looks at Harris and eye signals for him to stay as she is leaving.

"Alright, I will be here waiting for you." he says as she disappears out the door.

Marcus gets up from the chair and is walking from window to window and observing the street.

There is a silence, but Harris wasn't the shy one, he was used to asking uncomfortable questions, this was his job. "So, Marcus, how did the two of you meet?" he asks in a casual manner.

"It was by chance, and a good one. One morning, I was walking to get my coffee and she was just there, and things changed for me." Marcus says heartfelt.

"I understand exactly what you mean; she is one special and unique woman with a unique energy. You would be hard pressed to find another woman like her; she's one of a kind. She knows how to communicate, she is funny, sharp, and she will run circles around people; never underestimate Jacqueline." Harris says.

"Jacqueline? Oh... so you know the *real* Penny?" Marcus says and realized that he needs to stop being surprised, "She wasn't Penny when you met her... hmm." Marcus stops his wandering and walks up to Harris and waits to hear more.

"Penny got her name from me." Harris replies unexpectedly, "After our run in the Balkan war, we were targets, so I helped Jacqueline to change her name, and then she moved to the States, that is all I can say."

Marcus was listening intently; that name had haunted him since he had tried to track her down after Howard's passing. He made a promise and it was something he had intended to keep. It was too much of a coincidence, and the last time he spoke with Howard was when he heard that name, "So, where was her husband... Howard... killed?" Marcus probes by threading carefully.

"In Mafraq..." Harris says and gets quiet for a minute and observes Marcus, "How did you know his name?"

Marcus knew now, for certain, that this was Howard Grant's Jackie.

"Well, she mentioned it to me in passing." he says as it was common knowledge, "So tell me..."

Harris stops him by interjecting, "Well... If you want to know more you will have to ask her when she gets back." he says smugly while pointing towards the door where she had left. Harris was still bothered that Marcus had asked the front desk about him. He was quickly assessing Marcus by watching him and how he was carrying himself. "So, you two met over coffee, but let's be real here, you are no boy scout, are you?" Harris says with a superior tone.

"No, I wouldn't say that." Marcus replies and wasn't sure where this was heading.

"OK, so before we get any further here, tell me what I need to know so we can get over the pleasantries. Jail time?" Harris continues and it gets quiet. "I figured as much... what do you know, I mean, what's your expertise? I mean you are here, and you asked about me, and that is for a reason, so we should get good use of your talents, don't you think?" Harris looks at him waiting for an intelligent answer.

Marcus thinks about what to say, his options, and whether to lie or be straight forward. Harris seems to already see straight through him, so he goes with the truth, "I killed a person." Marcus says and leaves it at that.

"OK, so you did time. Did you get wiser in jail or was that also a waste?" Harris goes on in the same superior tone.

"I got a degree in computer systems while I was waiting." Marcus says and is careful to not offend Harris despite of how he felt as all he cared about was getting closer to Penny and the information she is holding on to.

"OK, so there is a brain besides muscles." Harris scoffs. In the same moment there is a knock on the door. Harris turns around and opens it, and Penny is back. She hands the computer to Harris, he takes it and puts it down on the table, and she immediately notices an awkward silence.

"You know, Penny, your friend here is no novice." Harris says and Penny watches Marcus as she listens to the tapping from Harris typing on the computer.

Marcus knows he needs to break the ice and avoid the conversation all together and bridge it back to the present moment. "So, what are we dealing with here?" Marcus asks Harris.

"I tell you it's something I have never seen before, or even thought was plausible or that someone would think of." Harris says and looks up from the computer then he moves back a step. "It's ready Penn, go ahead and retrieve the information." he says and watches her walk up to the desk. He glances over at Marcus and can see that he was emotionally vested in Penny, and that was all because of coffee.

Marcus pulls out his phone, he scrolls over the pictures, he finds a picture of Bradford. It was an older military picture.

He walks up to Harris, "Do you know this man?" Marcus asks, and hands him the phone.

Harris looks at the picture, he gives a puzzled look and figured that it was Bradford. He hands the phone back, "Bradford?" he responds guessing at the same time questioning it.

Marcus looks surprised at him, "How did you know?" he wasn't sure how it was possible, "Who are you?" Marcus is now taking a step back as he is not sure what to expect. Who was this man, he knew about Bradford, and yet it was information only few privy people really had insight to.

Harris walks up to Penny as she was logged into the system at the bank. "Let me borrow the computer for a second." he says to her, and she gets up from the chair and lets Harris take the seat.

Marcus looks over Harris' shoulder as he is pulling up a file with pictures, he can see him skim through pictures of different events, war zones, pictures of people, and, suddenly, he slows down and stops on a picture of the military that includes men in Middle Eastern clothing. He points at the picture, exclaims excitedly and stunned at the same time, "I knew I had seen him before; he has these distinguished eyes." Harris turns to Marcus, "When was the last time you saw him?" he asks with a now serious tone to the voice.

Marcus doesn't need time to think and quickly responds, "It was in Geneva... he walked into the same hotel we stayed at." and he points at Penny. "I'm certain that he stayed there." he continues.

Time was working against them, Harris knew that, and he looks at Penny, "We are going to do a 'fly by fuck you in a ghost rider style'." he says and starts to grin to relax everyone, but he knew that there was going to be surprises and wasn't sure when they would be knocking on their whereabouts. "We will have to work fast, are up to the challenge?" he says and looks at Marcus. Penny knows this will be a surprise sting and that was the best way to tackle this situation.

Marcus takes his seat in front of the computer and he thinks about what he needed to know. He starts to search for AVI files, and randomly starts to look at video and audio files. The time is ticking away, and Penny has fallen asleep in her clothes while Harris was stuck sitting in a chair with his feet kicked up and resting with one eye closed.

Marcus suddenly sees three people on the screen, and he is looking at the computer trying to figure out how to turn up the volume. He looks over at Harris and leans over and taps him on the leg.

Harris looks up, "Yes?" he says as he was expecting an answer.

"How do I turn on the volume on the computer?" he says as he was a little embarrassed that he was unable to figure it out.

Harris gets up from his seat and takes a step over at the computer, "What did you find?" he asks curiously.

"There is a footage here from 4 months ago, and it is on a Sunday evening in what looks like a conference room..." he says as he wasn't sure what the discovery was.

Harris turns up the sound and is listening to the conversation, one man spoke with a broken English accent, not American, but English. "Can we get a better picture of the three individuals?" Harris asks.

Marcus is trying to zoom in, but the picture gets grainer. As Marcus works to try and improve the picture, Harris is intently listening to the audio of a conversation between two of the individuals.

"What are we looking at, the time frame for having the plan in place?" asks one of the men.

"Oh, I think possibly two to three months. Who are you having retrieve these documents? I cannot come back to the US, it's too dangerous, and too many questions in customs." replies the man with the broken English accent.

"We will have someone within our company to come and pick it up." the man replies.

"Very good, I will have the plan for the US banks and the European banks, but, understand the rules and the execution of the plan are two part; not the same for them, because they are different markets. Maybe a little easier in Europe than in US, but I have a plan already. Very easy, but we need someone with people skills in the US." The man with the broken English accent says as he looks at the other two men, waiting for an answer.

"John will be the contact person who they are going to speak with in the US." The man nods in John's direction concluding.

"Can you give us an idea what it will look like, the plan I mean?" John asks.

"Well, the American member banks have a different way of doing business. Here, you are looking at someone's credit score... and you call it their FICO score... before you are lending money to a person. The European member banks, well they look to see if you are working, assets and debts, and collateral. No scores in Europe, just ability to pay back. So, in Europe we can simply falsify data and present it. That way we can give loans to people, who do not qualify; that is why it will take a little bit of time. I need to get the right people into these banks to handle that part." The man with the broken English accent finishes.

"Well how about the American banks, how do we get through the barriers here?" John continues to ask.

"Stop it there!" Penny exclaims, as she shot straight up in the bed and startled both Harris and Marcus. They turn around quickly and look surprised. They should have expected that she wasn't really sleeping. She recognized the sound of the voices.

"Man, you scared me, I'm not young anymore, you have to watch my ticker." Harris says as he gives off a grin. Penny smirks back at him, and she knew that it would take more to kill him then simply startling him, despite of his wounds from the war he was still walking strong.

She gets out of bed and straightens her clothes, and walks up to the desk, "What did you find?" she asks curiously as she leans over Marcus' shoulder and looks down on the computer.

"There were some AVI files that I had Harris help me to turn on the sound for... and what you heard was a conversation between two people from your company, I think." he says unsure.

She looks down on the screen, "Can you see who they are?" she says as she looks at Marcus and he looks at her with a questioning look on his face. "I mean, can we get a close up?" she says as she looks back at the screen to figure out where this was recorded.

"No, I just tried it with Harris. This is an AVI not a jpeg, it will just be grainer the more the picture is zoomed in, but these two..." and Marcus points at the two individuals, "...one is named John and I believe they work for your company." he continues.

"Do you have a location where this was recorded?" she asks.

Marcus looks over the file logs of the different locations, "Dallas." he says as he looks at the screen, and then he looks up at Penny who was standing behind him and had a concerned look on her face. "Who are they?" he asks as this didn't look as something that came as a surprise.

"Taytum and Neal." she says under her breath, as she was getting a clearer picture.

"Did you say Taytum? Is his name John Taytum?" Marcus says surprised and points at John on the screen.

Penny takes a step back and looks at Harris, "I guess this confirms it really." he says with a demeanor that it's better knowing the devil you're working against instead of being kept in the dark.

"Hold on, hold on here, will you!" Marcus says as he holds out his hand, he was feeling left out of the conversation.

"Why, are you surprised?" Penny says as she looks at him. "Your Captain told you about Taytum and Bradford. What is it that I don't know about Bradford, Marcus?"

He looks down and gives off an awkward smile, and then back at Harris.

There is an awkward moment of a silence, then she continues, "OK... what else is there that I need to know?" she says as she watches Marcus sit and screw himself into the seat.

"Bradford." he says as it was some kind of code word.

"What about him?" Harris asks.

"Bradford was the troop who went rogue in Mafraq that I was working on to get turned over to the authorities. He was selling the equipment and weaponry to terrorist organizations and said he lost them in the desert to cover it up." Marcus says as it was still bothering him.

Penny is thinking back to her time in Mafraq herself, and she can't say for sure if this Bradford was the man her husband was looking for. She continues to listen and take mental notes. "Well, go ahead and download the AVIs, we may need them later." she orders in a disinterested way.

"Well, it's not over yet. Remember Blue Ginger?" Harris says.

"Blue Ginger, what is that?" Marcus interjects into the conversation.

Penny looks at Harris and contemplates if she needed Marcus or if she wanted to do this alone.

"We are meeting Bradford at the Blue Ginger tomorrow." she says, and looks over at the time, it was past midnight. "Let me correct myself, today." she says and sighs as she yawns and stretches her arms into the air. "Listen..." she walks up to the desk and closes the lid to the computer and hands it over to Harris, then continues. "...I need to get back to my room and get some sleep before shit hits the fan again."

Marcus and Harris look at each other, then Harris looks at Penny and says, "Listen, Penny..." he pauses, "...we could use some back up..." and he looks at her as if this wasn't such a bad idea, and the next moment he turns to Marcus to let him know that he was agreeing to let him join them.

She sighs surrendering, "OK." and turns around and pulls the door open and walks out.

Harris grabs Marcus by his shoulders, "I will call you when we head out." and follows Penny in tow.

CHAPTER 21

BRADFORD wakes up and looks over the time, it was early. He stares up at the ceiling, it was still dark outside and the street-lights were making moving shadows on the wall. He leans over to the side table and grabs his laptop and turns it on. He had a lot of work ahead of him, and then he had promised to help Afifi with his situation and track down the Englishman.

He reaches down to the floor and grabs his pants and pulls out the address. Next, he gives the pillows a push behind his back, to make a back support against the headboard, and pulls the computer up on his lap. He ponders for a second on where he should start to look and what he needed. Afifi had mentioned that the man was an MI6 agent.

Bradford opens the internet program and types in the FBI's login page then enters credentials. He watches the page load slowly, and then he looks over at the name he had on the note with the address, "Harris P. Anthony... Who is this man?" he utters out loud to himself. There are a few hits and he look over them, then he looks at the address, Haddington, Scotland. "Edinburgh?" He looks over at the locations, and there, at the very end of the list, he finds a possible match. He clicks on it, and the page is pending, and, after several long moments, it finally displays. He sees the picture of Harris' estate that is attached to the file, he cross references it to a former British Prime Minister from the early 1900's. He continues to scroll down and there is a picture of Harris. It wasn't very clear and Afifi had not provided any photographs, so this was going to be a guessing game to figure out where this was taken, but he could tell it was a war zone.

He pulls the phone off the nightstand, scrolls down on the list of names, selects one, then waits as the phone rings. Suddenly, he hears a voice as the call is answered. "Hey, I need the chopper in the air... I need a surveillance shot of 55.9559° N 2.6378°W," Bradford says with a stern voice.

"Yes, Sir, 55.9559° N 2.6378°W. Copy that." and the man disconnects the call.

Bradford continues to read the bio of Harris and realizes that he had been in the Balkan war, and that was where Afifi had operated supplying the militia with weaponry. There was no mention of a woman anywhere, so she was clearly not a spouse. So, who was this woman who had ghosted Afifi? That was the question that made things more interesting.

HARRIS IS LOOKING AT THE PHONE, it was already 9 am. He submerges his hands into the sink and lets his cupped palms fill up with water and then splashes it on his face, rejuvenating his face and washing away any leftover good mornings. He looks out of the bathroom as he grabs for a hand towel and views Penny laying on the bed and cling to the cover with one leg poking outside the cover. He smiles, she was something else this girl, and that alone was an understatement.

He dries his face and stops himself for a second before he turns off the light and exits the bathroom. As he walks back to bed, he grabs the laptop, and then opens the blinds to let in some natural sunlight in. He carefully crawls back in bed, being careful not to wake her up, and turns on the computer. The route to the Blue Ginger had to be carefully planned, as Bradford was unpredictable. There had to be a Plan B set up before they left the hotel.

Bradford was not working alone, that much he knew, and Harris wasn't sure what to expect, but he was damned certain he wouldn't be caught by surprise; it was going to be the other way around. He remembers the safe house he had on Sutherland Avenue, and that had been something that was a hiding place is plain sight.

Edward was his trusted MI6 partner and he had let his house become a safe haven for hiding people, it was a risky business, but they were both working for MI6, and that was risky in itself; this was ultimately their secret. However, this was years ago, and he remembered Edward falling ill, he was diagnosed with leukemia. No treatment had worked, and he wasn't getting better, they had thought he would have five years, but he didn't reach his third year as he passed away. Edward had been his wingman, and, then, one day he was on his own.

Harris shakes his head to get his focus back on what he had to do. He had kept in touch with Edward's widow, and she still accommodated him when he needed, and it had been a minute since he had had to use this safe haven.

Penny is starting to move around in the bed, and she rolls over and the light hits her, then she slowly starts to open her eyes. She quickly shields her face with her hand, then looks up at Harris. "What time is it?" she asks, and her voice sounded raspy and dry.

"Time for breakfast." Harris says as he is tapping on the computer.

Penny rolls back over to the other side of the bed and sits up, she was tired, but she needed to wake up. She looks to her right, and the pillows were tempting her to go back to bed.

"Don't think about that, we have work to do... Bradford." he says to remind her. She nods agreeing then gets off the bed and walks to the bathroom and closes the door.

Harris grabs the receiver off the phone and dials Marcus' room, "Weaver." he says as soon as the person on the other side answers. "Meet us downstairs in two hours." he continues and hangs up. Harris then calls out to Penny, "We are meeting Marcus downstairs in two hours, so let's get ready." He does not get a response, so he gets up and walks over to the bathroom and knocks on the door. "Penny did you hear?" he calls out again. Still not hearing a reply he opens the door and listens to the sound of water running in the shower. "Hey, Penny!" he calls out to get her attention.

"Yeah, what's going on?" she calls back.

"Did you hear what I said? We are meeting Marcus downstairs in two hours." he repeats himself.

"Oh... OK." she says, and he can hear her not being too enthusiastic about it.

"Oh, come on now... stop rolling those beautiful green eyes." he says and gives up a laugh to ease the tone to the conversation.

Penny continues to shower and grins, Harris knew her better than she had expected. She had to accept Marcus tagging along because Harris had made the decision, and for whatever reason, he had a reason, she just didn't know what it was.

MARCUS WAS GETTING READY and he looks down on his phone, he was pondering on whether he needed to give Q a heads up on what was going on. He starts to text him, and then he stops himself, as much as he wanted to let him know, this was probably not the best idea. If Bradford saw too many familiar faces it would scare him off. Bradford knew that he was wanted person, and, despite him being in London, he knew that nothing was a safe bet. Marcus knew his mindset as they had been in the same squad. Being under his command, it was a given how he operated, both physically and mentally.

Marcus walks up to the window and opens the drapes, and the sunlight hits his eyes and he quickly turns around. He needed to have a minute to get adjusted to the light.

Marcus' phone starts to vibrate on the desk. As he walks back over to the desk he grabs it and looks at it; there was a text from Q, and his thoughts were that even he had crossed his mind.

"What's new?" he reads. To think that Q was anything but direct was an understatement, he cut through the bullshit pleasantries and went for the core.

"I'll let you know, when I have something." Marcus responds and puts the phone down and walks into the bathroom to get cleaned up. He, like many others, did his best thinking on the throne.

CHAPTER 22

HARRIS AND PENNY are taking the elevator down to the lobby, and, as they walk out, they are met by Marcus who's been waiting for them. They nod acknowledging to each other but are not saying a word.

Harris walks up to the front desk, "Has my car arrived?" he asks

The clerk acknowledges him by raising his hand to give him a second. He looks over at the valet boy and he signals, and watches the valet give a hand signal that it was ready. "Yes, Mr. Benjamin…" he says and points at the valet's directions.

Harris walks up to Penny and Marcus, who are waiting for him, "Marcus, you will be driving…" he pauses and gives a quick look at Penny and Marcus. "I'll give directions." Harris continues as he had everything planned; they are both nodding that it was understood, and with that he takes the lead and walks up to the valet boy and exchanges words that are indistinct for Penny.

They all get into the car and they start heading down towards Eastbourne Terrace. Penny is looking over her phone, "The meeting is set, he said he would be there in fifteen minutes." She looks up, "That means he must be close."

"OK, I want you to be on standby and keep the engine running." Harris looks at Marcus, and Marcus nods his head. "Turn to Eastbourne Terrace, make a right, then continue and make a left onto Bishops Bridge Road, take a right on Westbourne Terrace and cross the bridge... when you cross it make a left and you will end up on Harrow Road... as you continue to drive up Harrow you will see Blue Ginger on the right." Harris instructs Marcus.

Marcus notes the instructions mentally as he drives up the streets, swerving fast in the Land Rover, he is thinking of Bradford and where he could be, if he was just 15 minutes away. He passed the Blue Ginger, and Harris looks at him, "Good job, let scope the place if someone is watching and waiting" he says as he gives the both side of the street a quick look.
"Make a right here!" he exclaims and Marcus makes a quick turn into Amberly Road and parks in alley right behind the Blue Ginger.
Penny and Harris gets out.
"Stay here" Harris says before he shuts the door.

Penny walks down the sidewalk and make a left turn on to Harrow road, and before she knows it she's stepped through the blue door and the doorbell that sitting attached to the door chimes.

The blue ginger was giving off a distinct strong fragrant Indian culinary smell. She looks over at the dining room and she can see Bradford and before she proceeds to walk inside a man suddenly appears from the back.

"Ya madame", he says as he smiles while his teeth look like they had seen better days.

"I see my party... thank you" she says and points at Bradford's direction and smiles back at him bashfully.

She walks towards Bradford as she scopes the place; there was just an old man sitting at a table pushing a piece of naan bread into a bowl, and fishing up something looking like a curry and putting it in his mouth. She watched the man in slow motion as she was thinking how to tackle this meeting. She felt she was walking in daze, with no plan, and in her mind the plan was in ongoing development as she was feeling the energy rise.

Bradford was sitting at a table by the far-left wall, and when she gets up to the table she can see his face exuberate this arrogant look over it.

"Penny, or should I say Jacqueline?" Bradford greets her snidely with a grin.

"What do you want Bradford?", she pauses, "I know all about you, there's no secrets" she states as the cat was out of the bag, and sits down across from him.

He looks at her with a confident demeanor as if he had this, "Then hand it over and we can walk away in one piece".

Penny was not the one that you'd push over and she wouldn't roll, no she was the one in charge of this cat and mouse game. Suddenly their conversation is interrupted by the doorbell chime, and they both look over at who was entering, and her eyes meets Harris. He looks over and proceeds to the counter and disappears behind the wall, and she turns her attention back to Bradford.

"What are you gonna do? You can't open it." Penny says as she was buying herself some time.
"OK, then you're going with me, and you're gonna to open it." he says as he points at the door.
"Why do you think I would go anywhere with you, and secondly hand over this information to you...tell me why you need it?" Penny was waiting for an intelligent answer, something she could believe in, but, it was shining with its absence.
"...that's what I thought" she says as she knew he couldn't tell her.

Bradford looks around, as he didn't need a second set of ears listening to the conversation, and he leans into the middle of the table. He looks at Penny threatening and says firmly, "Stop fucking with me, this isn't a game".
Penny wasn't intimidate or afraid, she was ready to deal with this head on.
"First, you have to go through me, and who's playing? What have you been smokin', you must have lost your damn mind" Penny says, and looks over at Harris direction and she still can't see him, and looks back at Bradford.
"You are playing with the wrong person! If you know me that well, then you know that I don't let people tell me what to do, Seels" she says as she emphasizes on his first name, and turns her ice queen facial expression at him, and gives off an evil grin.

He knew he had underestimated the situation. This wasn't going to be easy, not as easy as he had expected it to be.

"Well I can't protect you now" he says and leans back acting comfortable, but Penny knew this was just a smoke and mirror. "Protect me? Huh? Protect me, I should be the one telling you that" and she gets up from her chair and is ready to walk away when Bradford stands up and stops her as he grabs her by the arm and pulls her close.

"Jacqueline, don't do this" he says with a whispering tone and a last warning.

Penny yanks her arm free, "Penny for you... and I'm sorry" she pauses and looks at him with disgust "...not sorry, to say that it's the last time I am wasting my time on you. Take a last look, this will be the last you'll see of me".

Penny can't wait to leave his presence fast enough, as she is getting more agitated by the moment, and she walks with rapid steps up to the entrance, and disappears behind the wall.

Bradford is left standing by the table, and the old man has turned his head and is looking at Bradford with an empty stare. He gives the man a glaring stare and the man turns around and faces his plate again. All Bradford can do is to sit down and ponder on he what he was going to do, he had expected this to be easy, but he had misjudged the whole thing. His men were right, she was slippery, and the white glove treatment had not helped, he had no other choice but to handle this differently.

Bradford is waiting for Penny to come through the entrance and walk out, but the more time goes by he is getting concerned. Bradford throws down 3 quid for the drink, and walks up to the entrance, it was staring empty.

A lady emerges from the back of the counter, Bradford turns around.
"Madame" he says, and walks up to the counter.
"Yes" she responds.
"Where is the woman that walked up here just a moment ago?" he asks.
"Woman, no woman here" she says in broken English.
"Yes, yes, of course" Bradford says and understands now that she had left through the back.

Bradford walks to the back where the bathrooms were located, and he see the emergency exit. The door was cracked, it hadn't closed properly. He walks up and pushes the door open, it led out to a back alley, he continues to walk through the gate that leads out to the street, it was Amberly Road.
"Damn!" he exclaims.
He pulls up his phone and looks over the contacts before he places the phone to his ear.
"I'm on Amberly Road, half a block down, come and get me" he says and closes his phone.
"I'll get you Jacqueline, one way or another" he murmurs to himself.

CHAPTER 23

MARCUS SPEEDS DOWN FOSCOTE MEWS passing cars
parked on the right and the street is narrow and Marcus wasn't
used to be driving on the wrong side of the road, but he stood
alert of unexpected things to appear. The street ends up on
Sutherland Avenue.

"Make a right", Harris commands and Marcus is on autopilot,
just doing what he was told, "What's next" he says as he
wanted to be prepared for the next unexpected call.

"Look for number 21" Harris says as he seemed not too familiar
with the location.

All the house's looked the same, they were white washed
townhomes along the street with planted medians, and cars
parked on the wrong side Penny observed, *better him then me*,
she was thinking while she was sitting in the backseat
watching the townhomes wiz by.

"Sutherland Ave 21." Marcus reads out loud and stops abruptly
and pulls over to the curb. Harris looks at both, "...this is a pit
stop, we'll see how long we will be here", and he exits the car.

Marcus turns off the engine, pulls out the key, and watches Penny step out of the car and get up on the curb. He had parked by a bus stop sign; the building was having a basement and four stories Penny could tell. The entrance portrayed modest roman pillars framing the front door. Harris grabs Penny by the shoulder and leans into her ear, "This is best kept secret in London" he say whispering, and pushes the cast iron gate open.

Harris takes the lead as Penny and Marcus follows.

He pushes the doorbell, and there is a moment of wait, then the door suddenly opens up, an older lady answers the door.

"Oh, you made it, I didn't know what to think when you called me. I have everything set up, come inside." the lady says and waves with her hand invitingly to Harris.

"Thank you dear, I wasn't sure whether I would need to come here today or not. I needed to have this option open" he says in a concerned and cautious manner as he cradles her by the shoulder.

The lady shows them into a room with a large fireplace, a chaise lounge were situated by the fire place and a cat was resting peacefully curled up.

"Well, I don't know if you are staying or not but if you do then you have to figure out the sleeping arrangements" she says as she is circling her index finger at them, and she takes a seat in the winged armed chair.

"I'll have tea shortly...if you like." she says as she looks at Harris, "I put the kettle to go in the kitchen just before you arrived" she continues.

He nods agreeing without saying anything, and he looks over at the picture frames on the mantlepiece.

"I see you are looking at you and Ed, that were the good ol' days," the old lady says as she looks over to her right for something, and then she leans down and fetches her walking stick.

The old lady grabs the stick and pushes herself back up from her seat, at that very same moment the whistle on the tea kettle can be heard from the back of the house.

"I think I will go into the kitchen" she says and starts to shuffle her feet as she uses the stick to balance herself.
Penny elbows Marcus to follow her lead.

Harris lingers in the front room, and his thoughts were going back to the time how Ed and he had met, and how their friendship had developed by helping each other out.
The days of being a radio pirate king on the open seas by the Dutch coast were over after the ship had been sunk, and in the next he was recruited by MI6; this was how Ed and he had met.

Harris knowledge and access to people made him the perfect infiltrator, and he was placed to spy on a company in Switzerland that was selling transmitters and timers to a middle eastern dictator.

So being in the middle of this situation brought memories back and he was pondering carefully the best way to blow this wide open and still stay in the background. He had his own demons out there looking for him, so the less that he was in the spotlight the easier he could contain the situation.

Harris snaps out of his thoughts and looks over at the doorway, and back at the window they were all gone but he could hear voice from the back of the house.

He walks to the back and into the kitchen, the old lady is making the tea ready and her back is facing them all, and without forewarning, "Oh you finally decided to join us." she says in a cockney accent.

She turns around and looks at Harris, the lady seems to have eyes in her back, and she shuffles her feet sideways as she pulls out the tea pot.

Harris and Marcus sits down at the table, while they watch Penny shadowing the lady at the kitchen counter.
The old lady turns around and looks straight at Marcus, "How about you lad, do you want a cup too or are you one of those coffee drinkers?"

"Yes, ma'am, tea, and make it strong please." Marcus replies.

"Well there is no such thing such as a weak tea. A weak tea is like sipping bathwater, well, depends on how much of a muddy affair you are, before getting in." the lady says and gives up a laugh. There was no doubt about this lady's sense of humor, dry like an Englishman in the Sahara, but so entertaining.

Marcus couldn't wait for the tea to be ready he was curious and wanted to inquire about her relationship with Harris, but he was going to be diplomatic and make it conversational.

The lady prepares the tea in the porcelain tea pot, she pulls out cups and saucers from the cupboard, and Penny can see that the lady's hand is shaking. She steps in and grabs the cups and places them. She looks at Penny, "Thank you lassie." she says and shuffles her back to the table while Penny grabs the tray.

The lady takes her seat at the kitchen table across from Harris, and you can hear the sound of a tired body as she sits down with a vocal sigh. She looks a bit worn. Penny places the cups on the table and grabs the porcelain tea pot and start pouring it.

"So how long have you guys had this friendship?" Penny asks in a casual way of conversation, she looks at Harris then back at the lady, and sits down next to him.

Marcus was thinking how connected he felt with Penny, like she could hear his thoughts.
The lady takes sip of her tea, "Well..." she starts and then interrupts herself, "Oh I forgot the milk." she bursts out.

Penny gets up, "Let me fetch it for you. Where can I find it?" she asks with a voice of reassurance.

"Oh, in the ice box, luv."

Penny walks up to the refrigerator and grabs the milk which is contained in a small glass bottle.

"Thank you dear" the old lady says and her eyes glow with this happy and endearing look as she pours the milk into the cup. A sigh of relief can be heard as the lady stirs the milk into the tea. She takes another sip and she give out a pleasurable exhale of a tea done right. "Now, what was the question dear?" she asks Penny.

Marcus jumps in, "How long have you know Harris?" The lady looks at Harris as she is waiting for him to say something.

"Oh,... ahh, yeah that was the question." she says and sips on the tea again as she wanted to avoid the question all together. "Well, you see, my late husband Ed and Harris" and she points at Harris "... they were born right after the second world war, they grew up together in Scotland and both went to Aberdeen University. After Harris had published a book that was pretty controversial he became involved with MI6, or as they called it now, SIS. My husband was already working for MI6, so that is how their brotherly bond got stronger as they were both working at the same firm."

The lady pauses and takes a bigger sip of her tea. She continues, "Well... my Ed passed away a few years ago from cancer." she pauses briefly, "I am now alone in this house, but I still keep it going as if nothing has changed," the lady says and sips again.

"Yes, Harris and Ed were doing things differently, and with Harris being in media and having access to MI6 and other governmental institutions, they helped a lot of people by their ingenuities."

"So, this is Ed and Harris' safe house hiding in plain sight then?" Marcus gestures with his hand downwards as his comments and confirms at the same time.

"You can say that. There's no secret as one in plain sight; seems inconspicuous and too good to be true," and she looks at Harris.
"Thank you..." he says by moving his lips soundless, and he places his hand on hers.

"Thank you for sharing the story with us." Marcus says and takes a sip on his tea. He looks over at his phone and he receives a message from Q.

"Harris told me that you saved his life" she says as she looks at Penny, "...strange world, small world, things turns into full circle, it's like fate." the lady says and waits for Penny to say something.

Penny takes a sip on her cup of tea and smile and looks at Harris while patting him on the back. There was no need for words, they had a history unlike any other.

Marcus is absorbed by his text and Harris is watching him. "That seems intense..." he says, and Marcus looks up from the phone.
"I have received not so good news" he responds, and it gets quiet and they are all looking at each other expecting more information.

"I think there is someone you should meet" Marcus says while he looks down at the message.

"Why?" Penny says questioning and not happy about involving another party into this.

"You'll understand, but it is important for you two to be aware that this is not as simple as you want to believe it is" he says concerned.

"I never thought this was anything simple" Harris says and takes a large gulp of the tea, "Who is this Q" he continues and looks at the old lady as he sensed she was not just a spectator but she listened well.

"Q, is short for Quentin, he was the my superior in the army. He knows Bradford, and all too well. I don't want to tell you much more, I need it to come from him, rather than me" Marcus says in a cautious way.

Harris looks over at the standing grandfather clock that is located right behind Marcus, and he watches the heavy weight arm on the inside of the glass go from side to side, as he thinks about what had been said.

He can hear the clock make its tick tock sound, even if was ever so subtle, but, he could still hear it. There was something that Marcus had said, and the tone he had used, he knew that he had to find out for himself who Quentin was, he had to meet him.

"OK", Harris says out loud and sits straight up in his seat.
"OK what?" Penny says and turns to him with a tense look.
"OK, set up the meeting" Harris continues and looks at Penny. Penny grabs the spoon and twirls it into the cup, and watches the rings form on the surface and as if this was an omen, things would now start to spin faster and faster.

Marcus is consumed by texting and in the next moment he looks up.

"It's done…" he says, "…he will meet you at the Golden Horseshoe casino in 2 hrs., it is located next to the Bayswater station".

"OK, you can take us there… I know where that is" Harris says with familiarity in his voice, it was located with a lot of foot traffic, and one could easily disappear without much notice. "Wait", Penny says and grabs a hold of Harris arm, "…you don't know anything about him…" Harris looks at Penny and moves her bang out of her forehead, "I am not worried because you are going with me" he says and winks at her.

CHAPTER 24

BRADFORD IS LOOKING OUT the car window while the
driver is taking him back to the hotel, he needed to get his
belongings as he had promise Victor that he was going take
care of business up north. He had already placed the Augusta
in the air to surveil the area in Haddington, now he had to get
up there to clean up the situation.
Bradford looks down at this phone, he wants to call Penny as
they had unfinished business, but something tells him to hold
off.

The driver pulls up to the hotel, "Sir" he says to get Bradford's
attention.
Bradford looks up and looks at the driver who is pointing his
finger to his right. He looks out the window and realizes that
they had arrived, he acknowledges his que.
He grabs his coat, and exits the car and walks up to the curb,
he gives a quick look around, and walks up the three steps and
inside.

Q LEAVES HIS PLACE ON PORTOBELLO ROAD, and walks down to Notting Hill Gate station.

The sun is slowly setting, and he knows by the time he has reached Bayswater it will be dark.

He suddenly feels his phone vibrate and pulls it out of his pocket, it is a private incoming call, he doesn't answer and lets it go to voice mail, if it was important they would leave a message.

He has a sharp eye as he walks with steady steps, he registers the surrounding as if he had an internal camera that took pictures. He was like this walking bionic military troop, his skills were unnerving as only a few were in the know of his ability, one of those few were Bradford.

Q couldn't help thinking about how they'd met, and what he needed to do.

They both had enlisted at the same time but ended up in different platoons, and despite of it all they had promised each other loyalty. They were both loyal military to the state, but Q had realized that his loyalty was different from Bradford's idea of what loyalty was; it was not for him or the state but to himself. He had acclaimed self-serving purposes, and there was the ending of their relationship, to Q it was, however Bradford was unaware of the revelation that he had had.

Q didn't know where Bradford was, but he knew how to get a message to him. He had gone through his records of who his minions were and had little faith in them as most of them had left or been discharged on bad terms.

There was one particular person who had grown close to

Bradford and had his loyalty, his communications specialist. He was Mr. Grayson, and had taken the fall for Bradford's shady behaviors, and what he had suspected had manifested into reality. The loyalty Bradford had wanted from Q, he had received from Grayson. It was convenient as Grayson no longer served in the military, so he was a sort of an 'outside the circle' person who had insight of many things.

Grayson had been under surveillance by the F.B.I. Nothing unusual had surfaced or had been a concern, not until this whole financial Watergate situation had come to light accidentally.
Bradford had reached out to Grayson and their conversations had been all in code. The old code language that Q was all too familiar with and this was how he had been involved with the whole Bradford situation. To encrypt the language and then it was wide open chase amongst them to catch Bradford.
What had been a simple extraction operation of catching Bradford for his involvement in Jordan, now it involved civilians and they had been affected.

There was this jigsaw puzzle that FBI had been working on with a cartel of 13, and oddly enough there was a connection to Bradford, they knew that much. The only reason they had not snatch him up was because they needed more information that would hold up in court. Suspicions and hunches wouldn't hold up against a judge, it would be dismissed, and Bradford would walk free and vanish deep into the rabbit hole.

Q walks through the turnstiles and down into the underground at Notting Hill Gate station. Thoughts were occupying his mind, but he would not allow that to distract his focus of what he had to do and his assignment to finish it.

The train races in to the station and the doors opens up and Q watches people getting off with determined steps as they all had places to go to, and plans to be executed. They were no different from him although his were of a different caliber.
 Q was feeling he was on his way too, but wasn't sure where his destination would end, as he had been on this journey for a while and felt old and tired. He was hoping that the meeting he had set up with Marcus would lead to tie the loose ends to the saga he had been involuntarily dragged into.

The ride was making a few stops all while Q was contemplating on the meeting and he watched the name of each station, until they reached Bayswater.

He steps out and walks up the stairs slowly while making sure no one was following him. He stops at the top and make people pass him, as he watches each individuals carefully.
Once the crowd got thicker at the entrance he makes a quick right exit move and disappears in to the crowd and with a few steps he was inside the Golden Horseshoe casino. He could hear the shuffling of card, the roulette table ball run circles, and then, the click of falling into a slot.

He walks up to the bar, there is already two individuals having their drinks. He sits down and waits and pulls up his phone. Marcus had left him a text message, "Package delivered".
Q lifts his hand to get the bartenders attention.
"One Scotch, please".
"On the rocks?" the bartender asks as he pours the drink.
Q nods, "yes...please".

Harris sits and watches the interaction between the bartender and Q, and he knows he was the VIP he was there to meet.
He turns to Penny, "I believe we have arrived" he says to her and she looks at his eyes speaking a language only they knew.

Penny grabs her cocktail napkin and pulls out her pen, and writes "find me at the tables", and gets up from her seat and walks up to Q and drops off the folded napkin next to his drink.

Q turns his head watching Penny walking off and gives her a wondersome look and turns back to nurturing his drink.
He casually looks at the folded napkin, and takes another sip of the drink before he unfolds it.
Harris watches him read the note, while making no sudden moves but instead takes a sip of his drink and puts it back on the napkin and says unexpected.
"Yea...Marcus said you had some information you wanted to share" he utters casually as he looks into the mirror behind the bar straight at Q.

He looks up from the napkin, and leans his head to the left, and gives a casual look at his 6 and takes another sip of his drink.
"Yea, he said that about you too; that the information we had we should compare..." he pause and continues "... and we would catch our man" he responds as he rubs his thumbs on the rim of the glass.

Harris gets up from his seat, and throws down a few quid's on the counter, and walks off to meet up with Penny who are already playing the black jacks.

CHAPTER 25

'You are playing with the wrong person! If you know me that well, then you know that I don't let people tell me what to do, Seel?'

The words were echoing inside Bradford's head as he was speeding down the highway, on his way to Edinburgh.
What did she know he wasn't aware of?

'Protect me? Protect me? Protect me?' He was shaking his head as he was thinking of what he knew, what he was guilty of; he was responsible for her husband's death.
His thoughts recollected that he'd followed her back to Heidelberg and watched over the situation, and then she'd disappeared without a moment's notice.

The voice of Penny and her sharp response; *'Huh? Protect me, I should be the one telling you that',* gave him an eerie feeling that was crawling up his spine, and yet he coveted her.
She had disappeared for a decade, been under the radar under

a different name, and lived a life away from anyone that knew her, but she had surfaced unexpectedly due to his situation.

The trip to Edinburgh was 8 hrs. The time was ticking along imperceptibly hour after hour, until he realized he was close to Scarborough. He made a quick decision to steer off to the North Sea coast to have a late snack.

This was a low pay capital, but they had the most spectacular cliffs, and ancient castles, and the best fish and chips.
Just the thought of the fish was making Bradford hungry.

He realizes when his eyes hits the dashboard that he was almost on empty as he was driving towards Scarborough. He needed gas that he knew for sure and it was just a few miles up the road.

He's slowing down on A64, and starts to scope for a gas station, suddenly his eyes hit the towering Shell sign as he is getting closer to the town. He comes up to the corner of St James Rd. and there on the left the Shell station was emerging. It was having two pumps conveniently, easy to enter from both directions he thought as he assessed the area like a scout.

He pulls in and stops at one of the gasoline pumps and gets out. A man from inside the shop comes out with short skipping steps, and a direct demeanor. He is dressed in a mechanic overall and waves his hand as he hollers at him in norther English accent.
"I got that!" and Bradford looks over his shoulder as the man steps in and takes away the pump handle from him.

Bradford observes the short man in a measuring way and can see a sowed in name tag saying 'Joe', as he is looking over at sky. The weather is looking gloomy, and is about to change. "There is trouble brewing" he mutters as he continues filling up the tank, "...a storm is coming in, I hope you have a place to stay overnight" he says and glances over at Bradford, and suddenly the handle clicks off. The tank was full, and Bradford was ready to move on. The man pulls out the pump handle and puts it back on the base and puts the gas cap back on. Bradford watches the man and follows him back into the store to pay.

The man walks behind the counter, and he can hear his finger press the buttons that determined his price, and then he pulls the lever. A ripping sound follows, and then the amount was displayed on top of the register. This was an antique register that still did its job, determining the debt, and then releasing the customer from their monies. The true 1800 century debt collector that once it was paid, it was put behind. Bradford accumulate debt but of a different sort, the kind where the price was too high and impossible to pay by currency, but instead with his life.

Bradford looks over at the cash register display to see how much he owed him. He breaks the silence as he looks down at his rolled up wadded bills and pulls out an amount that was more than enough that was owed and hands it over. "Where can one get a late evening snack around her Joe?" he says as he puts the rest of the money back in his front pocket.

"Well" he looks up from counting the bills and gives off a look that he was thinking, and continues "..you can get some fish

and chips down at Nellies…down at the marina" Joe responds
as he finishing counting the paper bills and pushes a button on
the cash register, and it opens up. He gathers the change, and
is about to hand it to Bradford when he holds out his hand in a
rejecting fashion, "…consider it tip" he says and takes his
recommendation on Nellies place.

THE DOOR BELL CHIMES on the yellow painted building by
the marina as Bradford walks through the door of Nellie's. He
walks up to the counter and an older lady emerges from
behind,

"We are closing for the day" she says as she couldn't care less
that he was standing there as a customer.
"Closing?" and he looks around as he wasn't sure as he was
watching people sitting down and eating their dinners.
"yes, closing…did I stutter?" she says as she is giving him a
dumbfounded look and then she has a realization, "oh you are
one of those" and she waves her hand in a dismissing way, "out
of towners" she continues in a negative discouraging tone and
bends back down as she continues to talk to Bradford but is not
bothered to give him the courtesy to look at him.
"You don't know our weather pattern here, look out the
window. What do you see?" she says with a heavy voice
sounding old and tired.
Bradford doesn't say anything, but instead looks out and can
see the waves coming in strong and washing the sides of the
walls by the marina, and up on the side walk.
He could tell this was a bad time to try to enjoy the coast,
everything had been bad since this situation started and this
was an omen of what to come, he wasn't superstitious but
couldn't help to think that something was working against him.

He would need to find a place to stay the night and this was not looking promising.

BACK AT THE OFFICE IN SEATTLE Spencer is walking by Penny's office, and he looks over at Julia's desk, she was sitting and doing filing. Spencer ponders for a second, and walks up to her desk.

"Julia," he says, and she jumps in her seat.
"Oh I didn't mean to scare you" he says apologetic, "Have you heard from Penny" he says as he points his finger at her office. Julia looks over at her door, "No, actually. She normally is good at keeping in touch and now...I don't know" she says and looks at Spencer both surprised and concerned.
"I figured, I have a bad feeling as this is not her MO" he says and walks off in deeper thoughts.

Spencer is back in his office and sits down in his chair, leans back and swings slowly around looking at the computer as he was thinking. Where was Penny that was the question.
He needed to know when she last entered the system or if she had used the system, and what program she had touched last. *'Who better than Edwin would know'* he says out loud as he sits straight up and leans forward. He grabs the receiver and pushed three-digit extension.
"Edwin...in my office stat" he says stressed and puts the receiver back on the base.

Spencer was not just a simple man; he was an ex-marine and had a law degree. He could smell trouble from afar and now was the time his senses were shark like. In the midst of his thoughts there was a knock on the door.

"Come in!" Spencer exclaims out loud. Edwin enters the office, and he looks surprised.

"What's the urgency, you sounded like something was on fire." Edwin says in a serious manner while he was throwing jokes.

"Penny" Spencer says and looks at Edwin to see if that was going to resonate waves that he would be able to pick up on.

"Yea, what about her" he says equally as nonchalant.

"I need you to tell me when she was on the system last...nae, in fact I want you to show me at your office" he says as he stands up and pushes the chair out.

"Right now?" Edwin ask and he knew there was no hiding now he was going to have to come clean about it, even if his job was going to be in jeopardy.

"Is there a problem?" he says and waits for an answer, "Ok then" and he points at the door.

Edwin walks up to the door and pulls it open, and then hesitates.

"We need to talk" he says to Spencer.

Spencer looks at Edwin and understand that he knows more than he is saying.

"Ok...let's sit down "Spencer says as he points at the sitting area facing the corner windows.

Edwin sits down with a heavy sigh and closes his hands as his looks up at Spencer with a guilty face of knowledge that he should have been privy to.

"What is it that you are not telling me?" Spencer asks.

"Hmmm...Penny called me one early morning, and asked me if

she could access the system, the surveillance system. I told her I could get in trouble, she promised me I would lose my job if I didn't help" Edwin says guilty.

"So, do you know what she was looking for?"
"I looked through the downloaded files, it was all AVI and MPEG's", Edwin continues.
"What was on them, because I assume you wanted to know." Spencer calls him on it.
Edwin nods agreeing, "Yes, I did view them" and stops.
"OK, so spit it out..."

"There were conversations from the corporate office, in the conference room, Neal and Taytum talking to some guy" Edwin says as if it was innocent.
"I see, ok.... I need you to get back to your office and send me the files" Spencer says as he gets up from the seating area and walks back to his desk.

Edwin gets it; that was his queue, the conversation was over, and he gets up from the seat, and exits the office.

CHAPTER 26

Q FOLLOWS HARRIS and meet up with him at the roulette table where he is keeping Penny company.

"What do you have for me?" Q says while he is looking where he is placing his bet.

"I got the information you are looking for" Harris replies as he is leaning over the table and puts down his bet.

"What's your plans?" Q asks curiously, and glances over at Penny who is standing on the other side of Harris. He knew he had seen her before but could not place her, there was something familiar over her.

"Do you know what it is... what I mean is, do you know the content of it?" Harris asks in a probing way, he had to be sure that he was the right person Marcus had sent and not some mole sent by Bradford, and his eyes were following the ball run along the roulette wheel.

"The Feds are involved in this" Q says with a serious tone.

"OK" Harris acknowledges, and puts down a new bet.

"Well, it's some serious stuff, and it involves institutes both here and over the other side of the pond" he continues.

"If you hand it to me I can take care of it" Q says reassuring and looks at Harris.

He looks at Q and he wasn't going to trust anyone at this point. "I tell you what, I will give you Bradford and stop this whole madness" Harris says concluding, "...but it will be my way" he says.

Q leans down places another bet on the table, on top of Harris and says, "OK, we will work together on this one." The bet he placed was a sign that this was a joint effort, he wanted to stop anything from metastasize like a cancer, and Bradford had become an infection, like a decease and he was a lose canon.

"We will be heading back to Scotland, where I can control the situation" he pauses, "... I know he will follow, and I hunt better on my own territory" he says and nudges Penny giving her heads up that they were leaving.

Penny turns to Q and, at that moment it comes to her, that she knows who he is, and her face changes. He looks at her with an intensity as he knew her but could not place her. His mind was moving in slow motion as he tried to figure it out before she was out of his sight indefinitely.

Harris follows her out the door and they quickly make a left turn and down into the Underground.

Q is still left inside the casino, standing at the roulette table. He pulls up his phone, and text Marcus a message, "Do you know who Penny is?"

HARRIS AND PENNY EXIT THE PADDINGTON STATION and they walk back to the hotel.

The valet greets them with a nodding motion of acknowledgement.

Back at the room Harris is starting to pack up and looks over at Penny.
"You know it's better if we catch him or we will continue to be a target for him" he says as this was no other way to do it.
"...and how are you going to do that" she says discouraged,

She was exposed now, and it was just a matter of time before Q also knew who she was, but she intended to be gone far away by that time.

IT HAD BECOME LATE in the afternoon and the sun had almost set, and Harris knew that they travelled better in the dark and that was his plan for now.
"We are going to go home" Harris says as he look at Penny.
"Home, as in Scotland home?" she looks at him like a question mark.

"Yes, I know myself around there" ... he says victoriously "I doubt he does" he continues with confidence in his tone.
"What about Marcus?" Penny say inquiring.
"What about him?" He replies as it was obvious, at least to him.
"Are we doing this alone or ..." she stops in midsentence.
"Yes, Marcus is going along, I better have him closer than not knowing what he is up to. I don't know if I trust him yet." he says and makes it an out of discussion debate.

Penny says nothing more of it, he had made up his mind and she trusted his instinct.

"Why don't you check on Marcus and let him know…" he stops and looks at Penny who is in deep thoughts.
"What are you thinking about luv" he says endearing, while he can tell Penny is contemplating on something.

"I just have a bad feeling about this, that's all. Something in my gut just is uneasy" she says and as she can't get rid of it.

There is a knock on the door, and Penny looks at Harris with a concern, she knew they weren't expecting anyone. He nods at her to get up from the bed and answer the door.
She walks slowly up to the door and looks in the cat eye.
Marcus, she looks over at Harris, as she opens the door.

"Hey… what took you so long?" he asks and continues to enter the room.

"You are ready!" Harris exclaims as he stands up and continues to pack up his belongings.
"Yes, I travel light" Marcus responds.

Harris looks at Penny and his thought crossed him that they sure did have something in common, both being light travelers.
"You didn't tell me where we are going" Marcus says curiously as he looks for Penny and meets her eyes looking for some answers.

"We are going to familiar territories" he says as he wasn't going to say much more and continues to have his eyes on the bag he was packing.

"OK", Marcus respond with a subtle tone, as he got the hint, he would know in good time.

"We are going to go when the sun has set" he says as he was closing the bag. He walks up to the window and looks out, "in about 30 minutes."

It is quiet in the room, almost awkwardly and then Harris says; "I told Q that I was going to give him Bradford".
Marcus is in deep thoughts when he hears Harris, and turns his way, "Say again" as Marcus couldn't believe what he was hearing.
Harris looks at him, "I told him we are going to hand Bradford over...I think that is a good bargain, don't you?" he responds and awaits his reaction.

"How are we going to do that, we don't even know where he is" Marcus says as he was clueless what Harris was playing on and looking both at Penny and Harris.

"I know we don't, but, there is a past between him and Penny, something unfinished" he says as he wasn't sure what it was, but with the interaction between her and Bradford was clearly stating that they had met before. "He will come for her" he says and points at Penny.

Marcus looks over at Penny, "What's going on with Bradford?" and he waits for an answer. She gives up a sigh and a tired look, "I met him on the plane over to London" she says as it really wasn't a big deal. She wasn't going to give him anything else, he was her past.

"That's it?" he says and looks surprised as he was expecting something worse and gives up a laugh. "I guess you are heartbreaker" he finishes.

Harris wasn't ready to tell Marcus what his suspicions were but it was clearly from way past before his time.

"So where are we heading" Marcus continues.
"To the Scotsman" Harris says and it comes out cryptic.
"Who is that?" Marcus says.

"Marcus!" Penny says with a superior tone, "It's a newspaper."
"OK, so you are going to blow this wide open, but giving attention to the matter...I'm just guessing here" he says as he wasn't sure and yet he was good at putting two and two together. "Do you have someone one the inside?" he continues.

"You'll see... eventually" is all Harris says.
He picks up the phone, "This is Benjamin, can I have the car pulled up...I'll be down in 10 minutes" and he puts the receiver back on the base.

Harris gives a look around if he was missing something, then he looks at Marcus and Penny, "are you guys ready?" he asks at the same time he gives off the marching orders that they were leaving.

DOWN AT THE FRONT DESK James are meeting them, "I heard you were departing" he says as he was relieved that this time it had been a more of a quiet event.
The clerk behind the counter hands Harris the bill, James interjects and grabs it.
"This one is on the house" he says, "You make sure you come by again when you are in town" he continues as he shakes Harris hand.

"You can count on it" and Harris gives off a smile, turns around and walks out.

CHAPTER 27

PENNY IS SITTING IN THE BACK SEAT and looking out the
window as they are going through the dark wet streets of
London. The street lights are dim and a fog is building up she
can tell as it was rising from the ground.

She knew they were soon going to hit the highway and then it
was just the headlights that was going to be their guide
through the night.

Penny closes her eyes are she falls into deep sleep. She was
dreaming of being back in Sarajevo. Her body being buried in a
coffin with multiple dead body stacked on top of her, trapped
and alive despite of it all. "Howard, Howard where are you
Howard" she says in her sleep.

Marcus looks over and watches her talk in her sleep. His
thoughts goes back to the picture he had been given by Q, she
was the one in Mafraq on the picture that was dated.
His gut feeling told him he was on the right track; he was

putting two and two together. He was certain she was Jackie, Jacqueline Grant, Howards Spouse, except she had not said it.

BRADFORD IS DRIVING up B6370, he knew he had almost reached his destination. It was dark and the only thing that lit up the road was his head lights. He was tired but he was almost there. He had received directions to look for Heather's Lodge.

He passes it, and slams on the break and comes to a full stop 50 feet away. He gives a quick look in the back-view mirror, and puts the car in reverse, and looks at the sign as he makes a right-hand turn into a dirt road that was leading up to the estate. The winy road had pothole puddles and the sound of splash could be heard against the wheelhouse, and the pressure of the tires were making mud sounds mixed with gravel as it rolled over the dirt. Bradford is slowing down, and he finally reaches the alley of trees. He suddenly catches a glimpse of a car in the dark, he was not alone. He was told that there wouldn't be anyone here, the estate was deemed deserted by his pilot.

Bradford quickly turns off his headlights, and slowly pulls over to the right and parks in between the trees. It wasn't a good sign, he needed to secure the location and he could only do that by foot.

He gets out of the car, hunches down and closes the doors quietly. He holds his hand over the Bowie 9' combat knife that is tucked in his side pocket. He was still very much wired like the military he trained to be, it was like the zebra's stripes who would never erase, it was part of who he was.

He moves along the brush like a leopard, stealthy and quick. There was only one person in the driver seat he could tell. The person was leaning backwards in the seat he could tell by the sideview mirror and wasn't moving instead seemed to be out.

Bradford sticks his head up and looks inside the back through the window; there was a sniper rifle, and small black duffle bag. This was not someone with friendly intent, he knew that much, but he could also not ignore it whoever he was.

Bradford was there to do a job and this was an obstacle he had to eliminate, but why was the person here.

He hunches down and sneaks up to the driver side door. He places his hand on the door handle as he takes a deep breath and prepares himself mentally and pulls the door open, and the person turns around quickly and gives off a surprised look. In the next moment the nine inches of the blade had penetrated the side of the man's neck and Bradford rips the knife in a motion as he cuts off the vocal cords and sheers off the front of the throat and the blood starts to pool out of the flesh wound and the mouth. His head tilts to the right and his body falls out of the seat.

Bradford moves away to avoid being stained by the blood flow. "Damn" he exclaims softly, he turns around and looks over the seat and out through the other window, and then to the right and left. He was alone, and his surrounding was completely still.

He reaches inside the back and pulls out the duffle bag. He unzips it, and rummage through it, there is a plane ticket, a roll of cash and a small book, maroon colored outside and the lettering is in Cyrillic.

Bradford closes the door, and swiftly moves back to his car. He reaches inside and pulls up his phone, and dials Afifi's number. He returns to the dead body as the phone rings and then,

"Alo salam" (hello), Afifi says tired as he is yawning.
"Man komak niaz aram (I need help) Bradford responds whispering.
"Sa'at chand ast?" (what time is it?) Afifi continues.
"Late...tell me who else is looking for your person?"
"Chi? (What?) What do you mean?" he asks confused and is now sitting up in the bed.
"There is... let me rephrase there was a man waiting..." he says irritated.
"Koja?" (Where?)
"Here... on the trail up to the house! I am not sure who he was, but there is a sniper rifle in the back of the car he was in, and a duffle bag" Bradford says irritated.

"I can only think of one...but it doesn't matter now, you take care of it.. where is the man?" Afifi asks inquisitively.
"I put him to sleep" Bradford says heartless.
"Hold on" and Bradford opens the book, and he can see it's a passport.
"Are you still there?" Bradford calls out to Afifi.

"Yes, yes..." Afifi responds tiresome and is ready to go back to bed.

"Do you know anyone from…" and he stops and reads out loud, "…from Croatia?" he says cautiously, and continues to read the name, "Igor Kazsic".

"No, and why do you say Croatia, and who this Igor whatever his last name was?" Afifi asks as he is getting nervous.

His problem he had stemmed from Croatia and Serbia. That there was someone from Croatia watching the same house he had sent Seels was something he did not expect.

"I'm holding the man's passport" he says and waits for an answer that would not be another question.

"I need you to get rid of him, and I will make some calls. What was his name again?"

"Igor Kazsic", he blurs out as to him this meant nothing anymore and he didn't have time to do any research. He was no longer a person of interest, as he was eliminated.

Afifi had hung up and Bradford was sitting by the side of the car with his own thoughts watching over at the man that was slumped over, he needed to remove him off the road.

He moves swiftly back to his car and drags the him further into the embankment by the road and covers him with greeneries from the ground to make it look part of the surroundings.

HARRIS STOPS in Nottingham to get gas, he still had 6 hours to go, and sometimes after midnight they were going to reach Edinburgh, and another hour to Haddington. The darkness protected them; this was Harris protection, the only way to reach the house without being seen.

He looks over at his phone and scrolls down on the list of

contacts, and hits Montgomery.

He keeps walking back and forth as the phone rings, and then voicemail. Montgomery was not at the office.

"Monty, it's Harris. I will be in the office tomorrow, I have two visitors with me, make sure you have badges ready for us", and he disconnects the phone.

He gets back into the car and he can see that both Marcus and Penny are asleep, and it was going to be a minute before they would wake up. He starts the car and gets back on the road.

Q LOOKS AT HIS PHONE there was an incoming message, from Marcus.

He was hoping for an answer to his question, and as soon his eyes hit the words, *"I think she's Jackie"*, he catches himself think out loud, "Jackie. Jacqueline, could it really be....".

Howards spouse had disappeared, completely wiped herself. It was a long shot, but he had nothing else, he had to follow the lead.

He needed more information, a recent picture of her, all they had was old pictures from the military base.

"The bank!" he exclaims.

He looks over the time, there was a 7 hour time difference, that meant that he had a chance to check it out.

Q gets on the computer and sends a message, *"Hammonds, give me a call"*, and he leans back in the chair, with his hands intertwined resting on his chest thinking what if this really was true, he would be able to solve the bombing in Mafraq, or get closer to the truth.

There was so many things spinning in his head; Bradford, the past, the present, all seem to come back to same starting point. It was a sordid mess, all about money, weapons and some devious mind with no regards to innocent third parties.

His thoughts get interrupted by a car alarm outside, he gets up from his chair and walks up to the draped window. He separates the drape apart with his index finger, gives a quick look. The street was empty and only a couple was walking pass, and the lights blinking from a car.

He walks back to his chair when the phone goes off, and he looks over and it recognizes the number.

"What took you so long" he says and laughs out loud. *"Listen Q, I have a job to do. I am not like some, on a permanent vacation"* she says.

"OK Hammonds, calm down. I need a favor" he says as apologetic as he can be.

"Yea, favor? I think that is all I have been doing" she says snarky.

"Is F.B.I. not treating you well?" Q asks as if it was a privilege to work for the firm, "...maybe you need a vacation after all, or a break in what you are doing".

"Listen, get to the point, I have work to do" she continues and wants to get moving.

"I have a person of interest at a bank; Penny Bridge at PegC. I need a recent picture, I had hoped you could get that for me" he says with a serious tone.

"*What is this all about, you have to give me something more than that*" she says as she was now showing interest in helping, and Q picks up on it.

"Penny Bridge, is what I can tell you, and why this sudden deep interest of her, what do you know that I don't?" he asks as he wanted some information now,

"*Bradford*" she says with a cryptic tone.

"Yea, he is here" he responds with the same enigmatic tone.

"*...that may be so, but he has a contact here...that he contacted just hours ago*" she says.
"Ok, and did her name come up?
"*No*" she says with a cutting tone.
"Damn, who did he reach out to?" Q is getting concerned that this was just the beginning of something grueling to happen.

"*Grayson, the military communications specialist, do you remember*" she says as she knew that Q had knowledge of the part he had played in Bradford's platoon. "*He took the heat for Bradford's covert operation*" she finishes.

"Not surprising...so what was the conversation about?"
"*...to eliminate a female 'trouble maker' he called her*" and he could hear that she did not know who she was.

"..so you think Penny Bridge is the person because I asked about her?" he asks as he wanted to find out if she was trying to put two and two together.

"Well, I don't normally get favors like these at the same time I have a female Jane Doe that I need to protect and I can't find her" she says frustrated and helpless.

Q sits down in the chair and places his left hand over his mouth as he sighs and fears that this may as well be connected but he was contemplating on whether he was going to disclose what he knew.

"What's going on Q, what is it that you are not telling me. I know there is something that you are withholding" she continues to push for more information.

"Ok," he pauses, "this has to stay between us" he says adamantly.
There is a moment of silence, *"OK, you got it"*.

"I think Penny Bridge is Jacqueline Grant, Howards Grant's spouse" he says factually.

"The Howard, from Mafraq bombing?" she questions shocked.
A silence creeped up on both ends of the line, it was as if they were thinking in sync.

"I can't be for sure; I need a recent picture" Q breaks the silence.
"I understand.." she says as she is thinking. *"Do you think this situation with her has something to do with the 'cartel 13?"* she says inquisitively.
"I don't know for sure, but..." and he stops in midsentence. "I

know that Bradford is on the run".

"*I will pay the bank a visit but keep me posted what you find out*" she says, and the call is disconnected.

CHAPTER 28

THE CAR ROLLS ON TO THE ESTATE, and the gravel can be heard pushing away underneath the car. Harris comes to a full stop and he looks over at both, they are still asleep.

Harris taps Penny on the leg, "Hey luv...we're home" he says with a quiet voice. In the next Marcus moves around and starts to wake up. He looks out, and doesn't recognize himself, he looks over at Harris.
"Where are we?" he asks as he is continuing waking up by rubbing his eyes.
"We are 'home'" Harris states welcoming.

Penny slowly wakes up and looks at Harris. She nods with her eyes squinting, and stretches her arms up in the air while giving up a growling sound.

She opens up the door, and sits for a moment as she feels the cool breeze hit her face, she closes her eyes. She's tired, and the cool air is crawling in-between the layers of her clothes, and she is getting goosebumps on her arms. She puts one foot down on the gravel and then the next, she gives up another stretch and gets out of her seat. The sound of gravel can be heard crushing under her feet as she walks to the back of the car. Marcus follows Harris and walks to the back and opens the hatch.

Harris grabs his gear, a long envelope shaped carrying cases, he hands one case to Marcus, and he knew what that was. Under the tarp there was ammunition in small metal boxes.

Penny grabs a metal box and pulls it out, and she reaches for her backpack. She gives a quick look around before she shuts the hatch.

Harris has already managed to get to the front door, all while Marcus is keeping a watchful eye as he is waiting for Penny to reach the door. They all enter the house, and Penny shuts the door behind them, an echo follows as the large heavy oak doors slams shut.

It had been a minute since Penny had visited Harris, but she still felt overwhelmed by the architecture that was something she couldn't get over.

Penny walks over to the large room that is both functions as a study and office. The fireplace was lit, and the burning logs were making crackling sounds

"Were we expected?" Penny says surprised and points at the fireplace.
"I had my housekeeper come by and set it for us" Harris says.

The house was large and could feel drafty, and it would take a while to bring it up to temperature.

Marcus looks around and observes the multiple computers facing each other on the desk, one on each end. Penny places her backpack on the chair adjacent to the desk, and from her side pocket she pulls out her USB key and hands the key to Harris.

"I already have it" he says surprised.

"Plug it in, humor me, and let me know when it is ready, I have to enter the password." she says as there was something about the key that gave her the feeling that there was more than met the eye at the first glance

Penny pulls out her firearm from her belt and places it on the table and watches Harris being absorbed in front of the computer.

She starts to stretch her tired body, and, at the same time, he waves his hand for her to come over. Penny moves over to the computer and enters the code that she had memorized, JO962. The file opens up and as Penny walks away Harris calls out to her.

"Did you see this?" he asks as he was watching the screen intently.

"What!" she exclaims.

"No, come over here, let me show you" he says in a more serious tone than he was back in London. He sits down in the chair and points at the screen, "...there..." Penny looks and tries to figure out what he is pointing at and shrugs her shoulder, "...and...what is it?" she ask as she wasn't sure what he was asking about.

"...there is a document hidden here inside the key, inside the file, and because you sent the file that was encrypted and it was not translating. It was only available through the hardware.

The conversation peaked Marcus ears and he pulls his attention away from the window.

"What is it that we are missing?" Marcus says questioning, and rests his hands on the hips.

Harris points at a blue underlined word, "this is a link" he says as he looks at both of them, "...an Easter Egg" he continues. He highlights the word and right clicks on it, and it links it to a website, but the address is untraceable .

The window opens up to an excel sheet with 200 account numbers, and names of 13 individuals.

"What is this?" Penny says confused and ridges were forming on her forehead as she was confused and concerned at the same time.

"It looks like account numbers, and names of people, but not any ordinary people" he says almost triumphant, and gets up from his seat and walks over the computer on the opposite side of the desk. "Let me show you."

He starts to pull up jpeg files while Penny and Marcus is standing behind him and watching the process.

A library of pictures are slowly forming on the screen. He turns around the swivel chair and says; "This is '13'", and both of them gives back an expression of being uninspired, at the same time their faces look puzzled.

"13, OK, we can all count, what's the big deal." she says and started to get inpatient.

Harris points at the chairs by the fireplace, "both, sit down...let me explain" he says as there was a backstory that had to be heard. He rolls his swivel chair to the seating area.

"These individuals are part of a group, you can call it a cartel if you so like" he says as he leans back in the chair.
Marcus looks at Penny, and back at Harris, this got more interesting by the minute.

"So why does the file contain this hidden file, and who was it for?" Marcus asks as this was something of importance.
"That is a good question, why would they place this file with these accounts in an Easter egg fashion?" Harris questions.
"Unless this is what Bradford is wanting!" Penny exclaims.
"Look at the names..." Harris pauses, "Victor Afifi" he says and waits for an reaction.

"I have not heard that name since Mafraq when I was working on a case..."Marcus stops himself.
"So you know this individual?" Penny ask out loud in a direct manner.
"I would not say I know him. I know about him, and what he does" he says almost innocent.

Harris looks at Marcus and then at Penny, "Ok, let me fill you in Pen, these guys here are the 'Underworld'...Afifi is a middle eastern mercenary. He was the one that was funneling weaponry to the Balkan war" and before he can continue, Marcus fills in.
"Yea, he is not playing that guy, he was turning a troop against us and we lost weapons and equipment" he finishes the ugly

truth of who he was.

Penny is no longer listening to either Harris or Marcus, and
she gets up and starts to walk away.
"Where are you going?" Marcus hollers at her, and Harris stops
him from getting up.
"I think she has some thinking to do, this is how she process
information" Harris states.

Penny was repeating the words in her head, '*I have not heard
that name since Mafraq when I was working on a case*'.
She thinks back, Howards was working on case, and he had
one person who he trusted the most, more so than her, or
maybe this was his way to protect her. She knew that he had
had a partner by name Weaver, but he also called him the
Aquarius.

She stops at the door way, something in her gut was starting to
churn, a feeling she had had before, the intuitive side was
making it to the surface. She turns around abruptly, she had to
face this head on. The feeling she had, demanded that she did,
and she couldn't hold back any longer.
The person she was perceiving as Marcus was the very same
person her husband had worked with, that was what her gut-
wrenching feeling was telling her.

"Do you know who I am?" she says and interrupts the
conversation between Harris and Marcus.
"Who are you talking to?" Harris ask confused.
"Marcus" she says direct.
"Yea,... Penny..." he says hesitantly.
"No, I am asking again, do you know who I am?" she says now

with a more stern tone and she was making certain of that the message was delivered that she was not playing games. "Jacqueline" he responds confessional. Harris is stone faced as he didn't know what to expect, he had seen her like this before and it had not turn out for the best.

"Listen" Marcus says with a compassionate tone, "I made a promise to Howard, that I would look after you if something happened to him, and I couldn't find you..." he finishes. He had figured out that she was Jackie, but he had hoped to have kept this ordeal on a downlow.

Harris looks at both of them, "So ... you are the covert that Howard was working with, so ..." and he is being stopped in his midsentence. It was over, her agonizing feeling that had forced her to confront the intuition that was nagging at her, had almost diminished.
"Yes... this is Weaver, or the Aquarius that Howard called him" Penny says factually as she slowly is walking towards them. "So, who are you working for?" she continues.
"I already told you guys, I was sent to get the file...by Q".

"Who does Q work for?" Penny had been blindsided before and it was not going to happen again.
"He is a contractor like me, but he is working on bringing Bradford in..." He looks at her, as she wasn't buying it.
"Ok, Ok, the feds are involved" he says surrendering.
"That means that I am in deep shit" she says almost defeated under her breath.
"No, you are not" Harris says to her, and he turns to Marcus, "You are keeping this under lid, Penny needs to be protected...do you understand?" he says with firm tone.

Marcus nods agreeing, it was crystal clear that he was going to honor Howards request to protect her.

"So how are we going to catch Bradford?" he ask Harris.

"He is on his way" he responds and turns around and rolls back to the desk.

Penny looks up, "What do you mean" she says as this was the last thing she needed to hear.

"Listen both! He is not going to give up until he has the key and we need to get to the Scotsman, as we are not really safe here…" he has their attention, and they realize that he was serious.

"Yea, not even here, and this is a big place" he continues and his tone was getting more frustrated and annoyed by each response they could tell, his decision was final.

Not even Harris large estate was able to keep them out of harm's way from Bradford, and he could not forget the experience by the uninvited guest that came ready for him.

She looks over at the time, it was already 3.30 am, and Harris glances over at Penny.

"Ok, let's wrap this up, we need a few hours of sleep before we head into town." He says as he no longer could think straight, it had been intense for the past 16 hours, it was time to let matters marinate over a few hours with no talk. They just needed to close their eyes and try puzzle together the information and figure what was head and tail of it all.

"Ok I need a bed. Where's the nearest bed where I can rest this tired piece of flesh?" she says morbidly to Harris.

"Come on dear." Harris says and grins as he places his arm around Penny's shoulder. Penny is grabbing her backpack and grabs her steel off the desk and packs it.

Marcus follows their lead and, while he is walking, he is looking out the windows. He catches a glimpse of headlights but continues upstairs.

Harris leads Penny into one of the guest bedrooms, "Here... you can sleep in here, and I am not sure..." Harris pauses and nods his head towards Marcus.
No words are needed Penny knows already.

"The bathroom is over there." Harris points at the closed raised panel door.

Penny nods signaling that she recognizes it and she says out loud, "Yes... Marcus will sleep in this room tonight!" she is looking around in the room, but not looking at him. She drops the bag next to her side of the bed.

Harris says nothing else and leaves the room, and Marcus looks surprised at her and jumps as the door closes behind Harris.
He wasn't expecting the invite, "so...why are you asking me to stay here?" he says as they had not had the best interaction after all that had transpired.
"I don't like to be alone" she says with a quiet voice and pulls the blanket aside.

Marcus studies her every movement as she is getting ready for bed, now he was no longer viewing her as Penny, but as Jacqueline Grant, Howards Jackie.

CHAPTER 29

BRADFORD SITS IN THE CAR and watches the lights turn on the second floor.

"Oh, so he is home after all" he says concluding and looks down at his phone.

He had options he knew how to take him out. He looks back up and thumbs on the steering wheel with his left hand, as he views the large building of how it could be done.

He gives a quick glance into the back, there was a tarp covering something he could tell. He steers his look back at his phone, there was a message, '*you have everything you need, take care of it*'. That was all it said, Afifi was a man with few words.

Bradford turns around 180 degrees and reaches his arm out and grabs one of the corners and pulls the tarp off.

He looks at the parts, Afifi had certainly equipped him with options. It was a box of shell casings resting next to the rifle, it was printed '50 on the outside.

The rifle was lined up in parts and he would have to put it

together. He looks down at his phone, and responds to the text, '*I have it*'. This certainly gave him options and he knew what he needed to do and how.

He starts the car and turns it around and slowly drives back the way he came. The solution was staring him in the face, and he knew this was the only way.

THERE'S A KNOCK ON THE DOOR, Marcus wakes up startled, and he calls out. "We will be downstairs in 20 minutes." He looks over and Penny is nowhere to be found, her clothes from yesterday were lying on her side of the bed.
He hurries to get his pants on, then he stops for a second, and listens as he hears what sounds like running water. Marcus walks up to the bathroom door, he can hear Penny talking to herself in the shower, and he smiles. He gives one knock on the door before he enters.

"Hey, have you been up for a while or what?" Marcus says questioning in a casual way.

"Yeah, I mean no." she replies quickly, "what are you doing in here?" she continues irritated.

"Ok." he replies, "Which one is it, yes or no?" and he grins to himself, "...are you done yet?"

"Are you leaving yet?" she responds and stops the water, reaches her arm out to grab the towel and wraps it around here body. She moves the drape aside, "Your turn." she says a little bitchy and grins as she walks out of his sight. She pulls the door shut behind her and she leans against it. She smiles to herself, as much as she was annoyed by all that had transpired up to this point she was thinking was this too good to be true, could this be her new chapter in her life.

Penny realizes that she was standing completely bare, covered in a towel. There was no time to waste, she knew that she needed to hurry to get dressed before he got out.

She could feel that her pants were getting too big, so she grabs her hip hugging belt and tightens it up in the corset lining.

She picks up her backpack from the side of the bed, pulls out her gun, and puts it behind her back in her belt.
She looks over at the bathroom door, she was walks up and gives it a knock.
She opens it and sticks her head in, "Hey, I am going to go downstairs, step on it a little will you." she calls out to him and closes the door before Marcus has a chance to reply back.

Penny walks downstairs, and she can smell the aroma of coffee linger up the stair. She steps inside the kitchen quietly where she finds Harris standing at the counter sipping on a cup and turning a page in the daily newspaper.

"I figured you needed something to wake up your senses." Harris says as he hears her walking into the kitchen still looking down reading.

"Nothing escapes your hearing!" she says, "I told Marcus to step on it." she says while she pours some black coffee in an oversized teacup. She walks up to the window, she looks outside, and contemplates what she was going to find, "What did you do after we went to bed? Could you sleep?"

"I went to bed just like you did. Do you think I would manage to be up making you coffee if I was out playing?" he says jokingly.

"You never know Harris, you may be an old bat, but your bad habits die hard." she says with a little mischievousness. She knew Harris' weak spot, as she and Harris had a rendezvous back in the days. His fetish for a nice ass was his 'cup of tea', and he liked 'a good tea'... that he could spank.

"Ok, here I am." Marcus announces, and both Harris and Penny turn his way simultaneously.

"...And so you are." Penny says with a bit of a British accent and gives up a fake laugh, then she gets serious again, "Come on then, let's see if we can't catch something today." she says with a snide tone.

Harris rolls his eyes, "I wonder what side of the bed she rolled off of, did something happen last night, or was that the problem nothing happened?"

Marcus and Harris give up a laugh at Penny's expense. "Women!" Marcus says.

Harris corrects him, "Woman, as she is one of a kind!"

Harris hands Marcus the keys, "Here you go, time for you to get more practice how to drive on the opposite side of the road."

Marcus grabs the keys, and everyone heads out to the car. They all get into the Range Rover and prepare for their trip to Harris' office. Penny enters the back but says nothing of the fact that Marcus is driving.

"Ok, I want you to get back on the A1 and then we are going to head to town; my office is located on Thistle St. in Edinburg. It will be about a half hour drive." Harris says and then looks at Penny, "Are you alright?" as he notices that she is quiet.
Penny just nods agreeing.

Marcus starts the car and looks straight ahead, and he can't help to notice the car.
He points and asks, "Is that your car?"
Harris looks and shakes his head, the car was sitting on the back road to the estate.
Marcus drives into the direction of where the car is sitting, and stops side by side.
He looks over at Harris, "Let's find out more" he says curiously.

The car was positioned off the road, and Marcus gets out with the engine still running. He looks in, and all he can see is a sniper rifle. As he walks around he can hear chopper blades in the distance.

He looks over at Harris and can see him get out, and watch the sky for the sound, and there in the distance Harris recognized the Augusta Helicopter from afar, and it was moving in closer in a much faster speed than he anticipated.
"Marcus!" he yells out loud, "Hurry get back in!"

Marcus runs back to the car and gets in, he puts the car into drive and steps on the gas, and unexpectedly he can see in the back view mirror the top floor being hit, the very room they had stayed was being disintegrated by rapid gun fire from the chopper.

"What the fuck is that?" Marcus exclaims questioning in a surprised way that was angrily shocking as he was driving off.

"I can only think of one person. Like I said, he was on his way." Harris says not surprised, and why would he be, he had sixth sense, like a blood hound he could smell it.

"Clearly", Penny fills in as the words comes out pondering. She knew this was far from over, she knew this already from the last conversation she had had with Bradford, even though she wanted to ignore the fact.

Penny is in deep thoughts when they are interrupted in the midst of it all by a large noise above her head. She looks out the window and rolls it down and sticks her head out and she can see the treetops sway and she realize the helicopter sound.

"They are above us" she says frantically.
"What the hell!" Marcus exclaims.
Harris knows his grounds better than anyone.
"Listen," he says commanding. "I want you to follow the trail and when the road splits make a swift left turn. The tree line will protect us and then, a small bridge will appear. I want you to stop under it" he continues. He had a plan B, Penny sensed.

The ride took them through windy roads, and unexpectedly the small stone bridge appeared. Marcus stops abruptly under it. It wasn't offering a two way, it was too narrow, just enough space to open the doors on each side.

Penny gets out of the car and watches Harris come around her side. There is a metal door facing her side. Harris pulls up a metal stick and pushes it into the door, and it opens.

Marcus looks at Penny and they both follow his lead. Harris is half running through the poorly lit tunnel, and Penny follows. She can barely see anything, but she hears her feet hit small puddles.

"Where are we going?" she utters as she is breathing heavily, and as she expects no one says anything.
Suddenly Harris stop and looks over at them catching up to him.
"OK guys, we just ran across the estate" he says, "...we are now entering a holy ground, I want you guys to just relax" he continues.

Harris opens the door, stone steps were appearing going up in a spiral shape. It was a sort of a medieval feel to it, she couldn't tell where it was going.
Then suddenly they are coming up to a small room, Harris flicks on the light. Penny recognizes whitewashed walls, and a coffin was placed across the rooms south wall. Marcus is hunching down as the room is not tall enough for him.

"Is this what I think it is", Penny says and an eerie feeling creep up. Marcus looks at Penny as he was expecting her to reveal it.
"This is the estates church, and we are under the altar right now" Harris confirms.
There are a few white washed steps up, and a flat door is hiding in the ceiling. Harris walks up the stairs as his hands are holding onto the steps to balance himself. He pushes the door up, and manages to stand straight up, and Penny follows Marcus.

They were standing behind the altar, and the stained-glass windows were staring them in the face. Harris makes a cross sign and kisses his hands up towards the window that depicts the face of Virgin Mary.

Harris turns to Penny and Marcus and with a low voice he says, "I have another vehicle that I keep here" and puts his finger to his mouth signaling to be silent.

Harris gives a quick look around the stone pillar, and waves with his hand for them to follow him.
Marcus signals to Penny to follow Harris as he wanted to protect her six.

As she follows Harris she scopes the inside of the church from left to right; it had stone floors with names etched into it, and to the sides of the exit door there were domed vaults with cast iron gates that housed coffins. What kind of church was this she was confused as she had never seen this before, except back in Sweden, and that was a medieval church.

At the end of the aisle Harris pushes the double doors open, and turns around to make sure he had Penny and Marcus with him.
He makes signs to move to the right, towards a row of sturdy bookshelves. Without a moment's notice and to Penny's eyes Harris motion in front of the shelf was completely unnoticeable as he magically makes one of the shelves move open.
A path with a set of steps appears.
Penny pulls Marcus closer, and as she carefully takes her steps down she notices the shelf close and the wall is sealed shut.
The path leads into garage like room, and another vehicle

appears being parked.

"What's this?" she says, and now she wanted to know what kind of place this was. Who had these kind of arrangements, there we still things she didn't know about Harris.

"I have parked another car here, well.." and he pauses as he gives admiring looks at the vehicle, "...shall we say for unexpected circumstance, being in the business I am one can never be too careful" he finishes and kneels down and grabs a set of keys placed under the car.

"What kind of car is this?" Marcus asks as he had never seen one like this before.

"A Jensen Interceptor", Harris says proudly, "Do you know how to drive one of these?" he asks Marcus.

Marcus looks pondering on it while scratching his chin.

"OK, I can see that I will drive it" Harris says concluding, and he opens the passenger side door and moves the seat forward for Penny to get in.

Harris gets inside the driver seat, and with a remote control he opens the doors that swing open and he starts the car.

Penny can tell by the sound of the engine that the look of the car gave off a deceptive impression.

Harris rolls out and the Penny views the church grounds, and she impulsively blurs out, "...who's church is this..."

"It belongs to the estate but it is a common church for the village", Harris responds.

"So the church really belongs to you?" Marcus asks stately.

Harris don't answer, and to Penny that was obvious without saying much.

"The church is located on the estate grounds, so technically yes" he says after much delay.

Penny gazes out the window viewing the country road as Harris and Marcus are talking about the horse powers of the vehicle and the specifics.
Penny were back reminiscing of Seattle, she wanted to go home, sleep in her own bed and wake up from this so-called dreaded nightmare of being chased, was she ever going to wake up.

CHAPTER 30

Edinburgh was like any ordinary city, but old with cobblestone roads.

Penny reads the street signs, they had ended up on George Street and almost as soon as they got on it, Harris made a left turn and then he stopped in front of a white building; 27 Thistle Street.

The street is narrow, and Marcus looks as to where they could park. He gives a quick look behind and is about to tell Harris his suggestion, when Harris opens a garage and backs in.

"well that works too" Marcus says out loud without argument.

Penny gets out of the vehicle and moves onto the sidewalk, and looks around to see if there are familiar faces on the street, all she sees are pedestrians walking by and a man standing by the Thistle Bar who is leaning against the wall and smoking. Harris exits the garage and has already reached the door to the building and has pulled it open. He makes a waving motion with his hand at them.

Hmm, when did they stop allowing smoking inside a bar in Scotland? One would think these citizens were born with cigarettes in their mouths. Penny's perceptive and analytical mind has risen from the back to the front of her mind. Well, she knows better than to ignore it, but she does have another agenda that is more pressing, and with that thought she dashes inside and closes the door and follows Marcus up the stairs.

When she walks through the door and she find Harris already tapping away on the computer.
"Ok, I see you are a step ahead of me", she says, and she takes a quick look around.
She looks over at Marcus who is standing at the other window facing the street.

Harris has been thinking about the incident that he had gone through before Penny had arrived. His mind is miles away; he looks out the window and starts to think back to the time when he had been hiding in a ditch, covered in human excrement on the outskirts of Sarajevo city. To say that he had been under a pile of manure would be kind, when the truth was really in the shits in so many ways, and this was all happening while watching high ranking military personnel execute innocent people, then dispose of them drop in mass graves.

"A 'Penny' for your thoughts." she says and suddenly Harris is brought back.

"Yes... no joke, really Penny, I was deep in my thoughts." He looks out the window and the man is still standing across the street smoking. "He has been there for a while, has he not

Penny?" Harris says, and Marcus nods agreeing from his position.

"Yes, I saw him when I walked in. I am not sure what he, or who he is waiting for." Penny says a little concerned.

"I need for you to sit down as there is something I need to tell you." Harris says with a much more serious tone and much deeper voice while he continues to keep one eye on the man on the street and the other on Penny.

"The other day I sat at my desk and I heard something outside the house, so I went to look..." Penny is about to say something, but Harris holds out his hand.
"Just listen, it was not Seels or any Middle Eastern group. What I found out was these individuals were Serbo-Croatians." He pauses, gives his full attention to the man on the street, and, before Penny tries to say anything, he again holds out his hand and continues.
"... that was the time I called and left you a message...I believe it was not a courtesy call, if you follow..." He states and gets quiet.
"Do you believe it's the leader that was put away?" she asks cautiously and quiets down into pondering thoughts.
She was looking down into the table and all those memories came to the forefront of her mind... memories of what had happened, and of almost being killed later on when they were leaving the city.

Penny turns her head to look outside, and the man has left. "I guess he left." Penny says and points out the window. She really doesn't want to bring back those memories.

"I understand you don't want to talk about it, but we can't avoid the subject as they came to our doorstep, maybe it was you who triggered it or maybe they have been staking out the place, and you coming was just a coincidence. What concerned me was that they had C-4 rigged explosives that they brought with them."

"Me? Why me?" she questions with distress in her voice. She couldn't take it anymore and didn't want to, she wanted to go home. She couldn't remember how many times she had uttered that before to herself, she wanted to stop it all. She walks over to the other side of the room, and plunk herself down in the dated arm chair and fold her right leg over the left and stairs into the pictures of Harris and another man. They look as if they were really close friends, and she glances over at Harris. "*Friends*", she utters to herself. Taytum and Bradford were friends and they had gone to the same school and they were now helping each other.

Penny calls out to Harris, "What's the purpose of having a file hidden among the rest of the document?" she asks cryptic.

Harris is pulling up a log of Universities and starts entering his credentials to get inside for more detailed information. He looks over at Penny, "Good question" he responds and moves his attention back to the screen.

Marcus is now standing behind Harris watching what he is looking at, "You really are a man with a world of knowledge." he says astound and puzzled at the same time.

"Come here Penny!" Harris calls out.

Penny pushes herself out of the chair and sits down in front of him.

"Listen guys...think about this for sec..." She says as she is trying to grab their attention.

Marcus and Harris are completely absorbed looking at the screen.

"Are you guys listening...?" she says now a little more demanding and impatient.

Harris and Marcus look up at her, "What did you say?" Harris asks apologetic.

"Really...I am trying to figure this whole situation and you are not listening" she says irritated.

"So are we..." Marcus replies sharp.

"OK, so tell me why is Bradford so adamant about this file? I like to hear your theory on that Mr. Weaver" she says snarky.

"Alright, alright..." Harris says and tries to intervene and stop any bickering that was about to surface and looks straight at her." What are you thinking of?" he asks now with a full ear.

Penny takes a seat at the desk and looks at Harris wondersome as she stays quiet for a moment. She had thought about this and yet not quite being able to understand it.

"OK" she says as she was ready to break it down in bits and pieces.

"Let's break it down from the beginning. I was given the assignment from Taytum. Bradford is involved in this situation that was unbeknownst to me. So, what is the relation with Taytum and Bradford?" She says as she was looking at them.

"Give me a pen and paper and let me draw a picture" she says as she sits straight up.

Penny starts to draw a form of a family tree shape diagram.

"So, let me draw first Taytum, and he is now associated with Bradford. What is the connection between them?" Penny says and now she looks at Marcus and then back at Harris.

"They went to the same school Q said" Marcus throws out. "What kind of school is the question." She says and looks at Harris, "Look up what you can find on that" she says delegating.

"What else do we have...oh yeah, who was the person who made the file, and let's take a closer look at the plot that the person concocted." She says as she continues to put down names and questions on the paper.
"Shariq Afifi" Marcus says as he is trying to help to build the picture of what she was trying to accomplish.

"...that's right, Shariq Afifi; that was the office I visited Bradford in..." she says and stops in her tracks. She looks at the picture she had created with names and taps the pen on her lips.

"...Harris do you know anything about Shariq..." and before he gets the chance to answer Marcus interjects, "He went to Oxford university, studied finance, and law. Q said he is considered to be shrewd and mastermind like"

They are all quiet as Penny is looking at the names on the paper.

"what we know is that Shariq was in our office in Dallas, and Taytum had him create the financial conspiracy, and Bradford is involved with Victor Afifi...would I assume that correctly?" she says and looks up at Harris.

"So, the question remains, what does the conspiracy has to do with the excel sheet with the names and the accounts" she says and now she is awaiting their answer.

Marcus is now resting his chin in his right hand as he had not thought of it the way Penny had broken it down.

Harris looks out the window in deep thoughts.

He looks back at Penny, "I think it is best that we head over to the Scotsman, there are more resources there where we can dig a little deeper and faster than we can do here" he says and shuts down his computer.

Suddenly there is a knock on the door. "Are you expecting visitors?" She pulls out the memory key and places it in her front pocket.

"No, and no one knows that I am here anyway besides the two of you." Harris says.

"..and the guy who was smoking outside..." Penny says.

He grabs the laptop and folds it closed. He grabs his bag by the chair and throws the laptop inside.

"Is there a way out besides the way we got in?" Marcus asks.

Harris pulls a book out of the bookshelf and it slides aside, "Old buildings are everywhere..." he says as he smiles confident.

Penny and Marcus look at each other and a sigh of relief comes over them at the same time.

There is another set of knocks on the door and this time harder. Marcus heads first down the spiral stairs and Penny follows. Harris shuts the bookshelf door at the same time the office door is kicked in and all he can see is the man's face from the opposite side of the street. He slides down the fireman's pole; he comes down to the lower level where he has another vehicle stored in his garage. They can hear rumbling from upstairs as someone is trying to break through the wall.

"How many cars do you have" Marcus ask surprised, he could only afford one and it was not in a caliber of any of the cars Harris was accustom to. He looks at Penny; what kind of people was she associated with. He started to like her and yet he didn't like her arrogant style that he had been exposed to, but that was who Penny was and he had to accept it or leave her be.

"What kind of car is this?" says Penny, who had not seen one like that before.

"Penny!" Marcus says with a superior tone, "It's a Maserati." he looks at her sideways, "...if you know what that is...?" he continues questioning.

"Well Weaver, I don't know what kind of car it is." Penny says with a sharp and snide remark, "...but I'm sure it will do the job of getting us out of here before they break through the wall." she says with her comedian snarky charm as she points her index finger in the direction of the door.

"OK, kids, stop bickering and get inside." Harris says annoyed and almost father figure like.

She gets inside and looks over at her right and there was the other car they arrived in.

Harris starts the car, he pushes the button inside the car to open the garage door, and before Penny knows it she is pushed back in the seat by the gravity created by the acceleration of the car as it leaves the building.

The car is going through the narrow streets of Edinburgh at raging speeds and Penny is trying to move around in the back seat. The car is sweeping the street in warped speed and Penny has never seen Harris drive like this before. She had seen him drive before, but not this aggressively.

The pedestrians crossing the streets were jumping out of the way as the car was racing down the narrow alley streets; bags and papers on the street were flying up in the air from the wind being created by the car screaming by.

Penny turns around and looks through the back window, "Someone is following us." she says.

"Tell me about it!" Harris responds and keeps one eye on the road and one on the rear-view mirror.

"Penny, hand me your piece!" Marcus exclaims.

She pulls her gun from her belt and gives it to Marcus. She grabs the memory key from her pocket, and she digs it into the seat where she is sitting.

"Ok, hold on to your seats!" Harris says as he makes a sharp right turn.

He comes up to the check point at the newspaper and shows his credentials; the man behind the glass opens up the gate and lowers the spike bar running across the entrance.

Penny turns around to see if they still have them on their tail, and they do.

The car has slowed down and is passing by the entrance to the building. She can see that the windows are heavily tinted, almost black. Who was driving the car Penny thinks to herself and she is getting goosebumps and chills all over her body like someone was walking over her grave.

Penny is feeling a small relief that they were on newspaper campus, but she knew that it is far from over.

"What is our next plan?" Marcus asks and looks over to Penny.

"I don't know yet, I don't know what Harris is thinking." she replies and looks at Harris.

"I don't even know yet, to be honest Penny..." he pauses, "... that is why we are here. My friends on the inside will help us figure out the best course of action on how to flush this story out into the open while keeping us safely out of the light."

"Well better to be in here than out there." she tries to sound encouraging, but she still feels a sense of being on uncharted territories as she didn't know who was coming after them. Was it Bradford's team player or was it the so called the Balkan frenemies who were going to settle the score in retaliation from the past?
Penny thought for a moment about how things had been for so

many years and then she began to reflect on how things had changed in just 10 days.

CHAPTER 31

HARRIS PULLS UP TO THE ENTRANCE of the papers'
garage; he rolls down the window and swipes his card, the
metal bar rises. He slowly drives the car down the spiral
entrance and into the underground garage.

"Harris, I need to make a call to the US." Penny says as she
couldn't help to think about Spencer and Julia and not to think
of Damien. She had been away from him too long and away
from home.

"Ok, you can do that when we get inside." he says as he pulls
out his phone and dials.

It is quiet in the car, Marcus and Penny are looking at each
other both waiting for the next orders, and as soon as Marcus is
about to say something, Harris raises up his finger as a sign to
wait.

"Hey Montgomery, your old jackal, it's Harris." says Harris as
he retracts his finger.

Penny is listening intently to the conversation.

"Yes, I am here.... mhmm, in the garage... Yes.... I have something that I want you to take a look at. Oh, before I forget, I have visitors with me... remember I left you a message... OK... I will take them there to get badges... I'll see you in your office shortly... Ok."
Harris looks at his phone and turns it off. Then he looks over to Penny, "We are in good hands luv." and he looks over at Marcus, "I bet you didn't expect this when you fell in love with this little lass." and his scoffs whispering.

Marcus looks surprised at Harris, '...*in love...*' was he reading his mind, had it been that obvious.

They all get out of the vehicle and Harris locks it by pressing the button on his key fob and the car dutifully responds with two chirps.

Marcus approaches Harris, "What did you mean by that?" Marcus says with a bit of an irritated tone.

Harris stops and turns around, "I want you to walk into this so-called relationship with your eyes wide open. I don't want you to think that it is going to be easy." Harris says.

"One would almost think you were jealous or that you are even in love with Penny." Marcus replies back in a bit of a snarky tone.

"I love Penny, but in a completely different way than you do, as I know Penny, and we have a history unlike yours. I would say I am protective of her. However, I know she is a big girl and can handle most things. I just want to warn you that she is not the kind of girl that you will ever have the upper hand on, in fact, she may ultimately have the upper hand on you!" and he gives up a laugh.

"What are you guys talking about?" Penny asks.

"Guy stuff..." Marcus replies back and looks at Harris at the same time.

They walk through the door into the building. A sign meets their eyes, 'Check with security for badge before continuing'.

"Ok, here we go." Harris says and takes them through the doors. A black man is sitting behind the desk, "Willie, my old fella! How have you been?" Harris greets him and shakes his hand.

"I can't complain, probably better than you." the man says and laughs in a deep baritone voice. Willie is 6'4", quite muscular with a chiseled look, a linebacker style sized. He's definitely someone who you wouldn't want to mess with him as he would easily have you down and pinned in a split second.
"Ok, so what do we got here Harris?" he asks.

"These are my two associates." Harris continues, "Can you get me two visitor's badges for them?" he says to Willie.

He measures Penny and Marcus with a quick, but intense look, and then, without looking at Harris, he asks, "So you are here to see Montgomery?"

"Yeah, as soon as we get these badges." Harris replies back with humorous tone.

319

James grabs the phone and pushes a button on the dialer pad, "I got visitors to see you Monty... yeah, that's right... What clearance level? Ok boss." he hangs up the handset.

"Ok, Harris." he says and hands him two badges and looks at Marcus with an investigating eye.

Penny and Marcus grab the badges and clip them onto their shirts.

"See you later Willie." Harris says as they exit through the door.

They walk through a long corridor where framed newspaper articles are lined up on the walls. The walk up to the elevator and Harris swipes his badge; the doors open up, he looks over to Penny and Marcus, "Your badges have the same clearance as mine does... just letting you know."

They walk into the elevator and Harris pushes the 2nd floor button. He looks at Marcus, "This is the only way in and out... the only way to get off these floors..." he pauses, "...it is their security."

The door opens up to the second floor, they walk right out onto the newspaper floor, there is a constant buzz in the air, and they notice that from down the walkway a man is approaching them.

"Harris!" the man exclaims and smiles. "Your old wolf, what do you got for me today?" He says and then looks over at Penny and Marcus with his arms folded over, "And who do we have here?"

Marcus stretches out his hand, "Marcus Scott." and shakes the man's hand.

"Montgomery." the man replies back. He looks over to Penny and says, "Harris... Harris, you sure have good taste in women I tell you!" he says and stretches out his hand to Penny while she gives him a strange look, "What's your name lass?" he says as if Penny was the fragile type and reaches out for her hand.

Penny places her hand in Montgomery's hand and gives him her interpretation of a male handshake, "Penny, my name is Penny." she says.

Montgomery gives Penny a second measuring look. "I like you Penny!" he says, "You are not what I expected...." he pauses, "...I like that!" and looks at her with a whole new set of eyes, "...hmm nothing like a wild card in the bunch of aces..."

Montgomery looks over to Harris, walks over to him, and grabs him by the shoulder, "Long time no see!" he says and starts to lead the way into his large office at the corner of the building.

Penny taps Harris on the shoulder, "I need to make that call now." she whispers to him, sounding a little desperate.

"Ok, give me a minute" he says.

Montgomery walks up to his desk, rumbles around grabbing for a pen and paper pad. He reaches for his glasses and puts on them on; he looks at Harris, "Whenever you are ready." and holds out his hands with pad in one hand and pen in the other.

"Penny needs to make a call overseas; do you have a line for that?" he asks Montgomery.

Montgomery picks up his phone and speaks into it, "George, can you come in here?" he looks over to Penny, "George will find you a secure international line that you can use."

Before Montgomery even finished his sentence George was standing in the doorway waiting for Penny.

"Take her to an ISL." Montgomery says.

George gives Montgomery a nod signaling understanding; no words were needed.

Penny walks up to George and neither says a word. She walks through the door and follows him to the phone.

In the office Harris, Marcus, and Montgomery are sitting down. Harris pulls out his laptop and opens up the pdf file that he copied to his hard drive.

Penny watches them through the window and see them talking.
She turns around and looks out on the news floor, and lets her eyes scan it. She views the busy operation of the paper and as her eyes are going from left to right, she suddenly halts in her tracks. She looks at the wall facing her, and the different time zones are displayed by the clocks lined up from west to east.

Penny looks at the pacific time, it was 8 am back in Seattle. She starts dialing Julia's number, it rings, and rings, and rings, and rings, suddenly Penny hears a voice sounding as if the person was sleeping.

"Hello." Julia's voice is faint.

"Julia, is it you?" Penny asks, "Julia, it's Penny, please wake up. Can you hear me?" Penny continues.

"Who is this? What time it is!?" Julia replies tired and yawns and she rolls over and looks at the time, it was 8 am. It was almost time for her to get up.
    "It's an Atlantic Ocean's difference." Penny says philosophical.

She can hear how Julia is trying to wake up. "Listen, Julia, I need for you to do something for me..." she pauses, "...are you listening?"

",,, yeah, yeah go ahead." Julia replies as she yawns and sits up in the bed.

"When you get into the office I need for you to go to Spencer and tell him that I need to speak with him. I will give him a call but make sure he is in his office.

"Ok, ok, I'll make sure he is in his office...but what time are you going to call?"

"It's 8 now... let's say 2 hrs. from now. So, get ready and get into the office" Penny directs in her boss like tone.

"I will, but...what is happening Penny? I am so confused" Julia says sounding concerned and oblivious.

"I can't talk, too many ears, but it will soon be over and then I can tell you... unless you hear it first elsewhere," she pauses and looks around, "just get going now" she says and finishes the call.

She knew that all this was too much for Julia to grasp over a phone call that she would have to sit down and tell her about it in small bits and pieces.

As Penny puts down the receiver George comes over, "I think they want you to join them" he says and points in the direction at the window.

"Oh..." Penny says, and she views the three of them motioning with their hands for her to come back into the room. She turns to George and smiles bashful as she squeezes out, "Thank you for letting me use the phone" and gives him a pat on the back and walks back into the office.

Montgomery stands up, "Penny come over her and sit down." he says and makes an inviting gesture.

Penny takes a seat in the accent chair that is sitting by the bookshelf and folds one leg over the other while biting on her pinky fingernail.

"Harris filled me in on the event and the documents you are in possession of." Montgomery says and pauses. "Wow, you sure have something pressing going on. So, let me know what is it exactly you want to happen? I know what we can make happen...but... are you ready for it, is my question." he continues.

Penny thinks to herself what if I don't say anything then what? What will the outcome be? It would affect a lot of people, or should I even care what happens to them? Penny turns and look at Marcus, and then at Harris. They are all looking at her for an answer.

"I want to blow this out of the water and have people held accountable!" she says with a confident voice, "I have more than one reason to reveal all this", she finishes her statement.

"Ok then, let's get started now, we have our work cut out for ourselves and we have to act fast!" Montgomery says.
"Hold on" Penny says as she is looking at Harris, and then back at Montgomery. "Did Harris tell you about my theory that we were crunching before we arrived?" she continues. She wasn't sure what had been said.

Marcus looks at Harris and then it was as if there was this elephant in the room that had appeared.
"What theory?" Montgomery says as he is resting his hand on his hips and looks over at Harris questioning.

"Well, we found an Easter egg hiding on the drive she picked up with an excel sheet hiding" Harris says confessional.

"So, what does this got to do with the plot we have right here?" Montgomery says clueless.
"Well, it's a long story...how much time do you got" Marcus says in a tiresome way.

"I have all the time you need" he responds and there is a silence, and Monty waits for someone to start to fill him in.
"Let's start hearing your theory Penny" he says as he looks at her.

Penny pulls out the paper she had started at the office before they had left, and she explains her thoughts around it.
"You are correct, there is something there that we need to

explore; how they are connected" he says and gets up from his seat and walks up to his desk.

CHAPTER 32

JULIA WALKS INTO THE OFFICE and she sits down at her desk. She glances over at the large oversize clock facing her on the wall, it was 9:30, and Spencer had not arrived.

She couldn't stop thinking of Penny, and the call. Julia knew this was beyond important and she was worried about Penny and what she had said her, and what she didn't say.

Suddenly the elevator chime went off, and the doors opened, people were exiting. Julia was expecting Spencer to stroll down any minute. She looked for him and at the same time the phone was ringing, and she kept ignoring it.
Finally she could no longer ignore the facts that no one was answering it.

"Julia speaking" she answers the phone as the doted secretary she was.
"*Yes, this is Agent Hammond for the FBI, I am looking for a Penny Bridge*" she says as this was business matters.

"Uhm, she is not in the office today. Can someone else help you?" she throws out as she did not want to give off any indication that something could not be resolved without Penny. "*Sure. Who else can I talk to?*" she asks, and at the same moment Spencer comes down the hallway.

"I believe I know the right person, just let me put you on a brief hold while I make sure he is in" Julia says in an helpful tone, and presses the hold button on the display.

"You are the one I need to talk to" Julia says as Spencer is coming down the hall.

"What's going on, you look like you did not have a good night's rest" he says as he stops in his tracks and sits down on the edge of her desk.

"I have FBI on the line, they want Penny" Julia says worried. Spencer look over at Penny's door wondersome and gets up from the desk and walks over to the it. He presses down the door handle and opens it, "I will take it in here... by the way, what's the name of the person?" he asks as if he missed the first time.

"Hammonds, Agent Hammonds" she repeats herself.

"OK", he says and gives her thumbs up as he turns around, gives the door a push and continues walking to the desk.

Julia gets back on the phone.

"Thank you for holding, I have found the person you need to speak to. I will transfer" she says before another response is uttered and transfers the line into Penny's office.

Julia turns around in her chair and she can see the door is cracked open, it never fully shut, and she can hear Spencer's voice answering, "*Spencer here*".

Julia turns around and watches the other employees, and then
she inconspicuously stands up, corrects her garments, and
walks up to the side of the door and stops. She can hear a
conversation, but it was from Spencer point of view *"How can I
help you"*. Suddenly unexpectedly the door is shut closed from
inside.

Julia walks over to the printer, and then back to her desk and
sits down. She glances over the time and now it was 09:55 and
Penny was about to call in 5 minutes. This was not good; Julia
starts to feel this sick feeling inside her stomach, and she rest
her elbows on the desk as she places her forehead in the palms
of her hands and shakes in disbelief.

"What's going on?" a voice utters.
Julia looks up and there was Edwin.
"What can I do for you...aren't you in the wrong department?"
she says, and puts her head back in the palm of her hands.
"I was looking for Spencer" he replies back and looks at her as
if she was this strange anomaly.
"OK, I let him know you were looking for him" she replies back
from her sitting position.

"Oh, ok" Edwin says lingers for a second and walks off. Julia
looks up from her position and yawns big.
The door opens at the same time, "Hey can you get a hold of
Penny?" he asks urgently.
Julia jumps startled in her seat as she wasn't expected sudden
interruption from him, and responds by rummage through her
desk for Penny's number, "give me a minute" she says as she
continues with the charade of looking all while knowing she
was going to call any minute. Spencer shuts the door to
Penny's office, and starts to walk over to this own office when

Julia calls out, "Edwin was asking for you".
Spencer waves with his hand as his way of acknowledging her
statement and continues into his office.

QUENTIN IS BUSY on his computer listening to audio
surveillance records of individuals in the Bradford's old crew
while a text message is coming in from Hammonds.

Q leans back in the desk chair and swing slowly as his hands
moves the bar on the timeline and shakes his head in
frustration. "Damn nothing...." he utters to himself, he glances
over at the names he had on his note pad in Alphabetic order,
A.L Gasparini, G.D Grayson "Ok let's do the G's..." he says
with a sort of disparaging tone.

He continues to go to the next file, "Oh no, I don't want to hear
you fucking this woman" he says as he laughs out loud, and
skips it over, and hits the next file.
'hey D' a male voice can be heard but it is overshadowed by the
busy background noise.
Q moves forward in his chair as the sound was familiar and
caught his attention. He leans over the laptop, and starts to
adjust the sound, and drown out the background sound to hear
the conversation clearer.
"Yea, what's going on" the other voice responds but in a
southern twang.
*"I got job for you... I need you to take care of it, make it look
like an accident, she needs to go. Clean it up nice and tight...
fireman style."* the man orders.
Q hits the space bar to pause the reel, "Bradford that mother
fucker... and Grant" Q stops himself as he leans back in the

chair thinking of the whole situation. Hammonds had mentioned something about a Jane Doe, could it this be it. He leans to his left and grabs the phone and recognize a new message. He opens it, "Hammonds!" he exclaims, *'Q, I am in. I am going to visit the bank later today'*

Q replies back, *'Just heard the audio on Jane Doe - It's trouble'*

PENNY IS LEANING OVER at Montgomery computer screen reading older news articles of the different individuals in the 'Cartel 13' and she inadvertently glances at the time in the lower right-hand corner. It was a few minutes after 10 am PST.

"Oh shoot, I need to make a call! " she exclaims and dashes towards the door and back out to the secured international line. She dials the number back to the office.

"Julia speaking" she hears on the other end.

"Julia, it's Penny" she says as she's catching her breath.

"Thank goodness, let me transfer" she says as if she was desperate.

The calls rings through to Spencer's office, and after the third ring she hears, "Penny, where are you?" she hears Spencer ask jovial.

"I am almost done, and on my way home" she says neutral.

"Almost done, what does that mean?" he asks as if he was clueless, and yet she knew that this was just the way he was. But the feeling she got was that something was different, and it was not going away.

"I believe this situation that Taytum and Neal put me in is not..." she stops herself.

"Is not what?" Spencer asks more interested, "...not on the

level?" he continues probing.

"What do you mean?" she now asks him, as if she was wearing his shoe acting oblivious.

"Listen, Edwin sent me the AVI files, I have pieced together my idea on what is going on...now fill me on the rest what you got" he says like he was her boss.

"I found something that is quite disturbing..." she continues, and lays out all the information, and her theory for Spencer. "So are you safe or do I need to send you escort back home" he says as he was protective of Penny. He felt compelled to keep her safe.

"No, I am ok... I am in good hands...I assure you" she adds, and he can hear the voice of confidence in Penny.

"OK, I am just saying...in case" he fills in.

Penny looks over at the glass window and she can see Montgomery and Harris talk and gesture.

"We need a headline." Harris says.

"OK!" Montgomery says pondering, "US Bank's Underhanded Plot in collusion with Cartel 13."

"That sounds great, but what should we do with the rest of the information Monty" He looks over at Harris with a facial expression that he was still mulling over it. "Remember the excel sheet?" Harris continues

Montgomery places the finger in the air, as he had just cracked an idea, "I do, I got that. You just start writing the article with Penny" he tells Harris.

Montgomery leaves the room and walks out to the floor; Penny watches him as he gathers his people and gives them orders.

She can overhear him, "Harris needs pictures of the cartel 13 and I have one more that needs to get into the paper for tomorrow, you let me know when you have it" he instructs the crew.

Harris begins, "Marcus do you have the download the AVI files and audio?" In the next moment Penny walks in.
"So what is the plan Harris?" she asks curiously.

Harris walks over to the desk, leans over, and starts to type on Montgomery's computer. He looks over at Penny, "We will create a news flash, place it on the internet, and in regular hard copy paper." Harris is completely in his element, his mind is working as his hands are gesturing, "On the internet we will add the AVI file so it will be a streamed constantly. I will have Marcus download what we have on AVI files from the bank's cameras and audio. Montgomery will have a first run edition preview of the newspaper, but we need to get the editors involved and get pictures of all the involved individuals, including Bradford and Shariq, as well as Neal and Taytum. That is what he is doing out there now." and points with his hands towards the window.

"So, it is important for us to get the story right. I will have Marcus run over to the news station to deliver it. The station runs a segment in the early morning where the largest papers in the country are examined for news almost before anyone else has had the chance to read them." Harris finishes.

"Hold on" Penny says with a collected tone in her voice.

"I thought this was what you wanted?" Marcus says confused.

Penny looks at Harris and at Marcus as this was going so fast and she was having second thoughts about it.

She had just got off the phone with Spencer. Something was feeling like a tower moment was to hit her and the change was going to be irreversible.

"It's going to be ok, you'll be able to go home, and things will be back to normal" Harris says.

"Really... is that what you think" she questions as she make a statement as the same time.

Penny walks over to Harris by the desk, "Ok, let's get it done" she says and pats him on the back. Harris smiles back, "You'll be ok lass".

BRADFORD SITS IN THE CAR and contemplates, he had missed his target and she was still out there somewhere, and the man that he was to eliminate had managed to escape out of his sight.

He knew that he had to call Afifi and let him know what had happened and this was not like him to not being able to clean things up. There was this feeling of a changed of the winds in his sails, he could feel it. He was so close to bring his life to the next level, but Penny was the one between him and his goal.

He needed to call Taytum to let him know, too many players were involved at this point.

He leans back in the seat and reclines it and opens his phone.

"Taytum! Seels here…" he calls out.

"What's going on. I haven't heard from you in a minute, something wrong?" Taytum says with an uncertainty in his voice.

"I've lost the device" and there is a pause as none of them were speaking, and Bradford continues,"… can you have your connection make another one?" he asks bashfully and embarrassed.

"You are saying that you were unable to extract the information?" Taytum asks and gets quiet as he was trying to think a way to get it done. The information he had managed to get on the device was belonging to the 13. He could consider himself a walking dead as he was expecting to be paid handsomely for the information he had intended to furnish to Seels.

"I never got a hold of the device; she is too slippery for my men and me" he says, and a heavy sigh can be heard.

"OK…" Taytum responds with a concern in his voice. It's quiet and then he continues.

"Let's not talk on this line. I need to get to a secure line, can't be too sure who's listening to this conversation. Let me call you back" he says, and the call is disconnected.

CHAPTER 33

HOURS HAVE PASSED and everyone has been working on
their tasks, when Montgomery comes in with the first edition of
the pictures. Harris is ready to hand him the article that he
and Penny have collaborated on. "Here you go." he says to
Montgomery and hands him the article.

He looks at it, "Harris, Harris, you still haven't lost you touch,
anal to the T, and, as usual, always a strong story!" he says
while looking over at him and smiling proudly about the
article's context.

"OK guys, this is what I need to do, I have to call Spencer now."
Penny says and is ready to walk off when Harris stops.

"Who is Spencer?"

"He's my boss over at the bank." she says.

"Is that wise...can we trust him?" Montgomery asks.

"I don't have much of a choice. I talked to him earlier, and he has seen the footage that we pulled, and I had to tell him what I knew. I need to give him heads up, that's the least I can do and it's right thing to do" she says as she felt this obligation to Spencer.

"Ok, then you" and Montgomery points at Harris, "...you need to get a hold of your contacts in MI5 because we have banks here in the UK that are affected by this, and she can then contact the FBI on her end. This is getting deeper than I thought it would." Montgomery says and he leaves the room to go back out on the floor. He hands over the article piece to his editorial team.

Penny walks along the window that was facing the floor and views the fast-paced operation. This was where her situation was being deciphered, analyzed and put together into plain English for the news reader to understand. It had to be done this way. While she paces back and forth she can hear Harris and Marcus working on the other avenues to saturate the story.

"Marcus, do you have the footage ready and downloaded?" Harris asks.

"Yes, it is almost done, I am going to clean up the audio and render it all together." he replies and pauses for a second, and then looks up from the screen, "Give me a few minutes and it will be ready." he continues.

"Ok, I have a package that I want you to deliver." Harris says as he pulls a few items off of his desk and then turns to Marcus, "I'll be back shortly, and, hopefully, that should be done." he continues as his points at the computer then heads out to see Montgomery.

Penny stands by the window as she watches Harris walk out to meet up with Montgomery. She continues to view him exchange papers and then Harris returns back into the office.

He digs out a manila envelope from the desk drawer and puts a large folded piece of paper into it, he writes down something on a piece of paper, and walks over to Marcus.
"Here you go." he says and holds out the keys to the car along with his swipe card to the building and garage.
"I want you to take this envelope to the news station. I have written down the address, it is really just around the corner, but I figure you can put it in this phone." Harris gives Marcus his phone, "It has GPS so you won't get lost." he says with a grin.

"You need to go to the front desk and then you will ask for the newsroom, request that someone comes out from that department, and hand the envelope over to them personally. Do not give it to anyone else!" he says with a calm collected tone.

"OK, I hear you." Marcus says and gives him a military salute jokingly and walks towards the door.

Before he reaches the door Harris says, "Go easy on it, I like to see myself driving it for a while." he laughs a little facetiously.

Marcus opens the door and there's Penny standing in front of him. He looks at her with concern in his face and walks out; she watches him walk away.

"So, did you send him for drop off now?" she asks Harris.

"Yes." he says and quiets down.

"Yes, and OK, that is all you guys are saying." she says with a concerned tone.

"My thoughts are that when we are done with this, there is still one more threat that we have to deal with." Harris says and quiets down.

Penny gets quiet as she has been so focused on getting this out of the way that she has buried the other incident in her subconscious mind. Stopping now to think, she is reminded of it as it comes rushing back to her.
"As long as we are in here, I intend to focus on getting this thing done first. When I have cleared that out of the way, I am going to focus on that," and then she points out the window.

As the day has slowly passed them by she'd barely noticed that the night had made its presence. She was made aware as she had walked over to the window where she paused her thoughts for work, the view of the night sky made a statement on its own that was noticeable. "It's like a blanket of diamonds..." She says to herself pondering.

She has a view of the check point and the street leading up to the newspaper campus. She leans both her hands onto the windowpane and feels her body feeling heavy and tired. She turns around and places her behind on the ledge of the window pane; she views the room by scoping it from one side to the other, and then her eyes end up resting on the people who are on the other side of the glass wall.

It's quiet in the room and there is this feeling of being in a space where time was not moving, like a waiting room. This was the first time that no words had been uttered in a while, and both Harris and Penny were in limbo mode; it was now a waiting game.

AGENT HAMMONDS STANDS BY the window in Spencer's office admiring the view of the space needle. The door opens and she turns around when she sees Spencer come in with stack of papers.

"Oh, what a day…" he expresses himself in a tiresome way.

"Is that right" she says as she was curious to what he meant.

"…putting out fires is never fun" he says as he looks down at the pile of documents he has brought back.

"…unless you are fireman" she responds jokingly.

" Maybe I need to change profession" he chuckles at the same time he is shaking his head. He gives his thumb a lick and start going through the papers rapidly and stops at one page.

He pulls one sheet of paper off the pile off and places it on the desk in front of him, and pushes is towards Hammonds.

"Here you go, this is the information you are looking for" he says as accommodating as he possibly can.

Hammonds walks up to the desk and pulls the paper and looks at it.

"So all I need to do is to request the images of these individuals that works here" and she points down with her finger to emphasize this particular location.

"Yes. Just walk down to the right and you'll find Julia and she will take you to Edwin. If you need anything else, just let me know" He hoped that this was the end of the inquire and that they were done with the conversation.

He had to talk to Penny again, he couldn't stop thinking about what she had told him, and he had to think twice who was working for him and against him.

THE WALL LIGHTS UP and she turns around to see a car pulling up to the check point. It looked like it was Marcus in the car, "I think Marcus is back." she says at the same time Montgomery comes running back inside the room.

"There is a phone call for you Penny." he is trying to catch his breath, "You can take it in here" and he points at the phone on the desk , "... line two." he says and closes the door.

Penny walks over to the desk and grabs the receiver off the phone then presses the button for line two. "This is Penny." she says with a soft-spoken voice.

"Penny, its Spencer." There is a stress in his voice that Penny has never heard before. "Penny, I have the FBI here. They were doing research on the employees of the bank and found your picture. Do you know what they are saying?" He pauses and continues

"...they are saying you are not Penny, in fact, they are saying you are Jacqueline Grant. I told them there is no such person working here. They insisted and pulled out a picture of you from a military camp." It gets quiet on both ends, "Penny, are you still there?" Spencer asks.

He had omitted to tell her deliberately on their previous phone call that he had spoken to Hammonds on the phone but on the other hand it had also been a very brief conversation he recalls, she was asking for access to the employee files and nothing had given him the inclination that it was about Penny. Well, Jacqueline, or whoever she was now.

"Yes, I am here... "she pauses for a second," ...and yes, they are correct." she says with a tired voice from years of fighting to hide her true identity.

"What's going on, and why am I just hearing about this now? Why did not tell me that when we spoke earlier. You didn't think you could come to me with this? Spencer says disappointed and continues," Let me tell you" and then he stops abruptly, and she can hear a second voice in the background. Spencer is quiet and then he utters, "We've figured out that Taytum is playing a dangerous game."

"Well you are not alone having that perception, by just looking at the information there is more than meets the eye in that document I was picking up."
"What do you mean?" Spencer ask curiously and calms down.
"There is something hidden in plain sight that we are trying to piece together and we are still waiting for information to be confirmed" she says, and she wasn't ready yet to tip her hand for anything.

"We are trying to get information about one Seels Bradford, American. Do you know that man?" Spencer asks.
The statement gets Penny's attention, what did he know and how did he know.

"Who told you about Bradford?" It gets quiet, and she is

waiting for Spencer to say something. "Well, I don't really know him, but he is the man in Geneva who handed me the file with the plan." She continues in a casually fashion. "...are you there?" she calls out to Spencer as he has said nothing.

"Well yeah, I was listening and thinking about this Bradford individual. They say he has been MIA, gone rouge on us. The US military they say..." He stops, and Penny can hear the heaviness in his voice, and he sighs.
"Who told you...F.B.I?" she continues.
"Well... I mean yea. It's not good, our bank is now involved in this because you are... and then we have this individual that is describe to me as being no altar boy exactly "
There is a silence on both ends, no matter how much she wanted to tell Spencer she couldn't, and this is how things had to be for now.

Spencer continues, "I can't talk any more about it now " he stops and with a lower tone in his voice he continues, "...and, just so you know... we are going to talk when you get back." he finishes.

"Ok.", Penny says.
At this point she couldn't give two fucks, she was going to get this done and then she was going home, sleeping in her own bed, taking walks and runs with Damien, and forgetting that any of this ever happened. She had made her mind up; she didn't care about her job anymore or anything else for that matter, except she wanted to stop this merry-go-around. She hangs up the receiver, looks over to Harris and their eyes meet.

Harris puts a pen behind his ear and walks up to Penny. "We are going to be ok, I promise you! Let's just get this cleared up and then we will have our Scotch ritual. After which, we will part ways and, maybe, we will meet again in another decade." he laughs while he grabs a hold of Penny, hugs her head, and rubs the top of it.

The phone rings again, Penny reaches for the receiver, and she rolls her eyes at Harris, "Spencer is persistent; man you have to give that to him." she says and shakes her head, "Yes, Spencer, what did I miss?" she says with a little bit of an attitude in her voice.

"Stvari nisu više još, dolazim po tebe i Harris" the man says on the other side.

Penny turns quickly around to Harris with a startled look in her face. The man hangs up the phone.

"What?" Harris asks and walks up to Penny. He grabs her by the shoulders while she is still holding the receiver. He takes the receiver from her and hangs it back up.

"He said, *'things are not finished, I am coming for you and Harris'*." she says with discouraged face.

"Who said that?" Harris ask much sterner this time.

"They spoke Serbo-Croatian." she blurs out. Penny moves Harris aside and walks up to her bag. She looks inside for her gun; she rummages through the bag and all she can find is her other loaded clips.

"He has it. Remember, you gave it to him when we were in the car." Harris says. He knows now that Penny is getting ready, both mentally and emotionally, for what's next.

Marcus suddenly comes through the door, "Wow, just love that car!" he says with a smile on his face. "What's the long face for?" he asks.

Harris says nothing and Penny turns around, "Good, you are back. Do you have the steel with you?" she asks.

"Yes, of course." he pulls it out and hands it to Penny and she packs it back on her.

Montgomery comes in, "Harris, I have a call for you out here on the secure line."

Harris leaves the room and, before he shuts the door, he turns around and says, "Behave now!"

Marcus walks up to Penny, "What's going on? I leave for a minute and things seem worse now than when I left."

"Do you recall the situation that happened earlier today?" Penny says and gives him a glaring look.

"Well, yeah, but..." Marcus stutters.

"That was our past, mines and Harris. It has resurrected again. If it wasn't enough that I have to deal with Bradford, there is now this, as well, that I have to deal with, and I don't even know how to get out this place in one piece." She says discouraged.

Penny looks back out the window; out there were bullets waiting for her, and with her name on it. She shakes her head; it was now just a matter of time.

Hours were passing by and Penny had found her a place to sleep on in Montgomery's office all while people were coming and going out of the office.

Marcus had been on the internet and pondered on what would be the best way to exit the building incognito.
Penny turns around on the couch and looks up at the back of Marcus.
He had been there for her the entire time, she needed to give him some slack she knew that, a second chance.

She moves her body up in a vertical position as she stretches her arms up in the arm, and presses her up from her position.

"What are you doing?" she asks sleepy as she slowly walked up to him

"Finding a way to get you and Harris out of this building and get us all back to the house safely." Marcus says. He pulls up a closed window where he had located a map of the area. "Look here..." he says to Penny, "...this is the place we are in now, if you look how we are located on the corner, however, there is an exit on the north side, whereas we came in through the west side." Marcus points out something that looks like a hedge and not an exit.

"Ok, so I am looking at a wall of greenery." she pauses, "A hedge!" Penny says with a tone of disbelief and sarcasm.

"Yes, and no." he says. "What you see is exactly what you said, that is what they want you to see..." he continues. He takes the map and switches to street level then he selects the camera angel and zooms in. "Do you see that?" he says and points at the hedge, to the corner where it has a mechanical device hidden in it.

"And you are sure?" Penny says.

Marcus looks at her with a facial expression that is telling her to stop doubting him. "I asked the guy at the checkpoint and he confirmed it, he said that they rarely use that gate." Marcus continues.

Harris walks in and gives a sigh with his whole body and then cracks a smile.

Marcus and Penny look like question marks, "What's with the contradicting expressions?" Marcus says.

"We finally got them!" He says and walks up to Penny, "They are rounding up the people on your list, Penny, throughout the UK, and, as we speak, they are also picking up all the others who are scattered around Europe." He says very excited. "If we turn on the TV we may have a glimpse of the arrests." he continues.

"Who are rounding them up?" she says as she was still not awake.

Harris goes up to the big screen TV, turns it on, and half a dozen screens are opening up on it. The stations were all covering the story. People shown being escorted out of buildings by Police.

"FBI in US and MI5 here and police in other places" Harris says proudly.

"Well, I be damned!" Marcus exclaims. However, for Penny this was one part of it, "What about 13?" she asks as this was far from over, not to mention the other nagging part. No one is saying anything,

"Well fuck this" she says out loud frustrated and starts to pull her stuff together. It was almost surreal that all this was going on right under their nose, Penny thinks to herself. She didn't need to see the conclusion, and it was in the works in her mind. CNN was going to show Taytum and Neal being escorted out of PEGC NA corporate office building in Texas. She didn't need to see the man who placed her in harm's way.

Harris walks up to Penny and stops her in her tracks and grabs her by the shoulders. "It will be alright; it will be alright I promise you" he whispers in her ear as he pulls her closer and embraces her. Penny leans on his shoulder for a minute, and then releases her from his grip and turns around, "I need to get home now, that's all to it" she says and shakes her head slowly as her mind was racing through down memory lane.

Harris and Marcus have turned their attention to the News on the different stations.

"I guess, now there will be an extensive investigation." Penny says annoyed and turns around and looks at both Harris and Marcus who are glued to the TV screens.

"It's far from over" she says as she watches the news channels lined up.

At that moment, she knew that there was no chance in hell she could hide from FBI. It was a given they would ask for her statement about what she was seeing. If was not a question about wanting, it was to cooperate or being subpoenaed and the latter was worse; that meant no freedom and all eyes was on her. It was as if matters just continued on in escalated matters. Penny was going from feeling lost and seeing no way out to being pissed off everything and everybody.

Harris continues to flip through the channels, and in every city there's the same scenario playing out, but only in different languages.

"Harris!" Penny exclaim, "I asked about the 13 and what about Bradford and Shariq?"

"Don't worry, I have SIS on them, and I am sure I will hear something soon." he says and tries to convey a calm to Penny, but, inside he had his own concerns. These concerns were not just about Bradford, they were also about the Balkan group that was now aware of their whereabouts. This was not over yet, not in a long shot.

Penny is walking towards the door, she was ready to leave with or without Harris and Marcus.

Suddenly there are rapid gunshots being heard in the building. They all jump up, and Penny reaches for her gun she had tucked inside her belt. She turns her head around and gives them a quick glance at Harris and Marcus who was now standing up.

"I told you!" she says to Harris while looking through the windows to see if the perpetrators were heading their way.

"Marcus, you have the keys to the car, I want you to take Penny with you." Harris says.

"No, you take Penny! I will take your car. They think you will be in that car. I'm going to take it from here, I'll get them off your trail. You two take another car and get to safety." he says with urgency.
Marcus turns to Penny and grabs her by the shoulder,
 "Now you know what you need to do, take a company vehicle, and leave. I have already showed you the way out from here."
He looks around and then down at her hand and grabs the gun from her.
Penny hands him her bag where the clips are located, "Take this." she says.

"I like how you think."

"There are four more clips and forty more rounds. I will hope that you use them, but wisely." she says as he dashes out the door.

She stops for a minute thinking and then she turns to Harris, "Now what?" she says as she throws her hands up in the air, and places her hands behind the head, as if things just got hopeless.

Harris smiles, "Did you think that you are the only one that goes packin' here?" he says and opens a drawer. "Montgomery may be the head of this department, but he is a crazy son of a bitch too!" Harris says.

Penny walks over to the desk with rapid steps; there is an arsenal of guns nicely laid out in a hidden, undetectable flat drawer.

"Damn!" Penny says, "He sure is under the radar about his personality, didn't expect that about him." she says astounded.

Penny starts to pick up different guns to find one that fits her, and there, a Colt 1911 Government Model was tucked in deepest into the drawer, she pulls it out and looks at it. She takes out the clip, looks at it to verify that it's loaded, and puts it back in. She checks the aim on it, and it has a nice feel to it, as if it was made for her.

Harris looks at Penny; "I assume you found what you like." he says and gives her a grin.

Penny looks back at him with a big smile, almost evil, as she is ready to kick some ass. She places it in her hip hugging belt; she grabs a second clip that is in the drawer and presses it down into one of her pockets. Penny feels better instantaneously; she is now ready to leave.

"We are going to take another way out." she says to Harris.

"I know." he says and gives her a double wink with his eyebrows.

She looks at him with her head bobbed to the side as she wonders how he knows.

Harris grabs his firearm, places it in a shoulder holster that is in the drawer and puts on the holster.

Marcus reaches the downstairs, and when he gets out of the elevator he hears a commotion by the security desk. He walks up slowly to the hallway and looks down to the security check point. He can see there are two individuals who are in midst of breaking down a door. He waits until he hears the door give in and the men have entered the room. Marcus runs with swift silent steps to the door; he looks in from the side of the door and he can see that they are covered in protective armor. The only areas that are still open are from the neck up and the legs down.

Marcus moves in quickly and fires first at their legs and then their heads. It goes so fast that James has not had time to react.

"Man, you just got here in time!" James says with relief.

Marcus says nothing, but hurries out the door, and down to the exit door that led out to the garage. He swiftly gets into the car, starts it, and races out of the garage at a rapid speed. The car has the feeling of flying out of the garage. He slams on the breaks and he looks in the rear-view mirror and sees the other vehicle waiting outside the gate for him, as if they expected him. He revs the engine as he views them, and without reacting he drives through the checkpoint and does not stop, breaking the wooden bar that spans across the exit. 'Oh, shit, Harry is going to be pissed!' Marcus thinks, "Well... it can't be helped." he says to himself, reassuring to himself.

Montgomery comes into the room; Penny and Harris are ready to leave.

"Ok." Harris says, "I need the keys to your car."

"Well, I figured as much, I just saw Marcus ram through the checkpoint with yours!" he says with a grin.

Harris shakes his head and gives Montgomery a less of a pleasing look.

"I think it is better if I put you in one of my newspaper vans to get you out." Montgomery says comforting. He goes up to his cabinet and pulls out a set of keys, "…and Harris, don't ram through the hedge gate please." he says pleading.

"Me… never!" he says factiously and smiles at Montgomery and then at Penny.

Harris and Penny are taking the equipment elevator down to the garage to reach the newspaper van.

Penny eyes the size of the van. "And I am supposed to sit where?" she says questioning.

"You can get into the back of the van, you will fit just fine." says Harris.

Unexpectedly a car comes around the corner fast with screeching tires, and the window rolled down and inch, and Penny yells at Harris to take cover. She pulls the gun out of her holster and she fires off round after round. She hits the edge of the window and it shatters, opening up completely to give her a clear view of the individuals inside, and she continues to fire her entire clip into the car. One round hits the passenger, but the driver keeps going.

Penny changes out the clip and starts to run across the stalls to catch up with the car as it is on its way out. She fires at the car and hits the tires, causing them to blow out. The car comes to a stop; Penny is completely exposed at this point.

The door on the driver's side opens up; Penny stops but keeps her target steady. A man comes out quickly, drawing his gun, but Penny empties the rest of the clip into him, ending it.

While Penny is standing there scanning for other potential targets, Harris has come around with the van, and the side door is opened. "Get in, Penny, get in!" he yells at her.

Penny jumps inside the van and pulls the side door shut. Harris speeds out of the garage, his driving is dicey. "Watch how you drive!" she calls out to Harris, "We don't want to attract attention!"

"It's not that easy with these fishbowl glasses on." he says annoyed and looks over to Penny.

Penny gets startled and hits her head in the roof, "Damn it Harris!" she bursts out. The top of her head is sore after the impact. Harris smiles at Penny almost apologetically.

Penny looks at Harris and it takes a moment before she starts to smile too, "You look ridiculous in that hat and glasses! Just so you know." she says and can't stop thinking of the ridiculous look.

"Well, that is good, because I will get no attention, then. I think that's enough attention what we just got from our uninvited friends. I just hope that with these Coke bottle bottoms for glasses I can still make out what the signs say!" he says.

It's a small delivery van and Penny is half lying down in the back; she moves her gun holster around and tucks the gun into her front pocket.

"You are moving around a lot in the back, I can hear you." Harris says, "I hope it is not too uncomfortable for you."

"No more uncomfortable than you are in those specs!" she says. Penny is annoyed with all the commotion and her head is hurting. She is talking to herself under her breath, 'You know what you need to do, take the company vehicle and leave...'

"What did you say?" Harris asks while facing forward and calling back to Penny at the same time.

"Oh, nothing." she replies back while her body bumps up and down as the van is driving through the parking lot and over the speed bumps. She looks over at her gun in the holster annoyed; she was out of bullets.

Harris looks over to the checkpoint and signals with his hand, and the guard opens up the gate, but only enough for the van to get out, and closes it almost immediately as the van goes through.

"OK, Penny, stay put where you are, we are entering the street." Harris says.

Penny leans her body against the wall that separates the front seats from the back of the van. The street is busy, and traffic is in rush hour mode. It's now been almost twenty-four hours since they left Harris office. Penny is thinking of Marcus and wondering where he is now.

"Are we going back to the house, I mean... we are going back to the house, correct?" Penny asks. As she asks, the notion of not being sure of anything anymore was made crystal clear. When and how she was going to make it, back home was the million-dollar question. Every time she tried something else surfaced and she wanted to stand up and scream like a child in a grocery store who wanted candy.

"Yes, that is my goal, and hopefully we can get there in one piece." he assures her and yet he is looking for surprises to surface.

CHAPTER 34

Marcus had a head start to get to the house and he noticed someone following him in hot pursuit. The car's windows were heavy tinted.

Marcus is on the A1 heading back towards the house in Haddington and thinking of a way to lose his follower.

Marcus sees an off ramp coming up, and, at the last minute, he makes a sharp turn to get off the freeway and onto the two-lane country road that led home. He could still see that he had the other car following right behind him.

"Man, that is one hell of a stubborn driver!" Marcus says annoyed.

"OK, let's see what this baby can do." He starts to speed up, faster than he has ever driven before in any car. Marcus presses on the gas and he feels the 460 horsepower under the hood kick in. The faster he drives the more he notices the leveling rear suspension.

He takes a quick look in the rear-view mirror, "OK, let's see if you can hang with me", he says out loud, and then he presses the speed up to 150 mph.

The other car is keeping up until they come to a curve. While Marcus easily controls his car, the car behind him loses traction and the rear of the car swings around dragging the car into the ditch.

Marcus slams on the breaks, and puts the car in reverse, He rolls back enough to see in his side view mirror a woman get out from the driver's seat, and a man from the passenger's seat. By the gesturing between the two individuals he can tell it wasn't good. Marcus smiles to himself, "That is a situation he can handle himself." he says and gives out a burst of laughter and drives off.

Marcus gets back to the house and parks the car close to the front door. He gets out and walks around the car to the front, and he notices a few scratches on the car from him driving through the checkpoint bar. He scratches himself on the back of his head, "He is not going to like this." he says to himself with a discourage look on his face. He continues to walk around the car to take a good look at what he has been driving. Hmm, I can see why Harris like his car, it's like a woman, nice ass, sharp curves, and fast; it has it all. Marcus takes a more intense look at the outside of the house.

Marcus comes to think that Harris had no pictures in the house of any females, or relatives. He must live here alone; no wonder he would pick a car like this. Marcus walks back to the car and pulls out the bag he got from Penny. As he is ready to enter the house he realizes that he doesn't have any key or code to the front door. He pushes the door handle down and the door is open.

While walking towards the office, Marcus can hear the sound of gravel under tires near the front. He walks into the office and drops the bag by the chair. He walks over to the window and he sees the newspaper van roll up. He waits to see who gets out; from the driver's side a man with a baseball cap and some ugly glasses steps out. He takes off the cap and glasses; it's Harris. Marcus starts to smile and shakes his head.

A moment later, Penny comes walking around the car from the passenger side.

"She is finally home." he says to himself with a sigh of relief.

The next moment Marcus hears the door open and he starts to walk towards them. "I'm glad you got here safe!" Harris comments.

"I don't know about safe, but I got myself here." he says with a less than jovial tone.

"Oh..." Harris pauses, "...you want to tell me about it?"

"I will tell you and Penny at the same time." Marcus says and rolls his eyes. "It was that good of a ride; well Penny probably had the most uncomfortable one of all of us!" he says and grabs Penny by the shoulder as she walks into the house, "She is a trooper though, my Penny, this is not our first rodeo!" and he laughs.

"Let's make it our last, will you." Penny replies without looking at Harris. She walks over to seat at the fireplace plunks down.

Harris just nods his head to the side and gives his version of an eye roll.

Marcus walks up to Penny and lifts Penny's feet off the chair and sits down opposite of her. He places her feet in his lap. "I know we are not safe here, maybe if we just plan to go home now" Marcus says suggesting, "you and me, let's go home Penny" he says with a more serious approach to the suggestion.

She's is tire he can tell, and he was in an unfamiliar territory.

"Well, Harris and I will make a good dinner for you... nothing Indian, I promise." and he looks at Harris and grins.

"Ok." she replies in an automatic fashion as she continues to just look out the window.

"Come with me Marcus." Harris says, "She just needs to relax a little; we got this."

Marcus follows Harris into the kitchen and they both walk up to the refrigerator to pull out ingredients for a meal. Marcus pulls out a whole chicken and puts it on the countertop. Harris hands him vegetables that he finds in the drawer.

Harris starts pulling out pots and pans, and places them on the stove. He walks around the kitchen island and grabs the vegetables then starts to clean them up.

There is this quiet moment in the kitchen and, now and then, Marcus looks down the hall to see what Penny is doing while he is cleaning the chicken. All he can see is her sitting in the chair. He looks up at Harris,

Harris stops chopping the vegetables and looks at Marcus, and then he looks over to see if Penny is still in her chair.
"What are you going to do with the upstairs room" he says questioning with a low voice.
"I'll have a handy man from the village come and take care of it" he says as he was continuously chopping away the ingredients.

"On my way here, it was not just a straight shoot." Marcus says.

"Oh, I never thought so, never, I knew that you would be going to have to work to get here." Harris pauses, "So did you get a good look at who it was or who they were?" he continues.

"Well, they ended up in the ditch on the corner of Luggate Burn and B6370."

"You know, that is not too far from the house." Harris says and looks up while he stops in his tracks.

"Oh, I know, believe me, I know." Marcus says agreeing.

Marcus finishes cutting up the chicken and he looks over at Harris, "Ok, let's get this meal in the pot. I want to see what the damage is upstairs for a second." he says.

Harris reaches under the counter, grabs two bowls, and slides one over to Marcus.

Marcus grabs the bowl and places the chicken in it. He washes his hands and the cutting board, and then puts it in the dishwasher. He seasons the chicken with salt and pepper, and then reaches out for the vegetables. Next to the stove there is an olive oil pitcher, he grabs it, and pours oil in both pots. He heats up the pots, drops the vegetables in the large pot, and places a few pieces of chicken in the other pot. He lowers the heat, places a lid halfway covering the pot, and walks up to Harris. Marcus has been watching Harris the entire time, he was on autopilot doing it all.

Penny gets up from her chair and she walks into the kitchen where she can smell something cooking. Her body is moving slow, it is getting more and more relaxed, the smell of real food makes her stomach growl, and she is ready to eat. She walks up to the stove and lifts the lid; she inhales the aroma from the steam slowly escaping the pot.

She suddenly hears glass breaking, "Harris, Marcus what are you guys doing?" she calls out. It is quiet, none of them answers. She calls out again, "Guys, what are you doing?" and she walks out towards the hallway. She gets halfway into the hall and sees glass on the carpet. She looks up and she sees the window has been broken. Before she can react, she has a large hunting knife at her neck and her right arm is pulled tightly behind her back.

She was now face to face with the ghost, it had started all over again, on peaceful territory.

There are two individuals standing in front of her with hooded faces and one holding her. "...and so, they were three." she says out loud almost in a crazy mannerism from an Agatha Christie story line.

"Zašto je tako luda i tako jebeno prekrasno u isto vrijeme?" (Why is she so crazy and so fucking beautiful at the same time?) one of the men in front of her tells the others as he walks back and forth, "Gotovo zločin ubiti nekoga poput nje," (Almost a crime to kill someone like her), he says.

She notes he is man, with a deep voice; they are all about six feet tall, the man holding her is more than six feet tall, and the man talking is Croatian, she can tell by his accent.

The man talking turns around to the one behind him. At that moment Penny gets a firm but painful grip on balls of the man who is holding her, he screams in pain, and starts to lower himself to the ground. As unexpected as she was when apprehended by him, she quickly recovers, gets out of his grip, grabs the knife out of his hand, and, in a split second, stabs him in the neck with two quick strokes; the first from the side and the second from the front.

The Croatian's reaction is not fast enough. By the time he has turned around he has walked into her knife.

From upstairs Harris and Marcus can hear the commotion going on downstairs. They look at each other and, in a split second, they are both running downstairs. When they get to the second set of stairs going down they find Penny with a hunting knife in her hand and three people on the floor. Both of them look at her and back at each other.

"Well, where were you guys?" she says and is almost hunched over.

Marcus shakes his head; "You are no Penny!" he says and looks at Harris, pauses for a second, "You got her that name?" while he looks at Harris and he points at her with his index finger, "What were you thinking of?" he continues and gives him a facial expression of 'unbelievable'. Marcus starts to look at the bodies then back to Harris, "Do you have a wheel barrel and a shovel?"

Harris says nothing and walks through the front door to the shed by the side of the house.

While in the house Marcus and Penny are having a quiet moment, "Well..." Penny starts to say.

"No..." Marcus stops her, "I don't want to know, or hear anything." he pauses, "I look at you and I think you need my help, and I turn my head around and find you here very capable of handling things on your own." he says clearly upset. "I don't need to do anything for you; I don't know who you are Penny?"

"How quick we forget...Weaver" she replies.

It is quiet for a second, "Oh, yeah..." he scoffs, "... and that name Penny sounds so innocent, but it is anything but innocent. You are something else, you know that!" he says and shakes his head in disbelief of what he has just seen, the commotion he heard, and the aftermath of it all that was displayed clearly on the floor. He was shaken up as he was supposed to protect her, and this was a close call.

They both get quiet and say nothing, because what was there to say. Penny knew how to take care of business when she was cornered, and she never asked this to happen. She did not provoke the situation; it was her or them in her mind.

The front door suddenly gets pushed in, and there's Harris with the wheel barrel and the shovel inside of it. "Ok..." Harris says, "Let's clean up and get this trash out of the house."

Harris and Marcus lift one of the heavy bodies into the wheel barrel.

"Let's go outside and find a spot where we can dispose of them." Harris looks at all three of the bodies, "...unless you want to take them to the taxidermist." he says sarcastically.

Harris hands Penny the shovel, "What..." she begins, "I have to dig the hole?"

"So, you want us to do it?" Harris says and looks at Marcus. They both give Penny the look and a quiet answer; they say nothing.

She looks at them for an answer, "Never mind, I will do it!" she says with a tired voice.

They walk out to a spot with many shade trees on a desolated area on the estate.

Penny starts to dig the hole, Marcus dumps one of the casualties on the ground, and then both Harris and Marcus walk back to the house.

They come back with another body and this one they can still hear is still breathing, "You may not want to drop him in, he is still alive." Marcus says to Penny.

"By the time he is in the ground he will not have much of a choice; I either bury them all together and clean this up so I can go home knowing that this is not going to follow me back home, or I keep him alive to satisfy you." she says snarky.

"Ok, never mind, forget I said anything." Marcus continues.

Marcus and Harris make the last trip back to the house and, when they get back, Penny has managed to dig a hole deep and wide enough for all three.

Penny rolls each body into the hole with her hands and she looks at Marcus, "You cover it now!" and hands him the shovel.

He looks at her surprised.

"I am not asking you; I am telling you!" she says and with those words she walks back to the house.

While walking back to the house she looks over the field, and in the distance she sees some flying object hovering between the trees. "Those damn drones are everywhere in the world." Penny says to herself and walks into the house.

Penny is in the kitchen when Harris and Marcus come back to the house. They enter through the front, and, when they get inside, they almost immediately step on the sordid floor.

"So, what do you want us to do with this?" Marcus says and points at the floor.

"I'll have my cleaning lady come tomorrow and she will take care of it." he says with no concern about it, "She will think I did some hunting, and I will get my ear chewed off by her, but she will take of it." he says.

They continue and walk into the kitchen.

Penny has taken the casserole off the stove and placed it on the center of the kitchen island.

Harris walks up to the counter by the window and brings the plates and utensils to the center of the island.

Penny start to serve them, one after another, and not much is being said just looks are exchanged. There is an awkward feeling in the air, and they are quietly enjoying the meal.

Suddenly Penny says, "So tell me, how common are drones in the UK?" she says in a curious way to break the silence.

"Drones?" Harris says questioning.

"Yeah, you know these small flying oversized bugs with a camera on their belly; a drone." Penny says again and now starts to think that maybe the drone back home was not something that belonged to kids at all.

"Well, let me say this, if you are talking about what I think you are talking about..." he says, pauses, and then takes a big bite of his food, "...that is not very common around here because people are not that sophisticated, they care more about their Whiskey and their cigars, if I can put it in a better way." Harris says and laughs while his body is moving up and down as if Penny had asked a silly question.

"Ok, I get it." and she starts to laugh with him. She leaves it at that, but she has not forgotten.

The sun has set, and it is getting dark outside, "I think we should make it an early night; it's been a crazy couple of days, and I think we all need some well-deserved rest." Harris says, gets up, and stretches his legs.

"I agree!" Marcus says. "That is something I have not been able to say in a long time." and he stretches out his body and arms.

"I will call Julia and Jennie and let them know that I am finally coming home." Penny says.

"How are you going to do that? Your phone is dead." Marcus says.

"Yeah, you are right. I will call them tomorrow from the airport. I'm going online to book a flight home and..."

"No, I am taking care of that!" Marcus says as he interrupts Penny.

"What do you mean?" she asks and looks surprised and questioning at the same time.

"Don't worry, I got this taken care of, you just go and take a shower and relax. In the morning we will go home together." Marcus says and brushes Penny on the side of her cheek.

Penny looks at him and has this sad look come over her face as is being in a need of a good cry to release her pent-up anxiety.

She gets up from her chair, places her plate in the sink, and walks upstairs.

Marcus and Harris are still in the kitchen and they are cleaning up.

"I want you to take care of Penny when you get back, promise me that." Harris says.

"Oh, I will take care of her." he says reassuring, "I won't let her out of my sight and I promise you this, she will not be Bridge for much longer." he says and smiles quietly.

Harris looks over at Marcus after hearing that, "Well, I'll be damned!" Harris blurts out astonished in a thick British accent and then smiles big and wide. He gives Marcus a good man slap on his back and grabs his arm. "You'll let me know when you have decided to get married, I want to be there for it!" he says encouraging.

Marcus and Harris finish the dishes and they both walk back to the office. Harris turns on the Blaupunkt Milano radio from the 1950's that is sitting on the opposite side of the room, and it starts playing piano jazz music. He pulls open the cabinet doors, which looks like a studio bar, and grabs the Macallan No.6. He pours a glass for each of them.

Marcus has plopped down in a comfortable seat by the fireplace.

Harris walks over to the Marcus. "Here's to you!" he says, hands him a glass, and lifts it up to salute him then continues, "...and to our friendship, as we have experienced some crazy events that have cemented our relationship from being complete strangers."

Marcus is moved by his words. "The same to you Harris! I could not have put it in a better way." and lifts his glass to salutes Harris without touching his glass, "To newfound friendship, untouchable!" Marcus finishes.

They sit quietly as there is nothing more to be said. All that can be heard is the music playing in the background. Harris opens a box of cigars; it says Ashton on the box. He faces Marcus and without saying anything Harris gives him a silent offering nudge to joining him.

Marcus grabs a cigar, the guillotine cutter, and prepares his cigar. He is really not a smoker of cigarettes or cigars, so this is something new. He'd seen others smoke cigars and now he was going to practice what he had previewed. He grabs the torch and lights his cigar while he puffs on it; he gives a sigh of relief and sinks deeper into the chair.

Harris is taking his turn with cutting and lighting his cigar. When he's done, both men just sit enjoy the simple things, the music that is filling the room. The sound of the music from the radio is changing their entire tune while they sip on their whiskey and puff away on their cigars. This is a moment long overdue, a moment of no interruptions, nothing except the man pleasures they have in front of them.

Suddenly this peacefulness is abruptly interrupted by the phone ringing, "That was short but sweet." Harris says and gets up and answers the phone.

"Yes, Montgomery..." he says, "...really, that is interesting..." he gives the cigar a puff "...and so there is no sign of Bradford, but you got Shariq?"

Harris looks over at Marcus and lifts his eyebrows in a reaction to good news.

Harris' facial expression changes as he is listening intently and thinking. "Ok, well I am glad we have resolved the matter in regard to everything else, but I will let Penny and Marcus know..." he pauses, "Ok, well... let me contact SIS and give them my information. They will have to 'tag' him." Harris finishes the conversation with those words, and he walks back to his seat while sipping on his whiskey. He sits down in the chair and folds one leg over the other.

"So, they have not found Bradford?" Marcus says.

"No, but they did find Shariq. I don't know where he is, but if I know a character like Bradford, he is not going to give up." Harris responds.

Marcus grabs the bag from next to the chair, the bag Penny gave him, and pulls out a cell phone from bag. He hands over the phone to Harris, "This is yours." he says.

Marcus then continues going through the bag and pulls out his own phone. He turns it on, there is not much charge left on it despite being turned off for two days. The phone vibrates for a new incoming text message, *'Where should we pick you up?'* Marcus does not know when this message was sent, so he responds back by dialing number on text message, "Marcus here." is all he says. "Ok... when was this message sent? ...Yes,

I would, and I will have a second passenger with me... At
Edinburgh Airport, yes Scotland... hold on a second..."

Marcus turns to Harris, "We are leaving early in the morning;
do you think you could drive us?"

Harris turns his head slowly towards Marcus, "No problem." he
pauses and looks at his cigar, and then takes a deep puff on it
and blows the smoke out, "I'll get you guys there, just get the
time." Harris says.

Marcus gets back to his phone conversation, "Ok, let's do it,...
at sun rise." Marcus says in a firm tone, looks at the phone,
and disconnects the call. The battery is low, and he shuts off
the phone.

He walks back to his seat, picks up his glass of whiskey, and
takes a sip. He sits down, reaches for his cigar, and takes a
long puff then blows the smoke straight up into the ceiling.
The cigar is strong, and it relaxes him.

Marcus looks at the time, "The hours are ticking away fast..."
he says while letting his head rest on the back of the chair, and
continues by looking at Harris, "...and I need to make sure I get
Penny up in time for us to leave before anything else happens.
We don't want to get stuck here with questions that we would
rather not have to answer." Marcus says tired and in a
comedic way to Harris. He gets up on his feet and puts out the
cigar in the ashtray by the side table.

"Oh, I hear you..." he sighs, "I hear you, and I will join you..."
Harris answers and drags his body out of the chair.

Marcus finishes his drink in one gulp, and it goes down smooth, leaving him feeling all warm inside. He walks upstairs and finds Penny on the bed with her clothes on, '*She must have got up here and just gone to bed without taking a shower, poor thing*' he thinks to himself.

Marcus starts to undress her by removing her pants. Penny doesn't fight it, she is completely out of it, and she doesn't recognize that she is being undressed. Marcus pulls the cover off the bed and moves Penny inside. He then gets himself undressed and lies down on the bed; he looks at his watch and sets the alarm for four am. He takes off his watch and puts it on the side table, and closes his eyes, and falls fast asleep.

This was all over now. There were going to be questions for Penny when she got back, but, at least, she didn't have to run anymore, she was finally going to go home, and she was going with Marcus.

Marcus' alarm goes off. Penny is moving around in the bed. Marcus grabs his watch and turns off the alarm. He leans over to Penny, "hey, it's time to wake up." he whispers in her ear.

Penny turns around and meets Marcus face. She grabs his scruffy face and gives him a friendly pat. She hugs him tired as she closes her eyes, and Marcus grabs Penny's hands and puts them together and says, "Listen, wake up. We have to get up, we have a plane to catch this morning." He walks over to the chair where he placed his clothes and starts to get dressed.

Penny is rolling around on the bed and then she notices that her pants are off, "Did I take these off?" she says confused.

Marcus looks over to Penny, "No, I did that, silly!" he says with a smile.

Penny is now lying on her back on the bed with her arms supporting her, she looks at Marcus and smiles back in a seductive way.

"No, that is not happening!" Marcus says as if he is talking to a child. He looks at Penny, "You need to get up so we can get going. Harris has promised to take us to the airport." he says, but this time with more of a demanding demeanor as he knows that seems to be the only thing that Penny responds to.

Penny jumps out bed and gets her pants on. She walks into the bathroom and starts freshens herself up.

Marcus walks in after Penny and grabs his toothbrush then starts brushing his teeth while he watches Penny from behind.

"So why is it that we are leaving this early, and what do you mean Harris is taking us to the airport?" Penny starts asking inquisitively.

Marcus points at his toothbrush and gives her the silent answer of 'unable to talk right now'. Marcus moves to the sink, spits, and rinses out his mouth. "I have a private jet taking us back to the States. I know you want to ask questions, but not now, let's just pack up, get out of here, and back home." he says and walks out to grab his backpack with his other things.

Penny is cleaning herself up and grabs her things and puts them in her pouch, goes back out into the room, and she looks for her backpack.

Marcus turns to Penny, "It is downstairs..." he pauses, "...your backpack is what I am referring to." and he turns around and walks towards the door.

Penny stops, "Marcus, should we not make the bed before we leave?" she says.

"Why, his cleaning lady comes tomorrow today, she will take care of it." he says as if he lived there as a full-time house guest.

Penny makes a funny face, "How do you know?" she asks him.

"Listen, I don't have time for Jeopardy now, let's go, he is waiting downstairs." Marcus says anxiously.

Penny grabs her pouch and puts her jacket on. She is ready to go; she gives the place a last look before she closes the door.

Downstairs Harris is ready and waiting, "OK luv, I am ready if you are." he says to Penny.

"We will soon see each other again, I promise." Penny says with a sentimental tone in her voice.

"I know we will." Harris replies and smiles at her.

Penny walks into the office, and over to the chair and grabs her bag off the floor. She places the pouch inside, and gives it a last look through to make sure that she had everything.

"Ok, let's not take any chances; we are taking the van, best way to hide you in case 'crazy' shows up." Harris says.

They all get into the news van; Penny and Marcus are sitting in the back while Harris drives them to the airport.

Arriving at the airport they get to the checkpoint at the private jet area. The plane is already waiting for them and the door is completely open.

Harris stops the van on the tarmac, gets out, and opens the side door. Marcus exits first, grabs his bag and Penny's bag. He reaches out his hand to her and helps her out.

Harris shuts the door and turns to Marcus "Let me know when you get home, you know what we talked about." and winks with his eye to him.

Marcus nods agreeing and turns towards the plane and walks up to the stairs where he is greeted by John, "Mr. Weaver, good to see that you are safe."

Penny hugs Harris and with half an ear she listens to the conversation that taking place between Marcus and the man on the plane's steps. She hurries after Marcus and walks up the stairs.

The man at the door greets Penny, "My name is John, and I will be at your service this morning. Can I take your bag?" he asks her.

Penny holds her backpack tight to her chest, "No thank you, I will be fine." she says gives off a suspicious and untrusting look.

She continues to walk onto the plane and John shuts the door behind her. Penny finds Marcus and she sits down facing him.

"Who is Mr. Weaver?" Penny says cryptic, while buckling herself up in the seat. Although she knew now that he was the covert person who had worked with her husband, she still didn't know who he was. Who was travelling with a Jet, and how could he afford that she asked herself. There was more beneath that surface that much she knew.

There was nowhere Marcus could hide, run, or go to avoid the question. She folds one leg over the other and folds her hands together, as she was demonstrating that she was waiting for the answer.

Marcus looks at her and he says and leans forward, "When we get back home I will tell you," and he looks over at side, and continues "...but not now as we have too many ears in this cabin." he says soft-spoken to her while the engines are revving up for take-off. He pulls back and moves his attention to the window and leans comfortably back against the seat.

The flight taxis out onto the runway and, in minutes, the jet is back in the air. The noise of the engines and air rushing by the cabin is making Penny sleepy. Soon, they both fall asleep.

CHAPTER 35

Marcus is nudged awake by John, "We are almost in New York. We are going land and fuel up, and then we will take off for the final destination".

"Ok." Marcus says and looks over at Penny, who is still sleeping.

He knew he was going to have to tell her everything if his idea of relationship was going to work. There was no trust between them, he had broken that, and he had to mend it. He was going to give it a try that was all he could do, but there was a possibility that once she found out it was over he thinks to himself.

As much as Penny thought things were over, and she was going to be safe just because she was home, that was a mistake. All she ever wanted was to forget all about it and what had happened, and so she did for a moment...

It's midmorning, around ten-ish and the Jet is descending down at Renton municipal airport.

A car is waiting for them on the tarmac.

Penny and Marcus unbuckles the seatbelt, look at each other, and looks spoke volumes.

Marcus leads the way to the exit door, and the plane comes to a halt. John stands ready to releases the door.

"Thank you" Marcus says to John.

"My pleasure" he responds while he gives Marcus a tap on his shoulder. There was this language between them Penny could tell that they had a history unlike any other.

Marcus places his arm around Penny, "We are taking you home first, I know you want to see Damien." he says and kisses her on her forehead.

Penny says nothing, instead just walks down the stairs and over the waiting car with Marcus on her tail.

They get into the car, it is quietly and she wants to ask the questions that she has been waiting to get answered, but, again, too many ears and nothing would really matter at this point. It would have to wait until they were home, she thought, and there was no one else besides them.

The car stops in front of Penny's house, the driver gets out, and he opens the door.

Marcus grabs their bags and gets out, Penny follows, and Marcus holds out his hand to Penny.

Penny keeps walking towards the door while Marcus is delayed talking to the driver. She looks over at him and realizes she doesn't have a key and that it is in her bag.

"Marcus, I need my bag." she calls out to him.

Marcus looks over and he waves at her then finishes the
conversation with the driver. He walks up and hands her the
bag.

Penny opens up the bag and on the inside there is another
pocket with her keys tucked safely inside.
She pulls out her keys and sticks her house key into the door,
and, when she opens it Damien is running towards her, with
his tail wagging, and jumping up and down.

Jennie comes walking through the living room. She says
nothing, just hugs Penny.
"I'm glad you are home and safe!" she looks over and there he
was. Jennie could feel she was the fifth wheel.
"We'll talk later. I am going to leave, and we'll catch up when
you have time. OK?" she says to Penny and walks out the door.

Penny just nods agreeing, "OK" and she watches the door close.

There was this awkward silence in the house even though she
was home and safe. Something still bothered her. She was
ready, didn't want to wait anymore.
She walks over to the patio door and opens it wide. She takes
one step outside and, with a deep breath; she inhales the crisp
and fresh smell of grass. She looks at it and sees that it is wet,
and this is what helps the perfume-like scent emanate from her
entire garden.

Damien is running around, and he has found a chew toy, he
lies down on the grass and starts to chew frantically; wagging
his tail constantly. It almost felt like a deja-vu.

I wish I was this content with what I had, or that my life was as easy as to be pleased by chewing on a stick, Penny thinks.

She suddenly feels her shoulder being touched by two strong hands, "You need a massage..." Marcus says and pauses, "...you are all tense, you need to relax you are home" he continues.

Penny turns around and walks up to the bag and grabs it and continues to walk back to the bedroom. Marcus follows her lead. She leaves the doors open to the back yard. She gets undressed while Marcus is watching her and throws her clothes into the hamper. She continues into the bathroom with her bag and starts to put her things back in their places.

Penny takes a good look in the mirror and she realizes that with being sleep deprived, tired, stressed, and hungry for the most part of the time that her face had aged. She knew that she needed to get her sleep and rejuvenate herself back to who she was. Penny did not see a happy and relaxed person; she saw a lot of work to get her back to where she was.

Penny turns on the shower, gets in, and, suddenly, feeling the water streaming down her face, she begins to cry. She was not crying out loud, just tears. Her way of releasing her stress, her anger, and she knows that she will need to get some counseling to get it all out of her system. As much as she wanted it to be forgotten, time with herself allowed all those memories crawl into the front of her mind and there was no escape.

She grabs her sponge and places a drop of shower gel on it, foams it up, and starts to rub her body down. She cleans herself from top to bottom. She rubs harder and harder until she is red all over. She washes her hair twice and the feeling of being burned out was prevalent. She knew that some much-needed time off from work was necessary. This was going to be a time that was about her and no one else.

Out in the bedroom Marcus has sat down on the chair in the corner with his hands folded together.

Penny steps out into the bedroom with her body wrapped in a towel.

Marcus stands up and walks towards her. He sits down on the bed and he pulls her closer to him.
"I am going to give you a massage to relax you." he says, and he pulls the comforter off the bed. He taps the bed with his hand and Penny understands what he wants her to do.

Penny drops the towel on the floor and lays her naked body on the bed face down.

Marcus walks into the bathroom and finds the massage gel, and brings it back out to the bedroom, where Penny is laying on her stomach waiting. He leans over to her to see if she is still awake and she has her eyes closed.

Marcus pours some gel into his hands and rubs them together, then slowly he places them on her back, and her body moves as if it was startled, she turns her head around, and closes her eyes again.

Marcus starts to rub her back gently and slowly; up and down her spine he lets the gel glide his hands as he spreads his fingers until he reaches her neck. His fingers and hands make circular motions and Penny beings to breath heavily as her muscles are tense the massage does feel painful. She is not fighting it, but she also does not know how to relax.

"Please take a deep breath and exhale. It will help you to relax." Marcus says.

Penny is exhaling every time Marcus rubs his fingers across her shoulder muscles and the more she does it, the more she relaxes.

He can finally sense through his fingertips how her muscles are getting softer and less tense. "Good, relax." he says and continues to rub her entire body; her lower back, her arms, and her legs.

Penny is getting sleepy again and when she finally is getting her hands massaged she intertwines her hands with Marcus' hands and does not let go.

Marcus stops and lies down next to her where he can see her face. He is facing the French doors, blocking the light coming through, and watches Penny lay there on her stomach.

Penny looks up at Marcus, moves little bit to the side, yes, she is naked, and it doesn't bother him. For him she is the most beautiful thing there is.

Marcus lets go of her hand and gets out of bed, he moves around towards the doors, and shuts the venetian blinds a little to block the direct sunlight enough so that is doesn't hit Penny directly in her eyes.

Marcus and Penny lay there together looking into each other's eyes.

"Who is Mr. Weaver?" Penny asks with a soft-spoken voice, she is not angry or upset; she is a tired woman who is done fighting, she just wants the truth.

Marcus gives a defeated look back at her, as this was the time for the truth to be revealed and there were no more excuses or delays on revealing what he was and who he was.

He looks at her, "I am not sure that you will like me after what I have to tell you..." he pauses and continues, "...I killed a man over 10 years ago and I have a felony record." he says and waits for a reaction, but instead it's quiet. Penny is not saying anything.
"I have done my time Penny, and I am trying to get back to normal life, to do what everyone else is doing." he says.

"So why were you carrying a folder with information on what I was doing and a picture with my face circled?" she says.

"When I got out of jail there was no one who wanted to hire me, so I was approached to do a simple extraction job. There was no killing involved, but it was also not easy or safe. I did the job it and it paid me handsomely. So, I continued to do small jobs that involved no one getting hurt and that was how I made my fortune." he says and looks down at her hand.

"Penny, I was hired to do a job, and it was supposed to be quick and fast money, but it was far from easy and..." he pauses, and that I had to make a choice... and I made the right one!"

Penny listens and thinks how to respond to all that, "I have a few things I need to settle before I can..." she stops herself, "Before you can be in a serious relationship... I understand you

have some unfinished business but give me some time...
please." he says as sincere as he can be.

"Time is all I have" she says, and Marcus kisses her hand as a
silent offer of gratitude.

"So, your name is not Marcus Scott, but Marcus Weaver?"
Penny asks and confirms at the same time.

"Yes." he answers and stairs up in the ceiling.

"OK." Penny says as she starts to digest what Marcus has told
her. "Penny Weaver." she says softly.

"What did you say?" he asks.

"I was just tasting my name, if, and that is if, we would be
something more than just what we are today."

Marcus gets into the bed a bit more comfortable, grabs a hold of
Penny, and moves her closer." I will wait for as long as I need
to." he says sincerely.

Damien comes walking into the room, he stands by the door,
and he whimpers. "I know, I know." Penny says and taps on
the bed. Damien comes running and jumps up on the bed.

Penny looks at Marcus, "I love to hear you say that. What I
would love to have done now is..." and she pauses, looks at
Damien, and then she looks at Marcus, "...something to eat."

Marcus asks, "Tell me what you would like to have, and I will
get it for us."

Penny thinks while she is looking up at the ceiling, she is pondering, something simple; no utensils needed, bare hands, "Pizza!" she blurts out.

"OK." Marcus smiles. "I will go and get pizza for us. What do you like?" he says while he gets his clothes back on.

"I'll take anything, oh, and when you are going, can you take Damien with you for a walk?" she says bashfully.

Marcus looks at Damien and then he looks at Penny, "You heard what your mommy said." he says and smile, "Do you wanna...?" he says to Damien.

Damien jumps off the bed and his tail wags fast and furious, whipping back and forth.

"Ok, where is your leash?" Marcus says to Damien.

Damien looks at Penny and then at Marcus, and waits.

"Go and get your leash." Penny commands Damien and he runs at once with those words and comes back prancing with his leash in his mouth.

Marcus puts on the harness and attaches the leash. He gives Penny a last look before he heads out the door and down the street to the local pizza place.

Penny lies in the bed with one leg wrapped over the cover sheet and is watching the sun through the blinds. '*Should I give this a chance?* she thinks. She turns around and faces the bathroom, '*Maybe I should get up and get dressed, and straighten out my hair before they get back* she continues in her mind..

Penny sits up in the bed and rests her hands on the bed. She lets her feet hit the floor; she contemplates what she is going to do, she looks into the bathroom. She gets up and walks into the bathroom, makes a right turn into the closet, and she starts to rummage through the hangers for something simple to wear. While she stands there, she feels someone watching her, she turns around, and there is Bradford. She gets startled to see him there; she is exposed in more ways than one.

"Well, have you figured out what to wear before your boyfriend comes back?" he says sarcastically.

"What the fuck do you want?" Penny says with a pissed off tone. She turns around, grabs a pair of underwear, and pulls them on and a t-shirt.
"I would leave if I was you, he doesn't take kindly to your presence." she says and walks by him.

Bradford grabs her arm and says, "Don't you worry about that, I have eyes in the sky." Penny looks at him and she knows at that moment that the drones were all his doing. "You didn't do as you were told; you didn't deliver." he says irritated.

"Deliver what? This whole thing was a well-planned plot and you had it all well figured out, but you thought I was some bimbo who did not know a damn thing." she says.

"No, I did know who you were, in fact I could have said that you were not the right person for the job, but I didn't want a 'bimbo'. I wanted for you to come and pick it up." he says with assured tone to his comment.

"Because?" she says.

"I could not wait to see what kind of woman worked in the company with a background like yours, Howards ex-wife. I was intrigued and I knew that you could protect the information." he pauses while he is walking back and forth, "I knew that there were others who wanted the information too..." and he turns his head towards the door and points, "...such as your boyfriend 'Weaver'. Q sent him that much I did know, and he wanted what you were carrying, but what I didn't know was your deeper involvement with him." he says.

"Well that is too fucking bad, isn't it Seels!" she says with cocky tone and walks by him.

"If you think that is too fucking bad, let me tell you something else that is too fucking bad; I don't leave tracks behind me."

"You think you didn't, but you did. They know that you went rouge and the Feds are looking for you. What I don't know is why you entered my house." she asks and continues to move things around on the living room table, "...that you don't leave tracks, what tracks would that be, you are here." she continues with a cocky attitude while keeping her back towards him.

"Well I will clean up after myself!" he says and gets quiet.

Penny stops, turns around, and, that moment, she is struck by a blunt object, is knocked out, and falls down on the floor.

Bradford starts to pour gasoline fuel by the doors and along the walls, and he walks out through the back-patio doors. He gives one last look inside, lights a match, and throws it inside.

The match hits the fuel, and explosive bursts of flames erupts. The fire grows fast and furious and it was spreading fast. Walls were engulfed by the voracious fire and the flames could be seen by the neighbors.

One pedestrian outside sees the flames bursting out the front door cracks and he pulls out his phone and starts dialing 911.

Down the street, Marcus is coming back with Pizza. He lets the leash go and throws the pizza on the ground as he runs to the house without hesitation. Both he and Damien are at the door at the same time. Damien is barking ferociously and people in the neighborhood start to gather around.

Marcus tries to open the door, but it's been locked from the inside.

Damien runs back and forth by the front windows and, without warning, his heavy pushes at the window cracks it wide open and flames are erupting through. Damien is not hesitating and jumps inside.

Marcus watches Damien and, at that moment, he finally breaks down the door with all his force and runs inside. The place is engulfed in flames; sirens can be heard outside. He calls out, "Penny, Penny, where are you?" he is holding his shirt over his face while the flames are now above him on the ceiling.

Marcus suddenly sees Penny on the floor in the middle of the living room and Damien is next to her licking her face.

Marcus suddenly hears the ceiling crack, he looks up, and, before he can move, he is buried under the rubble of the collapsing ceiling and the roof.

The fire department arrives, and two firemen jumps out of the truck with full face masks on and run toward the open front door. They make a quick assessment before going inside. They push through the flames to get to Penny, but don't see Marcus under the collapsed roof.

They get Penny outside; where one of the firemen rips off his helmet and starts to give her CPR. After a few minutes she finally comes back.

Penny looks up, her vision is blurry, "Marcus?" she says before she closes her eyes, and, in the distance, she can her someone call out, "Did you get the guy who went in?" and with those words everything turned black.

PENNY IS SLOWING WAKING UP in the hospital bed. She looks over at the doorway and she has a hard time differentiate who was standing there, her vision was severely blurred. The person took closer steps in her direction and could see she was slowly waking up and pushes the button for the nurse.

The nurse is walking in, and the person takes a step aside, and watches everything unfold from a distance as she was tending to Penny.

'*Who was that person that she was looking at, what did they want?* she was thinking, and she could feel a severe pain in the back of her head, and she closes her eyes in agonizing pain.

The nurse turns to the person and they exchange a few words, she can't understand what they are saying, but she can tell the person is a man.

The man is now standing next to her without saying anything, and she still has a difficult time to see clearly.

The man stays after the nurses are gone.
"Penny" the man says.
"Yes, do I know you?" she asks. She still couldn't make out his face.
"It's Dee" he says.
Penny is quiet and don't know what to say.

He grabs a chair and sits down next to her.
"I normally don't do these kinds of visits, but I believe you needed to hear this from me"

"What do you want" she says and moves her attention out towards the window and yet she can barely make out what was outside.
"Dee, continue to tell me what you were going to say and then leave" she says as this was the last person she wanted to see or hear from.

Dee continues to tell Penny about Damien and Marcus, and she lays there in the bed just hearing him talk, but not focusing on anything else and her tears start rolling down her cheeks.

"Baby... listen. You'll be alright" he says as comforting as he
can and yet he didn't know if she was listening.
She was hurt and understandably so, and he, well, he had also
hurt her in the past. This was the first time in years he had
seen her, and offering her comfort was probably not how he had
expected them to meet again or under these circumstances.

She'd lost the most important individual in her life, and the one
who caused this was still on the run.
He knew he needed to give her time, and today was not the day
to be invading her space as she needed time to come to terms of
what had happened.

Dee gets up from the chair and walks out the door. He walks
across the parking lot and gets into his truck, still thinking of
how the fire had started. Who did this?

The sound of a cell phone going off was interrupting his
thoughts.
"Hello" Dee answers the phone.
"Dee" he could hear from the other side.
"Yea, who's this?"
*"It's Bradford...listen don't worry about the assignment I gave
you, I took care of it myself"*
"What do you mean?" Dee asks.
"I pulled a fireman on it..." he responds riddle like and it gets
quiet, and Dee is waiting for more to come, then he looks at the
phone and can see that the call had been disconnected.

He looks back towards the hospital building, '*was that him?*' he
questions out loud as he couldn't stop thinking of the possibility
that Bradford was the culprit of what had happened to Penny.

He knew that he needed to go back another day. The need to make sure she was ok, and hopefully then she would accept his apology for what had happened in the past between them.

This was his hopes but, knowing Penny and how strong and independent she was, he wasn't sure. She had ghosted him permanently when they broke up, and this situation was merely serendipity.

Made in the USA
Las Vegas, NV
09 February 2022

43555859R00223